STRAYS

GARRETT LEIGH

"You are my dreams. I just never knew."

TABLE OF CONTENTS

LENNY

CHAPTER ONE

The policewoman slid a cup of grey tea across the interview table. "Tell me again, sir. How many times have you seen this man at your place of work?"

Lenny Mitchell sighed and dragged a hand through his electric-blue hair. "I *told* you. I don't know exactly. He's just there sometimes."

"Standing across the road? At the bus stop?"

"Yes."

"I see." The policewoman made a note. "Have you considered the possibility that the man you've described is simply catching the bus?"

Lenny levelled the woman with an acid glare. *Seriously?* "Catching the bus to where? My flat? So he can loiter there too? Or the club where I used to work so he can tell everyone he's my boyfriend like he did before?"

"Which club is that?"

"Shades, in Brent Cross."

"The strip club?"

"No, the *gay* club."

The policewoman jotted another note. "Okay, so you say this man has been present outside your home and your place of work, and that he's written you letters, and contacted you on social media. Do you have evidence of this? Copies of the letters? Screen shots?"

I'm such a fucking idiot. Lenny shook his head. "I deleted my Facebook and Twitter when he started harassing me, and the letters were taken from my flat."

"Taken?"

"Stolen, whatever."

"Did you report it?"

"No."

"And you haven't received any since?"

"*No.*"

The policewoman's left eyebrow twitched. "So you have no evidence to corroborate your story?"

"'My story'? I'm not making it up."

"I'm not saying you are, Mr. Mitchell, but without *evidence* there's little we can do if we find this man and he denies your allegations. Have you reported him to your landlord or your employer?"

"I don't know who my landlord is. I rent through an agency, and my tenancy is nearly up, anyway. And my previous employers at the club thought *I* was the fucking lunatic."

"What about your current employer? At the restaurant?"

"At Misfits?"

"Yes."

Lenny shrugged. "My bosses are really busy. I don't want to bother them."

The policewoman went back to her notes. "Okay, well . . . like I said before, without evidence and an ID for this man, there's not much we can do except give you some advice on staying safe."

Unbidden, the dull eyes that seemed to follow Lenny everywhere flashed into his mind, prickling his skin like tiny feather-drops of battery acid. "His name's Gareth. He told the bouncers at Shades when he was pretending to be my boyfriend. I wrote it down for you."

"Oh, yes, so you did." The policewoman cast another disinterested glance at the notebook Lenny had handed over, pages filled with the incidents and sightings, and plain freaky shit that had driven him from Croydon to Camden in the first place. "Well, this is all very helpful, Mr. Mitchell, but as I said—"

"Yeah, yeah. Take a leaflet and fuck off. I heard you."

The music in Misfits pumped a subtle, thudding beat, keeping time with Lenny's pulse as he rushed from table to table, pouring champagne and delivering towering burgers from the sizzling chargrill. He'd worked in quieter restaurants, but even on his worst day—and today was definitely among them—he couldn't deny that waiting tables at Camden's hottest food spot was almost as good as dancing up a storm at the club. The place buzzed, vibrant and frenetic, and four months into the job, it felt as much like home as anything had of late.

And the free ice cream helped with that. Midway through his shift, he took a break and loaded up with a bowl of Hackney-brown biscuit—a devilish mix of chocolate, caramel, and bourbon biscuits—and decamped to the bin yard to smoke a fag and catch some sun before the evening rush. He pulled out his phone and scanned the news website, but with no social media accounts to suck away the minutes, his cracked iPhone held little appeal.

He dropped it on the step beside him and finished up his ice cream, the last of his favourite flavour for a while, a fact that made his heart weep as he scraped the bowl clean. Misfits was famed for its burgers, but Lenny reckoned the ice cream—artisan-made at an East End dairy owned by the same company: Urban Soul—was its true gem. Where else could you get flavours like his beloved Hackney-brown biscuit, and Walthamstow's marmalade cream?

Lenny ate every drop and moved on to the jellybeans he'd stashed in his pocket. Staff got a free burger on every shift, but Lenny stuck to the sweet stuff. Craved it. Let the sugar carry him until it was time to go—

A movement in Lenny's peripheral vision cut his thoughts dead.

He's here.

It was always the same: Lenny glanced around, almost forgetting what he might find, and then the sensation of being watched slammed into him, and drove his stomach to his knees.

He's here.

Lenny stared hard at the vacant building behind the restaurant. The large bay window was now empty, but that didn't matter. It wouldn't be the next time he looked. Never was. His faithful tormentor always liked one last look before he scarpered back to whatever cave he'd crawled from.

This time was no different. Lenny forced himself to blink, holding his eyes shut for ten beats of his stampeding heart. Then he opened them and met the hollow gaze that had become his near-constant companion. Today, their encounter was brief. Another five beats and then the short, pasty man backed away from the window and disappeared into the depths of the empty shop.

And you still didn't take a photo, dickhead.

Damn it. On the restaurant floor such a thing was impossible, but the few times Lenny had found himself face-to-face with his stalker, his phone in his hand, the moment had passed before he'd pressed the button, like he was the one hypnotised by what he was seeing.

The irony was beyond fucking annoying. Lenny stood, the ice cream he'd eaten for dinner curdling in his churning stomach. Reason told him he should be used to this shit by now—ten months after it had first invaded his life—but it hadn't got any easier.

With weighted legs, Lenny trudged back inside and reclaimed his section twenty minutes early. The evening rush filled Misfits to the brim, turning every table ten times over, giving heart to the eclectic restaurant's reputation. But the buzz that had carried Lenny through lunchtime was long gone, replaced by jittery hands and a dry mouth. He made mistakes, took his orders wrong, and forgot the side dishes that earned him a bonus at the end of each month.

Eventually, his shift manager lost patience with him and ended his shift prematurely. For the first time ever, he was the team's weakest link. And despite the humiliation, he couldn't even go home, at least not sober. A bucket of rum and Coke was the only way he could face the dark alleyway that led to his Chalk Farm studio flat.

Lenny took a seat at the bar and drank through the tips he'd managed to make before his day had gone to shit. His fourth Sailor Jerry's was sliding down a treat when Ricky, the barman, set an envelope down in front of him. Lenny tilted his already booze-heavy head to one side. "What's this?"

"Dunno. Tash found it in the staff room with your name on. Figured you'd left it there."

Ricky went back to his work. Lenny stared at the envelope, the unease the rum had dulled reigniting with a vengeance. It was brown—*he* usually left white ones—but the writing was unmistakable. Perfect, like always, curved and script-like. With trepidation roiling in his gut, Lenny drew the envelope towards him. Experience told him he wouldn't find anything pleasant inside, but the masochist in him had to look.

He tore it open. At first glance, it appeared empty, but then a single nail clipping fell onto the bar—clean and neat, with tracings of the blue polish Lenny had worn on his toes until yesterday.

Fuck. Lenny's heart skipped a beat, and he spun around so fast he toppled from his stool, barely righting himself before he crashed to the floor. He scanned the restaurant, studying the yuppies, students, and tourists. There was no sign of a stained anorak and grubby jeans, but that did little to calm the panic fast rising in Lenny's chest.

He kicked his stool away. It clattered into the bar, and Ricky shot him a quizzical glance. His gaze was one Lenny knew well, but as his brain imploded—terror and rum melding in a sickening mix—all Lenny could see was another set of eyes.

He's here.

Lenny stumbled out of the restaurant and into the muggy night air. Every instinct screamed at him to run, but where would he go? His pockets were stuffed with the leaflets the police had given him, but what good were they now?

Despair washed over him. He dropped the leaflets onto a nearby bench and sat down. His back hit the dented metal with a thud that should've rattled his bones, but he felt nothing beyond the hopeless dread he'd lived with for so long. His trip to Kentish Town police station replayed in a loop in his head. *"We need evidence, Mr. Mitchell."* Lenny had some now—but *did* he? What use was a clipping of his own fucking toenail? *There might be fingerprints on the envelope.* But Lenny was too far gone to catch the rationale before it slipped through his fingers. Too drunk, too scared, it didn't matter, because whichever way he turned, he was fucked.

He's never going to stop.

Lenny leaned forward and dropped his head into his hands. The world around him spun. His heart beat an ominous tattoo, and only the rum still swirling in his veins gave him any reprieve.

A car stopped in front of him. A door slammed. Familiar voices echoed in his head, but he didn't look up. Couldn't, even when someone called his name. The bench shifted as someone sat down beside him. Lenny's pulse raced impossibly faster, and he braced himself for *those dirty fucking hands* finally touching his skin.

But they never came. Instead, warm fingers closed around his wrist, and a rough voice he'd heard somewhere before gently spoke his name.

"Lenny, mate? Do you need some help?"

CHAPTER TWO

rep, cook, clean, sleep. Prep, cook, clean, sleep. Rinse and repeat. The process was as natural as breathing, but as Nero Fierro moved from kitchen to kitchen within the Urban Soul empire, no two days were ever the same.

Today—a humid Tuesday morning in mid-July—found him holed up at the Stew Shack, an old pub in Greenwich that had been converted into a stew-and-ale bar, and wondering what the fuck he was going to cook for the evening rush. He studied the shelves in the dry store, half a mind on the pork shoulder and spicy chorizo he'd stashed in the walk-in fridge, the other half on the steamy day brewing outside. Summer at the Stew Shack meant heady, spicy stews cooked over the fire pit in the cobbled garden, a task he enjoyed, even if it did expose him to the curious eyes of the yuppies and hipsters he cooked for. Because that was what you found in Greenwich these days: yuppies, hipsters, and bloody tourists. *Fuck it. Let's blow their heads off.*

Nero grabbed paprika, chillies, and fennel seeds, and chucked them in the prep box under his arm, then went to the fridge and retrieved pork, chorizo, and peppers. He was bashing the shit out of a bulb of garlic when he sensed a presence behind him, felt a tingle on the back of his neck, and heard a chuckle he'd recognise anywhere on earth.

Cass.

Sure enough, Nero spun around and there he was—all lean, mean, six foot of Cass Pearson, Nero's boss and co-owner of the many restaurants Nero cooked in. He was also the closest thing to a best mate Nero had ever had. *First bloke you ever fancied too*—but Nero silenced that devil for today. He didn't see Cass that way anymore . . . at least, not often. Besides, Cass was taken not once, but twice, sharing his life with the two other men Nero happened to work for. *Lucky them.*

Nero turned back to his pestle and mortar. "What the fuck do you want?"

Cass rounded the counter and hopped up on the clean side opposite Nero. "Nice to see you too, mate."

"Yeah, yeah." Nero scowled. It *was* good to see Cass, though his surprise appearance was bound to mean a royal pain in Nero's arse. "What do you want?"

"I've got a job for you."

"Course you 'ave. Let me guess, you want me to go to Dagenham or some shit and set up a vegan cupcake shop?"

"Close. It's a bakery in Vauxhall—artisan, organic sourdough, all that hipster stuff you love."

"This is your idea?"

Cass snorted. "As if. I ain't the ideas man, you know that, but Tom and Jake are busy, so it's up to me to get it off the ground until they come along and change everything."

Sounds about right. Nero finished up the garlic and moved on to hacking up meat with his cleaver. "This what you've been doing with yourself lately? 'Cause I ain't seen you in the kitchen."

"I've been around."

"No, you haven't."

"Miss me?"

Nero turned away, because truth be told he *did* miss Cass, and the years of working long nights side by side seemed a lifetime ago. "What do you need me to do for this wanky bakery?"

Cass chuckled, unfazed as ever by Nero's lack of enthusiasm. "Help me build the kitchen, source the ovens, find a team. Maybe some menu development too?"

"What kind of menu?"

"Artisan sandwich shop by day, jazz café by night."

"Seriously?" Nero rolled his eyes. "Why can't you lot do one thing at a time?"

"Because it don't pay to leave a premises idle at night when it's working anyway. It's gonna be a twenty-four-hour operation once we get the bakery set up. Speaking of which, do you think you could nick some of the sourdough starter from here and brew a new one?"

"You want me to take a bucket of yeast home with me?" Cass's smirk said it all. Nero sighed. "Anything else?"

Cass's expression sobered. "Actually, there is something I wanted to ask you."

Nero had figured as much. Why else would Cass hoof it all the way down to Greenwich for a conversation he could've had over the phone? "Is it something that will piss me off more than babysitting a sourdough starter?"

"Probably. You might like it eventually, though. At least, I hope you will."

"Right. Pass me them onions." Nero retrieved his favourite knife while Cass emptied a bag of onions into his prep box. "Dunno what could be worse than a hipster bakery, unless you're about to suggest I teach school kids how to make sausages again."

Cass laughed. "To be fair, Tom didn't know how cabbage that was when he suggested it. You can't blame him for not knowing you'd never pass a CRB check."

Nero grunted and brought his cleaver down on his board with a brutal *thwack*. That particular incident was the only time he'd been thankful for his epic criminal record. Grubby hands and snotty noses? *Fuck that.* "Go on, then. Spit it out."

"I need you to take someone at Pippa's for me—one of the servers from Misfits."

"Take him?"

"Get him in there to work."

Nero tossed more meat in his pan. "I don't run Pippa's. Why don't you ask Steph? Sure she's got room for him on the bar."

"Actually, I was thinking he could go in the kitchen with you, if you agree to hold the place for a few weeks. Jimbo's got his holiday coming up, so I could use you there anyway."

Nero had been half expecting to spend the coming months at Pippa's, since Jimbo, the incumbent head chef, spent every summer surfing in Hawaii. "I can do that. What kind of background has this kid got? Has he done posh gastropub shit before?"

"He's never been in a kitchen."

Nero set his cleaver down. "Okay, you have my attention."

"I don't need your undivided attention, mate. Just asking you to do me a solid."

"By having some front-of-house knobber in the kitchen with me? Why would you ask me to do that?"

Cass said nothing, which said everything. Nero reclaimed his cleaver and finished hacking up the pork shoulder. "He's not going to be much good to anyone at Pippa's. Why can't Rascal's take him?"

"Is that where you'd go if you wanted to keep your head down?"

So this kid was in trouble? *Great.* But Cass had a point. Rascal's was Urban Soul's rowdy street-food canteen in South Bank—the last place anyone would go for a quiet life. "I suppose he could wash up."

"Or you could train him to commis for you. You said you needed a PA?"

"I was taking the piss," Nero said sourly. "Not asking for numpty to look after."

"So you'll do it?"

"Do I have a choice?"

"You've always got choices, Nero. You know that."

And there it was, the reason Nero could never refuse Cass: because without the opportunity that Urban Soul—that *Cass*—had given him, his choices would've been limited to the arsehole of nothing. "I'm not back at Pippa's till Friday. He could start after the weekend?"

Silence. Again. Nero eyed Cass, taking in the face and form of the friend he knew so well, but would never truly understand. "Fuck's sake, mate. What is it, eh? You want him in sooner? Fine. Say so. You know I'll do whatever you need."

"That's not why I'm asking you. I'm asking you to take him in because I think Pippa's is the safest place for him right now. Living and working there, he can stay indoors the whole time if he wants to."

Take him in ... living and working ... "You want him to live at the flat with me?"

"Yes."

"Why?"

"It's complicated, and I'm still trying to figure it out myself." Cass mussed his already messy hair, worrying it, tugging, in a way that left Nero torn between wanting to stop him and joining in. "All I know at the moment is that he's in trouble and I want to help."

Why? But Nero didn't ask this time. Didn't need to when the memory of Cass scooping him from the kerb outside Feltham YOI had yet to fade, even after all these years. "Another stray, eh?"

"One more can't hurt."

Nero let the idea percolate as he tumbled garlic onto the counter. "Shepherd's Bush isn't a world away from Camden. If he's in trouble there, it'll follow him."

"Would you leave London?"

"You did."

"I moved a twenty-minute train ride north to be with someone who loved me. It's not like that for Lenny. He's got no one, as far as I can tell."

Lenny. Nero turned the name over in his mind and tried to match it with the team he'd last worked with at Misfits, but came up blank. The fiery open kitchen at Misfits was his nemesis, and he kept his eyes down when he was there. Saved apologies later when he'd ripped someone's head off. "Babysitting at Pippa's, Vauxhall. Got it. Anywhere else you want me?"

"I want you everywhere, mate. You know that." Cass winked and slid off the counter, his smirk lightening the pensive air he'd arrived with. "But if you wouldn't mind settling for two for a while, I'd appreciate it."

"Pay rise in the post, is it?"

Cass shrugged. "If you want one. Tom said you told him to shove your promotion where the sun don't shine."

"I told him to stick his posh-twat titles up his arse. Never said I didn't want the dosh."

"You'll need to explain that to him when you see him then, 'cause he's kinda getting the feeling you still don't like him after all these years."

Nero scowled. How many times did he have to explain that he liked Cass's partner—lover—*whatever*—well enough, he just didn't . . . get him? Nah. Fuck that. Jake, Cass's second boyfriend and third link in the trio that ran Urban Soul, was waaay cooler than Tom. Nero loved him like a brother, even if Jake did call him a pirate cunt when his Tourette's was bad. "When do I get my lodger?"

"I'm not sure. I'll call you?"

"Yeah? You've been saying that shit for months, but my phone don't ring."

"Don't be a tart, mate. You could always call me."

True enough, but Nero rarely called anyone. "Guess I'll just sit by the phone, then, eh?"

"Got nothing better to do, I reckon, but Nero?"

"Yeah?"

"Keep Lenny close, if you can. Don't let him be scared."

CHAPTER THREE

Sunday night, Nero came home to find a skinny hood rat asleep on his couch. *Brilliant.* He shut the front door, and the kid jumped awake like a startled hare and slid off the couch in a heap of long, slender limbs.

"Easy, mate." Nero tossed his keys into the bowl and hung his coat on the hook. "You'll have to get used to me coming and going if you're gonna sleep there."

And sleep there, on the couch, he'd have to, 'cause as much as Nero loved Cass, he wasn't giving up his bed for anyone.

Lenny, Nero assumed, got slowly to his feet and then sat back on the couch. "Are you Nero?"

"Yup. Lenny?"

"Yeah."

Nero nodded and went to the kitchen, leaving Lenny to it. He had a sourdough starter to feed, goddamn it. He was adding flour to the bubbly mass when Lenny appeared in the kitchen doorway, platinum hair, as light as Nero's was dark, sticking up in every direction.

"How long have you lived here?"

Nero screwed the cap back onto the starter jar. "In Shepherd's Bush? Or this flat?"

"Um, both, I guess?"

Great. Lenny the Lodger was a nosy fucker. "I've lived here, in the flat, a couple of years. Since Cass stopped using it. Might as well, with Jimbo kipping with his bit of stuff down the road."

"Cass said you were his best friend."

"Did he now?" Nero opened the fridge. "You hungry?"

"Now? It's one o'clock in the morning."

"So? When do you think chefs eat if they're cooking every other arsehole's dinner?"

Lenny shrank back into the doorway, retracing the tentative steps he'd taken into the kitchen. "Oh, um . . . sorry. I hadn't thought of it like that. I'll get out of your way."

He disappeared. Bemused, Nero returned to his fridge rummaging, turning up eggs, potatoes, and a tired onion. A second raid revealed some manchego cheese. He fried up the spuds with the onions and added smoked paprika, then swirled in the eggs, leaving them to cook on a low heat while he chopped up the manchego. After sprinkling the cheese on top and flashing the omelette under the grill, dinner was done; a simple supper that was definitely enough for two.

Fuck's sake. Nero didn't have much of a conscience, but letting even a stranger go hungry was something he just couldn't do. He dished up and carried two plates to the living room, half expecting to find Lenny had gone back to sleep. But the kid was huddled on the couch, a coat bunched around his drawn-up knees.

Nero set the plates on the coffee table. "Ain't you got a duvet?"

"No."

"Why not?"

"Left it at my old place. Didn't want to go back there."

Ah. That was right. The kid was in trouble. Still, Nero was surprised Cass hadn't kitted him out before leaving him to Nero's mercy. "So you've left all your things behind?"

"Didn't have much, to be honest. The flat came furnished, and Cass took my books back to his house." Lenny shifted on the couch, making himself impossibly smaller. "He offered me some sheets and stuff, but I said no. He's done enough for me already."

"Yeah? Cass is like that. Grumpy twat, but he's a fucking old woman deep down—a nutty one, like his nana."

Lenny said nothing. His eyes drifted to the plates on the coffee table before he seemed to remember himself and his gaze returned to the floor. Nero regarded him, taking in his wild, bleached-blond hair and perfect eyebrows. His wide brown eyes and the freckles dusted across his nose. He had a perfect mouth too, curved with a full bottom lip—

Jesus, stop eye-fucking him. You've sworn off the boys, remember?

Nero swallowed. Truth be told, he'd never been *on* the boys, unless a few drunken fumbles with Cass *years* ago counted. There'd been no others he'd wanted enough to hook up with since. How could there be when up until this moment, Cass had been the most beautiful man he'd ever seen?

Whoa. It had been a long time since he'd dwelled on his attraction to Cass, but it didn't take a genius to figure it had been a hero complex. Cass had saved him and given him a life, a career, a purpose, and in return, Nero had fallen a little in love with him. *You sad fuck.* But Nero was over that now. Had been for yonks. Didn't even wank about it—

"Are you okay?"

"Hmm?" Nero returned to the present to find Lenny staring at him, his wide eyes wary. "Er, yeah. I made dinner. Eat up. I'll get you some bed stuff."

He stood abruptly and went to the airing cupboard, pulling out the spare duvet, a blanket, and a couple of pillows. At the back, he found a set of covers that looked like they belonged in a hotel, clearly left over from the days Tom—Cass's first fella—used to stay over.

Nero returned to the living room. Lenny was poking suspiciously at his slice of omelette. "Does this have meat in it?"

"Why?" Nero sat down. "You veggie?"

"Yes. I'm gluten intolerant too, unless it's biscuits. I can eat those."

"Fussy, are ya?"

Lenny snorted. "Nah, mate. Just misunderstood."

Nero absorbed Lenny's brief sass and matched it with his bleached hair, double pierced ears, and the scuffed Doc Martens tucked down by the side of the couch. "There ain't no meat in your supper, no gluten either, so unless you're one of them vegan loonies, you're good to go."

"Vegans aren't loonies. They're saving the world."

"Yeah, yeah." Nero set the pile of bedding on the arm of the couch. "You can have my bed any night I'm not here, but this should do you for now."

"I don't know how long I'm staying."

"Makes two of us. Eat up."

Nero grabbed his plate and sat in the armchair. He dug into his supper, making short work of it until he realised Lenny was frowning at his left hand. *Took him long enough.* Nero did his best to ignore it, but Lenny's attention made the stump of his missing finger throb, like it always did when someone noticed it for the first time, until the new person in his life trained themselves to studiously not look at it, at least until they got drunk and shouted their questions in Nero's face.

Suppressing a sigh, Nero put his plate on the table and toyed with the idea of stomping off to bed before Lenny reached the second stage of his morbid fascination, but something kept him in his seat as Lenny visibly forced himself to look away. And without Lenny's distracting gaze on him, memories, unbidden as always, came to Nero. Noises. Scents. Sensations he couldn't quite decipher. The phantom pain in his missing finger became excruciating as blackness filled his mind, clouding his vision. The cosy flat disappeared, and he was back in that cellar, dank and dark. He could even smell the cable binding his wrists, the rotting vegetables, and the smoke from his tormentor's pipe—tobacco smoke that fast became that of a burning bedsit in Bethnal Green, flashing blue lights, and more shackles on his wrists—

"That was really nice. Thank you."

Nero blinked. "What?"

"Supper. Anyone would think you were a chef."

The barest hint of a smile danced on Lenny's lips. Nero reached deep and forced a tight grin of his own, though given the way the light faded from Lenny's gaze it was apparently far from convincing. "Cass says you need a job. Asked me to train you in the kitchen downstairs. You up for that?"

Lenny shrugged. "Haven't got much choice. Got student loans coming out of my arse."

It was a tale Nero had heard before from the parade of students who floated through Urban Soul's various businesses every summer. "Where did you go to uni?"

"UCL, but I dropped out last year."

"What were you studying?"

"Medicine."

"Seriously?" Nero raised an eyebrow. "You don't look like a doctor."

"I'm not. I quit, remember? Didn't even make the first semester. And now I'm here."

It was on the tip of Nero's tongue to ask how the two things were connected, but he swallowed the question. Whatever had led Lenny to be sitting on his couch was none of his business. "Guess I'll see you in the morning, then."

He stood and took the supper plates to the kitchen, leaving them in the sink to deal with in the morning. It was his intention to head straight to bed, but something drew him back to the living room. He stopped in the doorway as Lenny curled up on the couch, his pale hair shimmering on the dark cushions, and was glad Lenny had buried his face in the back of the sofa. He'd expected to be indifferent to his new flatmate—or at least irritated as fuck by whatever bad habits he was bound to have—but he was oddly intrigued and wondered if Cass had been too. Then again, Cass had a nose for waifs and strays, *and* for trouble.

Nero's missing finger throbbed harder, and he was suddenly profoundly tired, like Lenny's woes had bled out of him and merged with Nero's dormant ghosts, sapping the life from both of them. *Fuck this.* He called time on his brooding and went to bed.

CHAPTER FOUR

Nero woke Lenny at dawn, shaking him far more gently than he ever had anyone else who'd had the misfortune to kip on his couch. "Up with yer. Come on. Got deliveries to put away."

"Wha—?" Lenny sat up, his hair a riot. "What time is it?"

"Time to work." Nero stomped to the kitchen and retrieved his cigarettes. He usually held out until after breakfast to light up, but something told him he'd be waiting awhile for Lenny to get going.

He stepped out onto the fire escape, blowing smoke into the clear morning sky. Below him the city was already awake and buzzing—buses, sirens, tradesmen shouting. In the distance, the fish supplier was idling at a red light. There went Nero's precious few moments of peace.

He stubbed out his half-finished fag. His head told him to go back inside, trudge downstairs, and sign for the three kilos of hake he'd ordered the day before, but he didn't move. For the first time ever he was in no hurry to get to the kitchen, his mind lingering on the blond stray on his couch. *"Keep Lenny close, if you can. Don't let him be scared."* What the fuck did that *mean*?

With a sigh, Nero went back inside. Lenny was in the bathroom, taming his wild hair, dressed only in a pair of jeans tight enough to make Nero's eyes water. He forced himself not to stare and pulled his phone from his pocket, firing a text to Cass. *Still waiting on your call . . .*

He watched the screen a moment, then remembered Cass wasn't downstairs making coffee and grilling bangers for breakfast, and was likely asleep. *Lucky him.* Nero pocketed his phone and knocked on the open bathroom door. "Get a shift on. You got whites?"

"Whites?"

"Chef whites."

"Oh." Lenny turned, revealing a skull tattoo on his chest and a pierced nipple. "I've got some old T-shirts?"

"What?"

"T-shirts," Lenny repeated. "I've got trackies too?"

Nero's mind slowed to a crawl as he stared at Lenny. He had a chest tattoo of his own, an intricate tiger and butterfly design that spanned his sternum, but Lenny's was far smaller and bolder, like a stamp of darkness over his heart, contrasted by his milk-pale skin.

Lenny stepped closer. "I can wear my Docs, though, right? I'm not putting my feet in any manky old boots like Deano's."

"Deano?"

"Kitchen manager at Misfits? Sorry, I thought you knew everyone. Cass told me you're the KM for the whole company."

Nero leaned on the doorframe, absorbing the faint heat from Lenny's body even though he was halfway sure he was imagining it. "Sounds like the kind of crap Tom would say."

"Does it? I've never met Tom."

"Lucky you."

"I heard he's pretty cool."

Cool wasn't a word Nero often associated with Tom Fearnes, though he couldn't deny the man possessed a poise and presence Nero had often envied. *And he shares Cass's bed.*

Lenny raised one of his perfect eyebrows. "You're not a morning person, are you?"

Perspective returned to Nero as abruptly as it had left him. He pushed himself off the doorframe. "I like mornings just fine. Are you ready?"

"Erm, I think so?"

"Good. Get some clothes on and meet me downstairs."

Nero fled the flat, changed into his whites in the staff room, then dashed to the kitchen to meet Fred, the perpetually cheerful fish man, who was waiting at the back door.

"Late today," Fred said. "Been out on the town?"

Nero grunted. "Chance would be a fine thing."

"You should be a fisherman, lad. Be done by lunchtime."

"I'd stink, though, eh? Besides, I don't like rain."

"You young'uns. Don't make 'em like they used to."

Nero signed for his order and bid Fred a good day. As the fish van disappeared, the meat lorry took its place, and so it went on until Nero had accepted four separate deliveries that all needed putting away. First, though, he had to find Lenny some clothes, 'cause there was no way he was spending the day with him wearing *those* jeans.

He left the stacks of boxes and crates and went to the staff changing room. In the spare lockers were various odds and sods of kitchen-wear. A white jacket seemed around Lenny's size, but the only trousers that weren't huge were women's—Debs's, if the pink animal print was anything to go by.

"Oooh, I like those. Are they yours?"

Nero glanced over his shoulder. Lenny stood in the doorway, hair tamed, a faded *Clockwork Orange* T-shirt covering his chest, and a healthy dose of— *Damn, is that eyeliner?* Nero grunted and turned back to the trousers. "They ain't mine. I can give you my spares if you want, but we'll have to tie you in with a cling-film belt."

"Sounds interesting." Lenny ventured into the staff room, his hand brushing Nero's arm as he passed. "And fun, but I'm happy enough in the pink."

He plucked the trousers from Nero's grasp and undid the button on his jeans. Nero backed away. "You're putting them on now?"

"Er . . . yeah? You're wearing yours?"

He had Nero there. "Right. Okay. Um. Here's a jacket for you. Meet me at the kitchen door when you're ready."

For the second time that day, Nero made his escape and retreated to the temporary safety of the kitchen. He began unpacking the vegetable delivery, setting aside what he'd need that day, and storing the rest in the walk-in fridge and dry storeroom. On his return trip, he passed the prep area to find Lenny frowning at a box of globe artichokes.

"What are these?"

"Artichokes."

"That some type of thistle?"

Nero reached carefully around Lenny and plucked an artichoke stem from the box. "What kind of thistles have you been eating?"

"I've never eaten anything that looks like that."

Cass had a talent for lacing his words with an innuendo so subtle Nero was never sure it was really there. Lenny, it seemed, played that particular game even better. Either that or his sinful jeans had gone to Nero's head.

Stop ogling him. What the fuck is wrong with you?

Nero dropped the artichoke and continued on his way. At the back door, he waited for Lenny to join him, sensing his presence behind him like a slow burning fire creeping up on him. "You gonna help me, or what?"

Silence. Nero forced himself to glance around again. Lenny was hovering by the fridge, a frown Nero would be proud of darkening his features. "Can't you just pass me stuff?"

"Pass you stuff?"

Lenny shrugged, all traces of his previous playfulness gone, even with the pink animal-print trousers hugging his slim waist. "I can put it away if you tell me where it goes."

In his head, Nero roared, like he would at any other fucker who didn't do as they were bloody told, but Cass's ominous words resonated, echoed, and despite the odd heat Lenny's presence seemed to stir, Nero felt chilled to the bone. *"Keep Lenny close, if you can. Don't let him be scared."*

Easier said than done when it was plain Lenny wasn't going to venture closer while Nero was at the back door. "Wait there."

Nero stepped over a box of venison and made short work of shoving the stacked deliveries through the door and into the kitchen. "There. How 'bout them apples? Can you work with me now?"

Lenny stared like Nero had grown horns, then a slow smile eclipsed the unsettling fear that had been there. "You're supposed to be a grumpy motherfucker."

"Cass tell you that too?"

"Maybe."

Nero's fingers itched to send Cass another abusive text, but, as per Cass's own kitchen rules, he'd left his phone in the staff room. "I ain't grumpy, just busy. Now you gonna help me, or what?"

Lenny shrugged. "Make me your bitch."

Only if you return the favour.

They packed the deliveries away, working in the companionable silence Nero preferred in the kitchen. The last box was the hake that Fred had brought. "Leave it there." Nero pointed at his bench. "I'll need it in a bit."

"Why? What are you making?"

"*Merluza a la gallega*, but don't worry about that right now. We've got shit to do before we start cooking."

Shit that entailed training Lenny to set up the kitchen, a ritual Nero usually conducted most days—whatever kitchen he was running—in relative solitude, no matter how late he'd been to bed the night before. Not today, though. Today, Lenny trailed behind him, asking a million questions Nero had never thought to ask when he'd followed Cass around this very kitchen too long ago for him to truly remember.

"What's that?" Lenny asked.

"A mixer."

"For cement?"

Nero scowled. "What do you think?"

Lenny peered into the giant mixing bowl. "There's one at Misfits for making the burger buns. It's not as big as this, though."

"This one's not staying here. We don't use it enough. I reckon it'll go to the new place in Vauxhall when it's set up."

"Jake said there'd be something new this year when he came in a few weeks ago."

"You know Jake, eh?"

"I've met him a few times. He asked me to paint the mural on the wall."

"That was you?" Nero pictured the geometric mural painted onto the bare bricks in the main dining area at Misfits. It had appeared overnight a month ago and no one seemed to know how. "Cass wouldn't tell me who did it."

"He doesn't know. Jake asked me not to tell anyone for a while. Said it made it cooler."

"So you told me?"

Lenny winced, mischief dancing in his eyes. "I didn't mean to."

"Your secret's safe with me," Nero said. "Okay, that's all the ovens on. I'm gonna light the grill. Reckon you can remember how to set up the steamers?"

Nero wouldn't have thought badly of Lenny if he couldn't, but Lenny sloped away to complete the task with a nonchalant shrug, and returned a few minutes later with a grin.

"Sorted?"

"Smashed it." Lenny's grin widened. "You'll be out of a job soon."

"That so? All right, then, let's get you prepping. See what you're made of."

Nero retrieved his box of hake and led Lenny to the prep area. "Blue knife and boards for fish prep. There's twenty fillets of hake in this box. They need pin boning with those tweezers, and cutting into three."

"Three?"

"Yeah, three, and they gotta be equal. Don't fuck it up."

"What happens if I do? Does it go in the bin like on the telly?"

Nero snorted. "No, mate. We don't chuck good food in the bin here. If you fuck up, we'll do something else with it, but that doesn't mean you can piss about. Just do as you're told; it ain't hard."

"Fair enough."

Lenny drew the box towards him, effectively turning his back on Nero, so Nero left him to it, ignoring the alien niggle of remorse in his gut. Cass had said to keep him close, not wrap him in cotton wool. Besides, Nero had a kitchen to run.

The rest of the morning was spent prepping and checking the kitchen was ready for the day ahead. Around ten, the rest of the team filtered in—chefs, kitchen porters, front-of-house staff. Lenny kept his head down, doing everything Nero asked of him with no fuckups Nero couldn't fix, and no one seemed to notice him until Debs, the sous chef, appeared at Nero's bench.

"Who's the new kid?"

"Lenny." Nero studied the spring onions he was charring on the grill. "Cass's mate."

Mate might've been pushing it, but it was good enough for Debs. Cass's reputation was fearsome, and *no one* fucked with him.

Debs hovered, though, understandably curious. "Where's he from?"

"Dunno."

"Is he a chef? Don't look like it, holding that knife."

Nero glanced at Lenny, who had moved on from massacring Nero's precious hake to butchering potatoes. "He's training."

"Shall I get him on puds with Spanks then?"

"He's gonna help me."

Debs's eyebrows shot up. "Help you? How's he going to do that if he hasn't got a clue what he's doing?"

"That's my problem, ain't it?"

Debs had never been good with Nero's bark. She backed away, hands raised. "Fair enough. Easy day for me, then. I'll help Jolen."

She drifted to the starters section, giving Lenny a tentative smile on her way. He responded with a friendly wink. Debs blushed. Nero stifled a growl and returned his attention to his work. Debs was a nice girl. If Lenny wanted to—

"Nero?"

"*What?*"

Lenny flinched. "Um . . . I'm done with spuds. Do you want me to wash up or something?"

"What?"

"Wash up," Lenny repeated. "Unless you need me to chop more stuff?"

Sensing Debs's gaze on them, Nero tossed the last of his charred onions into a bowl and chucked them in the blast chiller. "We're done for prep, unless we get a manic Monday. Go get a clean apron and wash your hands. You're staying with me."

Lenny did as he was told. While he was gone, Nero set about cooking breakfast for the team, an Urban Soul tradition, born of the Borough Market sausage sandwiches Cass was famous for, and the company ethos that no one worked a shift hungry.

Nero threw two dozen sausages on the grill. He was dishing up when Lenny returned. Nero thrust a stuffed bap at him. "Get that down yer. Service starts in twenty minutes."

"No, thanks."

"No?" Nero glanced around. The rest of the team had made typically short work of the free food. "On a diet, are you?"

"Very funny. Vegetarian, remember? I'm not putting pig bollocks in my mouth for breakfast, and I don't eat bread."

Lenny's tone was mild, but the niggling guilt Nero had carried all morning returned full force. "Didn't think you were serious about that shit."

"Why not? Not a crime, is it?"

"Erm . . . no?" Though it would be a cold day in hell before someone took Nero's homemade chorizo away from him. "Hang on."

Nero opened the upright fridge by the grill, searching for a gluten-free breakfast no creature had died for, but in a fridge loaded with steaks and chops, it was slim pickings. He grabbed a slab of halloumi cheese. "Go and ask Debs for a couple of field mushrooms."

Lenny sloped down to the starters section and returned with a handful of portobello mushrooms. Nero threw them on the vegetarian end of the grill, along with some sliced halloumi. "You eat green shit?"

Lenny scowled. "Not broccoli."

"Rocket?"

"I s'pose."

Nero grabbed a plate and pulled all the elements together for a breakfast of fat field mushrooms, grilled cheese, and rocket. He softened the blow of the bitter leaves with roasted garlic butter, and handed it over. "That's my best offer. Nosh it or toss it, I don't care. Be ready for service in ten."

"I don't know what that means." Lenny lifted his breakfast to his mouth and took a sinfully big bite. "I mean," he continued around chewing, "I know what noshing and tossing is, but I don't know how to be ready for service."

Noshing and tossing. Nero's brain caught up and heat bloomed in his gut. He snatched his fags from the side. "Don't be a dick. Just be ready."

He strode away, leaving Lenny to his breakfast, and went outside, sparking a smoke. Nearby, a few waitresses were doing the same, but Nero ignored them and stomped to an upturned beer crate in the corner of the yard. Debs and Spanks appeared at the back door, lighting up their own cigarettes, but they knew better than to approach him.

Nero closed his eyes, craving a stiff drink, or a spliff—anything to take the edge off what was fast turning out to be the most bizarrely tense Monday he could remember. Blood pumping, skin tingling, and his teeth worrying his bottom lip, he could barely focus now that he had the time to try. Stress came with the job, but angsting over a fake trainee chef who'd likely be gone by the end of the week? That was a new one, and he'd run out of time to brood on it. He smoked his cigarette down to the butt and tossed it away. It was time to cook.

Back inside, he hit the ground running. Monday was the slowest day of the week, but even a quiet Urban Soul restaurant brought its own brand of mayhem, and the ticket screen logged orders as fast as Nero barked instructions at Lenny. "Two duck, three lamb, and a seabass. Get the plates, I'll tell you what to put on them."

Lenny fetched the plates. Nero laid lamb steaks, sautéed potatoes, and grilled asparagus on three of them. "Pour over the jus and put them on the pass."

"Jus?"

"Gravy. It's here."

Lenny took the jug and carefully poured the sauce over the meat. "Done?"

"Done. Remember how you did it. You'll be plating the next ones on your own."

"What?"

Lenny looked alarmed, but Nero didn't much care. On his watch, chefs learned on the job. "Don't give me them eyes, mate. Concentrate, and put the food on the plates."

Echoing the way Cass had taught him, Nero kept his instructions minimal, a tactic that worked well until the first orders of the hake special came in. The dish was Spanish soul food at its best, and one Nero refused to tart up for Pippa's affluent clientele. No towers of garnish or drizzles of crap, just a sprinkle of parsley and it was done.

And then Lenny got hold of it.

Nero glared at the bowls of chorizo-spiced fish stew Lenny had set on the pass. "What the hell is that?"

"You tell me." Lenny wiped the rim of the fashionably wide bowls—about the only instruction he'd followed. "I don't speak Spanish."

"You don't speak English either, by the looks of it. And what the fuck is going on with that bread?"

"Jenga?" Lenny spread his hands, an impish grin curving his full lips. "You said it was important to make the food appear more intricate than the simple ingredients you put into it."

"When did I say that?"

"I'm paraphrasing. You actually said posh twats would eat pig shit if you garnished it with hipster micro-cress and charged them twenty quid."

That sounded closer to something Nero would say, but it didn't explain the adventure playground Lenny had constructed on Nero's precious hake dish. Orange zest, garlic, and chopped parsley stalks, there was even a nest of delicately shaved fennel roots. And it looked . . . bloody awesome.

"You would've thrown those orange shells out, right?" Lenny said. "The ones you juiced for the sauce? And the parsley stalks?"

Nero growled and turned back to the grill. "Sod it. Send it. And make sure each one going forward is exactly the same."

And so it went on. Lenny's lightly flamboyant touch graced every dish Nero sent his way, and after a while, it began to feel normal.

Halfway through, the floor manager, Steph, came into the kitchen and beckoned Nero away from the grill. "Two things: who's the cutie plating mains? What the hell is he doing to our menu? And why are you letting him?"

"That's three things," Nero snapped. "You gotta problem on the floor?"

"Not at all. I'm just curious. Cass never said anything about changing things up and you don't usually give a shit enough to bother."

The comment stung, but it was nothing Nero hadn't heard from her before, and really, who cared if she thought Nero's simplistic, peasant approach was lazy? She hadn't complained about . . . other things. "Lenny's helping me out for a while. A bit of fresh air to make up for my ambivalence, yeah? Now get out of the kitchen."

Steph scowled and flounced away, clearly knowing better than to argue with Nero when he had a grill full of meat he was itching to get back to. She'd likely moan to Tom about his attitude, but what else was new?

"Did I get you in trouble?" Lenny kept his gaze on the pea shoots he was draping artfully across a ginger beer–glazed pork chop as Nero returned to the grill. "She didn't look happy."

"She's never happy unless she's chewing my ear off. You sending that, or pissing about with it?"

"I'm sending it." Lenny called for service. The plates left the kitchen, and he joined Nero at the grill. "These are the last tables?"

"Till dinner time."

"Smashing." Lenny yawned. "I need a nap."

Nero snorted and laid steaks on the resting tray. "Good luck with that. You've got an hour before I need you back here to prep for dinner."

"Back? Where do you want me to go?"

"Wherever you want. Pub across the road does a cracking sarnie if you don't fancy eating with the riffraff later."

"I don't want to go to the pub."

Lenny snatched the tray of meat and returned to the pass. Nero eyed him, taking in the strain in his slim neck and slight tremor in his fingers as he plated up the final orders. *A pisshead, maybe?* But drunk chefs weren't safe in the kitchen, so Cass would've told Nero that. So what was it that weighed so heavily on Lenny's shoulders?

Nero didn't know why he cared, but he did. More than he'd cared about anything in a long time.

The afternoon passed in a blur of deep-cleaning equipment, prep, and serving up the staff dinner. Service flew by in another haze of Lenny's artistic anarchy, and before Nero knew it, his workday was over.

He left Lenny mopping the floor with Debs and Spanks and retreated to the office to record the wastage and complete the prep list for the following day. His phone buzzed as he was finishing up. He answered it with a grunt. "Bit late, ain't ya? He's been vandalising my plates all bloody night."

Cass chuckled. "You got him in the kitchen, then?"

"Yep. Kept him close. Had him plating on main line."

"He get on okay?"

"Not bad."

"But not great?"

"He ain't much of a cook, but he'll do." Nero absently shut down the wastage spreadsheet. "Might save you some dosh too. He's got a way with the scraps."

"That's good enough for me—" Cass yawned. "I'm glad he's well. He had me worried for a while."

"Yeah? And how's tricks at your end? You sound knackered. Two boys too much nookie after all?"

"Piss off, and no, it ain't that. I'm just tired, man. Swear down, the less I work, the longer I sleep. What's up with that?"

"Dunno. Got plenty for you to do here if you're bored, though."

"Very funny. I need you to come to Vauxhall this week. When are you free?"

Nero looked at the rota on the wall. "Wednesday? I finish at four."

"That's 'cause I'm covering dinner, you doughnut. What about Thursday? You're not in till five, right?"

"Why you askin' if you already know?"

"To give you a chance to duck out if you've got something better to do."

Nero didn't, though he had no real desire to tramp down to Vauxhall, even if it did mean spending time with Cass. "I'm in. What are we doing?"

"Oven planning. Tom found the firm to do it, you and I just need to decide where to put them."

"I don't know fuck all about bakery kitchens."

"You know more than me, and you've helped plan every kitchen we've ever done. I'm can't do this shit without you."

It was sweet of Cass to say, but he could likely do whatever he wanted without Nero's help. "What time do you want me?"

"Anytime, mate, but meet me at the warehouse at half nine."

After giving Nero the address, Cass hung up with another weary yawn. Nero pocketed his phone and pushed back his chair with a yawn of his own. Cass's fatigue had filtered through, and he'd had enough of Pippa's for one day.

And what a day it had been. The lights were off in the kitchen, so Nero bypassed the bar where the staff were sharing a drink, and went upstairs, grabbed his weed tin, and headed straight for the fire escape. In the balmy evening air, he rolled a spliff. He'd kind of promised Cass he wouldn't smoke weed on the fire escape anymore—*Tom* didn't like it—but he didn't care tonight. He lit up and blew herbal smoke to the inky night sky. Adrenaline and coffee were his best friends in the kitchen, but their combined buzz had long worn off by the end of the day, which made him all the more thankful that his bed couldn't be any closer.

The weed buzz kicked in. Nero closed his eyes and let it seep through him, warming him like gentle, creeping lava. A beer would've helped it along, but he'd neglected to snag one in his hurry for weed-laced solitude.

"Nero?"

Or not. Nero opened his eyes. Lenny was hovering by the door, clutching two bottles of beer, and wearing those damn jeans again. "What's up?"

"Nothin'. Brought you a beer. Debs said you drink Estrella."

"Cheers." Nero offered his joint. "Smoke?"

Lenny shook his head. "I don't want to come out."

"Fair enough." Nero stepped closer and claimed his beer, then, against his better judgement, held his spliff to Lenny's lips. "Blow it down your T-shirt or something."

Lenny took a deep drag and blew the smoke through the open door. "I haven't smoked weed in ages. Good job I'm still full from dinner or I'd be munching you out of house and home."

Still full? Nero had cooked summer squash risotto for staff tea—not for Lenny's benefit, of course—but Lenny had only eaten a small bowlful, and Nero'd had to leave the room to stop himself forcing more on him. *Boy's gotta eat.* "Can't eat what ain't there, mate. Think we ate the last of my stash yesterday. Haven't been shopping in yonks."

"Bet you don't have to much, though, right? Living above a restaurant must have its perks."

"Not really. Just means the twats downstairs bang on my door every time they run out of butter."

Lenny giggled, soft and light, like a feather that grazed Nero's soul, and took another drag on the joint. "Don't see how they dare. Everyone seems terrified of you."

"Yeah? Why are they so fucking annoying, then?"

"Aw, come on. You can't find *everyone* irritating."

"Give it a few days. You'll see." Nero brought the joint back to his own mouth. "Speaking of which, you're not on the rota yet 'cause I didn't know you were coming. Any days you can't do?"

Lenny snorted. "Not likely. My schedule's pretty blank."

"Don't spread that around. You'll end up working seven days a week if people figure out you ain't got nothing better to do."

"That's okay. I had fun today."

Bless him. Nero had heard that chestnut before from other rookie chefs who'd worked a couple of easy weekday shifts, only to find them weeping in the bogs by Saturday afternoon. "Leave it with me. I can have a word with Steph if you want some front-of-house shifts?"

"No!" Lenny shook his head. "I can't work out front. I can't . . . Fuck, I just can't, okay?"

"Suit yourself. Don't bother me." But as he said it, Nero realised it wasn't true. The fear in Lenny's previously playful gaze was back, and he didn't like it, and he liked the remorse that came next even less.

Lenny scrubbed a hand down his face. "Shit, I'm sorry. I'm in such a weird place right now, I don't know what's going on in my head."

"You might not figure it out stuck in that kitchen. It's sent far saner blokes than you round the bend."

"I don't mind being nuts. I . . ."

Nero waited, though his gut told him Lenny wouldn't finish the sentence.

"Aren't you going to ask me why I'm here?" Lenny said finally.

"You want to tell me?"

"No."

Nero finished his smoke and dropped it in his empty beer bottle. "Don't really matter, then, does it? Get some sleep, mate. My ugly mug's gonna be the first thing you see for the rest of the week. If fate wants us to talk, we'll talk."

CHAPTER FIVE

ero surveyed the exterior of the old warehouse in Vauxhall. The unit was close to the river, with good views over the water. If the finished bakery could bag some outside seating space, they'd be laughing. Or, at least, Urban Soul would.

He shoved open the rusty door, searching for Cass, who he was due to meet in twenty minutes, though he was almost certain that Cass would be late. Outside of the kitchen, Cass and mornings didn't get on, and Nero prepared himself to face the spooky inside of the derelict old warehouse alone. It didn't bode well that the place was unlocked—

"Morning, mate."

Nero jumped a mile. "You're not Cass."

Jake Thompson, Nero's third boss, grinned. "Nope. Good job too. Could you handle two—*crunchy twats*—of him?"

"Two crunchy twats? Probably not."

Jake's smile widened, reminding Nero that Cass wasn't the only owner of Urban Soul who was devilishly attractive. "Making fun of my tics again?"

"As if. Just don't call me a *pirate cunt*, eh?"

"Dick bag."

"Yeah, yeah." Nero punched Jake's arm. It was good to see him, and Jake's Tourette's aside, their foulmouthed exchange was fairly typical. "Where's Cass?"

"Fast asleep. His snooze button was doing my head in, so I switched it off and left him in bed. I did swipe his kitchen plans, though. Want to take a look?"

"Kitchen plans? Already? This place is a dump."

The warehouse was a shell of dust, rubbish, and broken glass. But it was the Urban Soul way to make something out of nothing, and Nero's curiosity outweighed his cynicism.

He took the plans from Jake and unrolled them on the floor, weighing them down with his phone and wallet. "Pizza ovens? How's that gonna work with a sandwich shop and a jazz café?"

"We scrapped the jazz café. Too poncy, even for Tom. I think the sandwich thing is a dead end too. The markups are too high."

The logic made sense. Sandwiches had to be fat to be good, which meant they were expensive to produce. Pizzas cost fuck all, especially if the dough was made in house, alongside a working bakery. *The mixers could go over there, the workbenches—*

Jake peered over Nero's shoulder. "You look like you're plotting."

"Me? Not really, mate. Just trying to get a feel for the place. I don't know much about pizzas."

"You know a lot about bread making, though, don't you? Cass told me you've worked in a big bakery before?"

Yeah . . . in prison. "I made cut-white loaves for Sunblest, not posh sourdough shit."

Jake clicked and shook his head. "Aw, don't give me that. You've developed all the bread recipes for the company so far, including a dozen sourdoughs, and you did the pizza bar at Rascal's. Cass's plans for this place are right up your street."

Nero couldn't deny that he did enjoy the art of bread making— real bread making, from scratch, with natural yeast and old-fashioned flour. It was an ancient art that was far better for his battered soul than dicing with chargrills and cleavers. Less dangerous for those around him too.

"There'll be a flat upstairs eventually."

"So?" Nero glanced up, half a mind on the Spanish pizzas he'd seen in Stockwell a few years ago. "Who the fuck wants to live in Vauxhall?"

"You, maybe?"

"Kicking me out of Pippa's?"

Jake chuckled. "It's not mine to boot you out of, but I wouldn't worry about that. We just want you to be happy. I know you haven't forgiven us for closing Pink's."

Nero pictured the tiny Covent Garden fish café that had been his pride and joy before a monumental hike in the rent had forced Urban Soul to pull the plug. "True that. And what you done with me since, eh? Got me running around like a fucking headless chicken."

"That's not—*waffle tits*—fair. You're the one who won't commit to anything."

Nero grunted. "You spend way too much time with Tom."

Jake flipped Nero the bird, his dark eyes shining with mirth, and Nero had to look away, unable to stomach the obvious love Jake had for both his partners. He didn't begrudge it, but he didn't get it. *Two soul mates? Seriously?* Cass deserved all the love in the world, but who the hell had time to do it twice?

Stop being a cunt. Just 'cause you're dead inside.

"Cass said you were brewing the sourdough," Jake said.

"Hmm?"

"Sourdough. Cass said you've started it."

Truth be told, it had slipped Nero's mind, and his first jar of bubbling yeast had died a death. "When do you think you'll need it?"

Jake rolled his eyes, and Nero couldn't tell if it was a tic or if Jake had seen straight through him. "The architect is coming next week, the builders at the end of the month. Tom wants it done in six weeks— which means the construction will take eight—so we've basically got three months until D-Day."

Three months was a long lead time for an Urban Soul project; they'd opened the Stew Shack in three weeks. Nero and Cass could handle the kitchen, but the rest? The recruitment? The branding? Nah. "Have you got a name yet?"

"Dude, we've barely got a concept. Cass reckons the food will do the talking, but you'd know that better than me."

Nero snorted. "Why don't he just call it Dolly's? After his nana?"

"'Cause what's dead stays dead."

Jake said it with a smile, but the words did odd things to Nero's gut. If the dead stayed dead, why did they haunt his dreams?

Despite the sunlight flooding in through the large windows, the warehouse grew suddenly dark, the cobwebs and dust suffocating. Nero shoved his tingling hands in his pockets. "I gotta go."

Jake stepped around him and gathered the plans from the gritty floor, passing Nero his wallet and phone. "Already? I was gonna buy you breakfast."

"No, thanks. Got shit to do."

Jake's facial expressions often bore no resemblance to his actual emotions, so it was hard to tell if he was offended, and Nero didn't much care. Jake was a mate, but Nero needed to *go*.

He left Jake in the warehouse and escaped outside, sucking down the muggy summer air until his head was spinning a little less, slowing to the dull carousel he'd lived with for as long as he could remember. *Idiot. Just get the fuck off already.*

If only it were that easy. Nero's phone rang as he crossed the road to the Tube station. He pulled it from his pocket and squinted through the bright sunlight at the screen. Pippa's. *Great.*

He took the call, steeling himself for a barrage of Steph's whinging. "What?"

A giggle-chuckle caught him off guard. "So you *are* always this grumpy?"

Nero stopped walking. "This again? I'm not bloody grumpy."

"Right." Lenny laughed harder. "You looked it this morning."

"Thought you were asleep."

"With you stomping around? Fuck no."

"Sorry."

"No, you're not."

And Nero wasn't. Lenny was on his couch. If he didn't like it, he could kip downstairs in the cellar, because there was *zero* chance of Nero disturbing him there. "What do you want?"

"Twenty fags. I was hoping you could bring me a box back. I'll give you the cash."

"Fine. I'll be half hour or so, though."

"I thought you'd be gone all day?"

"Bad luck." Nero checked his watch. Ten fifteen. He'd been with Jake less than an hour—hardly worth the trip, especially as he'd failed to give Jake much insight into where to place the giant bread ovens. "I won't be in long, if it's any consolation."

"Not really. Can I do anything for you in the flat?"

"Like what?"

"Dunno, washing or something?"

"Nah, mate. You're all right. See you soon."

"Bye, Nero."

Nero hung up and stared at his phone screen, wondering why Lenny's voice twisted his insides so much. He'd started walking again while they'd talked, but he drifted to a stop now, feeling somehow . . . lighter? *What the actual fuck?* Nero was used to trudging through life under a cloud of temper and sarcasm, his only shield between him and a world that had fucked him over more times than he could count, not spinning giddily because of the way a bloke he hardly knew said his name.

Still, the feathery skip in his chest was a welcome change from the usual dark stomp of reality, and Nero let it carry him home to Shepherd's Bush.

Inside Pippa's, he checked that the kitchen team was set up, then went upstairs. At first Lenny was nowhere to be seen, then Nero found him in the bathroom, sitting on the windowsill.

"What are you doing up there?"

"Catching the breeze."

"In here? The window's bigger in the bedroom."

"I wouldn't know, mate. I've never been in your boudoir."

Lenny's grin turned impish. Nero glared and left the room, intending to get straight on with his work, until he remembered the cigarettes in his pocket. *Fuck's sake.*

He went back to the bathroom. Lenny's grin remained, even as Nero tossed the box in his face. "Your eyes flash when you're pissed off."

"I'm not pissed off."

"No? Would hate to see you when you are, then." Lenny slid off the windowsill. "Thanks for the fags."

He slipped past Nero and disappeared into the living room. Nero breathed a strange sigh of relief and loss, but his conflicting emotions were short-lived. Lenny was back in a flash, brandishing a tenner and *still* that goddamned grin. "Thank you."

Nero took the money and stuffed it in his pocket, rummaging around for change. He found a quid and flipped it in Lenny's general direction. "No worries. I'm going downstairs, unless you need anything else?"

"Downstairs? To work? I thought you weren't in till five?"

"I'm not in the kitchen until five. Got plenty of shit to do before then."

"Like what?"

"What do you care?"

For a moment so brief Nero thought he'd imagined it, Lenny scowled, but then it was gone and he smiled again, though his eyes had lost much of their humour. "I was just being polite, mate. Don't mind me."

Lenny left the bathroom. A few seconds later, the door to the fire escape scraped open. Had Lenny ventured outside? If he had, it would be the first time he'd seen the sun since he'd been holed up at Pippa's.

The urge to go and check was strong. Nero pushed it down and left the flat, grabbing his clean whites on his way out.

Downstairs, he changed in the staff room, then trudged to the kitchen, claiming the back corner sequestered for menu development. His meeting with Jake replayed in his head, and lacking the inclination to hoof it across the city to Greenwich to pinch more of their sourdough starter, he got to work brewing a fresh one of his own. Flour, water, a handful of grapes to kick-start the fermentation process—there wasn't much to it, really. Nero mixed it up in a plastic oil drum and took it to the dry store. It would need culling and feeding every day, but for now, he was done.

Next up, he had to figure out what to do with it when it was ready. Urban Soul could dress any building up as some fancy hipster shite, but for it to mean something this time around, they'd need bread, and lots of it. Nero knocked up a rye dough and left it in the fridge to brew overnight. Then he threw together a simple white dough that he could divide and experiment with seeds and flavourings later when it had completed its first rise. He was mixing a batch of soda bread when Steph came to find him. "Heads-up. The boss is here."

Nero turned his back on her. *The boss* was code for the bloke who kept Cass and Jake on the straight and narrow, both at home and at work, and Steph had a penchant for crawling up his arse, all the while running around like God himself had come to call. *Idiot.* Despite Nero's grudging respect for Tom Fearnes, God, he was not.

"Afternoon, Nero."

Nero suppressed a sigh and tossed a glance over his shoulder. "Tom."

"Cheerful as ever, I see."

"I'm all right."

Tom chuckled, deep and low. "Good. That's what I came to find out."

"You came all the way down here to see little old me?"

"Actually, I was passing, but I would come and see you if you needed me to. You know I would."

Nero grunted. "Did someone get you a cuppa?"

Tom ventured closer and waved a mug. "What are you up to here? Is this for the Vauxhall project?"

"Yup. Sourdough won't be ready for a few weeks, but I've got farmhouse dough I can play around with."

"What's this?" Tom pointed to the loaves Nero had shaped during their short exchange.

"Soda bread."

"That's the one that doesn't need to rise before you bake it? The bicarb one?"

Nero nodded.

"And you'll use the sourdough for the pizzas?"

"Some incarnation of it."

"So, a bakery by day, pizza and beer by night . . ." Tom appeared to speak to himself.

Nero rolled his eyes and went back to his work. He'd danced this dance with Tom before. "It needs something else, though, right? You've done the street food and booze crack at Misfits."

"Do you think we can beat burgers and champagne?"

"Champagne is for arseholes."

Tom laughed. "Yeah, yeah. So what do you suggest? The pizza and beer concept works, but you're on point about it needing an extra layer."

"Why are you asking me? I'm just the hired help."

"You're far from the hired help, Nero. You're the backbone of this business."

"Piss off."

Tom sighed. "Suit yourself. I've got to go. Have a think on it and give me a call if you come up with anything good."

"What if I come up with something shit?"

"Call me then too. What you think is shit might be gold."

Tom left. Nero loaded his soda bread into the oven and considered the fact that neither Tom nor Jake had mentioned Lenny. Perhaps they didn't know about him, but that idea didn't sit well. Five years ago, Cass might have kept this from Tom, but things were different now, Cass was different, and the longer Nero thought on it, the more certain he became that Tom and Jake knew all about his bewitching lodger.

"Bewitching"? Enid Blyton now, are you? Nero had no idea, and he was no wiser when Lenny appeared in the kitchen ten minutes before evening service, dressed in his borrowed chef whites.

"What you doing down here?"

Lenny shrugged. "I'm bored. Figured I'd see if you needed a hand."

As it happened, the kitchen was a man down, meaning Nero had to spend the evening on the dessert section, a role he despised. "I don't need a hand, I need a hammer. Gotta spin some sugar."

Lenny frowned, and his perfect brows knotted. Nero looked closer, noting the dark fan of his thick lashes, set off by a subtle smudge of eyeliner. *Is that glitter on his cheeks?* Damn. Aside from his pathetic crush on Cass, Nero had always had a thing for blokes in makeup, and Lenny? Yeah, he was something else.

Not that Nero had a thing for him. No. Definitely not. *You hardly know him, dickhead.*

The order screen above the starter section beeped with the first order of the night. Nero jumped, though he often heard the automated system in his sleep. The kitchen, which had previously been in that odd lull before service—the calm before the storm—surged to life, and after a brief moment took Nero with it.

He turned his back on the counter full of half-finished bread products and beckoned Lenny to follow him. "You wanna help? Come with me. You can show me how to make Nana Dolly's trifle look pretty."

Lenny trailed Nero to the dessert counter. "Who's Nana Dolly?"

"Cass's nan."

"Is she nice?"

"She was. Been dead a few years now."

"Oh." Lenny watched Nero unload ceramic dishes from the upright fridge. "What about her trifle? Is it good?"

Nero shrugged. "If you like that kind of thing. I don't do puds."

"Why are you today?"

"'Cause that's my job, to fill in the gaps." Nero laid the trifles on the counter. "But I got you to help me, right? There's chocolate and shit over there. Do your worst."

Nero left Lenny to it and set about making sense of the rest of the dessert menu. Half an hour passed before he thought to check on Nana Dolly's trifles. Or, at least, Lenny's interpretation of them. "That a trifle or a stand at Chelsea Flower Show?"

Lenny poked out his tongue. "Piss off. You gave me free rein."

True enough, and Lenny had clearly taken his loose words to heart—chocolate, edible flowers, the bundles of spun sugar Nero had butchered earlier, it was all there. Arranged by anyone else, it would've looked like a dog's dinner, but Lenny's light touch had, as usual, produced something magical.

Nero sighed. "Stick them in the fridge and come whisk this meringue for me. It's doing my bloody head in."

Lenny did as he was told and took a balloon whisk to the bowl of egg whites and sugar Nero had been glaring at. Belying his slender wrists, he made short work of producing a cloud of snowy meringue. "What's this going to be?"

"Not sure yet." Nero tossed in corn flour, vanilla, and cider vinegar. "I've got about ten minutes to figure it out, though. Any ideas?"

So far, Lenny had showed little enthusiasm for the eclectic array of food he'd seen at Pippa's, only eating what Nero shoved in front of him, but he studied the bowl of sweet meringue mix with a new light in his eyes. "What's the meringue thing called that's all marshmallowy?"

"Pavlova?"

"Yeah, that's it. Can we make that?"

Cracking out the piping bag was one of Nero's least favourite kitchen tasks, but he couldn't think of a sensible reason to say no. He fetched the kit they needed and piped tiny individual meringues onto lined trays. Ten minutes in the oven and twenty to cool, and his part was done. Then he let Lenny loose with the decoration, a task that kept him occupied for more than an hour.

By then, Nero was distracted with running the rest of the dessert section, only yelling at Lenny when he needed an order of his precious pavlovas. Time slipped away, stolen by a busy dinner service, and it was gone nine when Steph came to the pass to ruin Nero's night.

"A guest wants to speak to you."

"Me? What the fuck for?"

"To tell you how awesome their meal was."

"Let 'em tell Debs. then. She probably cooked it."

Steph smirked. "Actually, they want to tell you how amazing your cheesecake was. Sorry."

Liar. Nero wiped his hands on his apron, then took it off in a halfhearted attempt to appear presentable as Steph disappeared briefly, only to reappear a few seconds later with the guest in tow.

The guest was a sweaty posh dude, half-sloshed and obsessed with touching Nero's arm. Nero shot Steph an irritated glare—*are you fucking kidding me?*—then dug deep for his most amiable smile. It took ten minutes to get rid of him, and even then Nero had to escort him back to his table. *Bellend.*

Nero returned to the kitchen, hoping Lenny hadn't been swamped by orders in his absence. But Lenny was nowhere to be seen when he reached the dessert section, and his pavlovas had gone AWOL too.

Fuck's sake. Nero growled and glared at the stacked screen of orders that had come on while he'd been gone: four tables, each wanting half a dozen desserts. Working through them kept Nero busy, but he couldn't help glancing over his shoulder every time he sensed movement behind him. An oven opened, a fridge slammed, the back door closed—Nero saw and heard it all, but there was no sign of Lenny.

The last order called for three of Lenny's pavlovas. He came up blank on the dessert section, so he called Debs to watch over his baked plums and went to the bigger walk-in units at the back of the kitchen.

He found Lenny in the last one, sitting on a box of lemons, his head in his hands. The tray of pavlovas was safely on the shelf behind him, but something stopped Nero grabbing them and leaving Lenny to whatever freak-out he was clearly having. Ice cream melting on Pippa's achingly trendy gooseberry crumble? Nero didn't give a shit.

He took a seat on a crate of sweet potatoes and nudged Lenny with his elbow. "Whatcha doing in here?"

"Nothin'."

"Uh-huh. Don't look like nothin'. I only hole up in here when I'm hanging out of my arse."

"You don't come to work hungover."

"What makes you think that? You think I'm some kind of saint?"

Lenny didn't deny it. "You love your job."

"I love a skinful too. Don't remember you having one anytime recently, though, so what the fuck are you doing in here?"

"Hiding."

"Standard. From who?"

Lenny shook his head and finally looked up. "I don't even know anymore. That man . . . I thought . . . But it wasn't, but I was in here before I realised, and then . . . shit, I couldn't come out."

It took Nero a few beats to process Lenny's convoluted stammer and match it with what little he knew about him. He was hiding from someone, that much was obvious. A dealer? A pimp? *Nah, he ain't the type*, but what?

Nero had enough demons of his own to keep his questions to himself. He laid a hand on Lenny's chilled arm. "If it's folk coming back-of-house you're worried about, it don't happen often."

"It's not just that. Being here, indoors all the time . . . it sounded like bliss when Cass offered it to me, but it's doing my head in. I can't breathe."

Cell walls Nero would never forget flashed into his mind, as stark and real as they'd ever been. And then the thick, choking smoke that had led him there. He took a deep, shaky breath. "The way I see it, you've got two options: fuck it and go outside anyway, or if you really can't—"

"I *can't*."

"Then you have to live the life you're stuck with. Me and Cass, we'll stand between you and any fucker comes near you, but we can't protect you from the gremlins in your brain. You gotta fight them on your own."

Nero stood, but Lenny's hand closed around his wrist. "Why are you nice to me?"

I have no idea. Nero pulled his arm from Lenny's grasp and retrieved the tray of pavlovas. "'Cause you're good at all the shit I can't be arsed with. See you back on the line."

Nero left Lenny in the fridge and dumped the pavlovas on Debs. Then, ignoring her glare, he stormed out to the bar and called Steph over. "No more guests in the kitchen."

"That bloke earlier was the local MP."

"Don't give a fuck. No one comes in the kitchen."

Steph raised an eyebrow. "We always let guests in the kitchen if they want to talk to the chef. Jimbo likes it."

"He's Australian. He likes people. I ain't, and I don't, so it's banned. Got it?"

He strode away without waiting for a reply. Steph was bound to grass him up to Tom—again—but who cared? Not Nero. Cass would back him on this. Always had, even without Lenny hiding in the fridge.

Nero returned to the dessert section and served up the last few tables. It crossed his mind that Lenny might retreat upstairs, but he was cleaning out the blast chiller when he smelled the curious, sweet scent he'd recognise anywhere. "All right?"

"Yeah." Lenny offered up a watery smile. "What do you need me to do?"

"Take the dirty shit to the pot wash. Clean the fridges down. Don't forget the door seals and the handles."

Lenny nodded and got to work. He didn't seem to want conversation, and that suited Nero just fine. Lenny's demons echoed his own, and he needed the quiet, subdued buzz of a closing-down kitchen to keep him sane. *Fire, smoke, blood. Fire, smoke, blood.*

Stop it.

Nero scrubbed the countertops hard enough to rattle his bones, but phantom pain in his hand remained.

Fuck this.

He abandoned his psychotic cleaning and retreated to the test area to check on his dough experiments. All seemed well. He was poking at a rye base when Lenny came to find him.

"I'm done."

"Good. You having a beer?"

Lenny chewed his bottom lip. "Are you?"

"Nah. Got shit to do."

"Like what?"

Nero gestured to the counter of risen bread dough. "Finding a home for this lot."

"Can't you put it in the fridge?"

"I didn't mean literally." Nero pulled the basic white bread dough towards him. "I've told you about the Vauxhall project?"

"Only that there is one. Not what it is."

"It's a bakery—a proper one—and a pizzeria. This lot is the start of it." Nero gestured at the array of dough on the counter. "There's more in the fridge."

"Wow." Lenny whistled. "I love pizza. Can't eat it anymore, though. Gives me a right bellyache."

"I might have an answer to that. Ever tried spelt?"

"Eh?"

Nero pointed at a nut-coloured dough. "It's not gluten-free, but it's easier to digest if you're . . . what's the word that ain't as bad as allergic?"

"Intolerant?"

"That's it. We've used it before in crackers at Bites."

"The snack company?"

"Yeah."

"Man, I forget how big Urban Soul is."

Nero grinned, and a little pride tickled his gut. He didn't own squat, but he'd helped develop every business to Urban Soul's name, and he couldn't deny he was proud of it.

Nor could he deny the warmth of Lenny's answering smile, or the way it seemed to pierce his soul, *or* his not-so-sudden need for a distraction. He grabbed the bowl of spelt dough and a bag of flour. "Roll yer sleeves up."

An hour or so later found them on the fire escape, drinking beer, smoking weed, and sampling the various spelt pizzas they'd cooked up.

Lenny was perched in the doorway, just his feet outside. "This is so good," he mumbled around a mouthful of red pepper and manchego calzone. "Do you always use Spanish ingredients?"

Nero shrugged, picking at the serrano ham and olive flatbread he'd made for himself. "Not on purpose. I guess I use what's familiar."

"You don't sound very Spanish."

"That's 'cause I was raised in Hackney."

"To Spanish parents?"

"My dad." The bread in Nero's mouth turned to dust. He put his plate down and reached for his beer. "He came over with my grandparents in the sixties."

"Are you close?"

"No. He died when I was seven."

"I'm sorry." Lenny swallowed the last of his supper. "So it was just you and your mum then?"

"Not for long." Nero dropped his empty beer bottle with a clatter and shoved his hands in his pockets.

"Oh." Lenny said nothing more for a long moment, then stood and took a hesitant step towards Nero, right up to the open door. It took an age for him to bring his other foot forward, and Nero's heart ached. He stood too, and wrapped his fingers around Lenny's slender wrist, putting himself between him and the outside world.

"What about you? Are you close to your parents?"

Lenny snorted softly. "No. They had my whole life mapped out for me, but I kinda ruined it when I dropped out of uni, dyed my hair blue, and told them I liked cock."

"'Liked'?"

"Still like, obviously, but either way, they weren't impressed. They moved to Saudi Arabia last year, and I couldn't give a shit."

"Do you have anyone else? Brothers and sisters?"

"Nope."

"Me neither."

"Guess we're both pretty sad, then."

"Speak for yourself, mate. I'm all right." Nero released Lenny's arm, slowly, like he was waking from the kind of dream he never had. "Want another beer?"

"I'll get it."

Lenny disappeared inside. He returned to the doorway a minute later with more beer and a jumbo packet of wine gums.

Nero waved them away, hoping Lenny might venture outside.

He didn't.

Nero rolled another spliff. Combined with the beer, he'd probably had enough, but the night air was warm and addictive, and so was Lenny's company. He watched through heavy eyelids as Lenny polished off his wine gums. "Sweet tooth?"

"Always. It's worse when I'm stoned, though." Lenny screwed up the packet and tossed it lazily over his shoulder, giggling as it ricocheted off the wall.

Nero chuckled. He'd been smoking weed so long he rarely experienced the side effects Lenny was enjoying now. "So, the spelt worked for you?"

"Huh?" Lenny blinked, then nodded as his weed-slowed brain seemed to catch up. "Yeah, I liked it. It was . . . nutty? But not bitter like brown bread is, you know? I hate that shit. My mum was obsessed with it when I was a kid. All my mates had white bread sarnies with plastic ham and Laughing Cow, and I had these hessian doorstops with beetroot in."

Nero laughed again, harder this time, a sensation he barely recognised. "She must've loved you a bit, then. I read somewhere that white bread is killing off the human race."

"Oh, it is. But I didn't give a shit when I was eight, I just wanted to fit in."

"And now?" Nero burned with curiosity. Lenny was like no one else he'd ever met, and he didn't strike Nero as a man who bothered much about conforming.

But the sudden shadows in Lenny's gaze made Nero wish he'd kept his bonehead questions to himself. Even Lenny's whisper-light sigh felt like a punch to the gut.

"I kinda found myself at uni," Lenny said. "All those years I'd wasted with my head in the books, treading the path other people had drawn for me, fell away. I met gay guys, trans guys, lesbians, and I felt . . . home, I guess. Clubbing, dancing, fucking around. No one cared who I was or where I came from. They saw me as I was in the moment—young, gay, and free. It was okay—it was *good*—to be different, you know?"

Nero nodded, though he had little understanding of the world Lenny described. Gay? Not quite. Free? Never. "How close to being a quack did you get?"

"Not very. I sacked it off a few months in."

"To do what?"

"To realise that prancing around, drawing attention to yourself, is as dangerous as killing yourself to fit in."

Lenny's tone was bleak. Nero's head wanted to ask more, but his heart said no. He passed the joint to Lenny, then slid down the wall, gazing out over Shepherd's Bush, mentally ticking off the landmarks that made up the skyline that was often his only companion on nights like these—the bookies, the laundrette, and the dodgy kebab van that parked up every night outside the pub. At 2 a.m. it was winding down, but there was still a crowd of late-night pissheads around it, queuing up for their dose of grease.

The sight sparked a vague idea in Nero's foggy brain. He chased it down, but it was gone before it became anything coherent. His eyelids grew heavier, and his bed called his name. Reluctantly, he forced himself upright, wobbling as the night of booze and biftas caught up with him.

Lenny smiled like a lazy cat. "All right?"

"Yup. I'm gonna sleep. You working tomorrow?"

"You tell me. You're the boss."

"So? I gave you the day off and you worked anyway. You're a fucking loose cannon."

Lenny shrugged. "Guess that means I'm working, then."

"You don't have to."

"I know, but I might as well. Got nothin' else to do. Night, mate."

Lenny stubbed the joint out and drifted away, leaving Nero to murmur his good night to a silhouette that seemed too ethereal to be real.

CHAPTER SIX

ero pried the tongs from Lenny's hand. "Seriously, take a night off."

"I don't want to." Lenny jumped, swiping at the tongs Nero held high above his head. "I'm learning, aren't I? I did all the grilling yesterday, and I didn't hear anyone complaining."

"That ain't the point." Though Lenny was right. He'd run the grill the previous day with the poise of a man who'd been doing it years, not weeks, and the only gripes had been Nero's own as he'd spent the entire service dressing plates with the artistic flair Pippa's guests had come to expect since Lenny's arrival. "You've worked every service since . . . shit, I don't know when."

"So have you."

"No, I haven't."

"Yes, you have, 'cause when you're not in here cooking, you're doing shit for Cass."

Another point to Lenny. Nero was so busy his brain hurt, but he liked it that way. Meant he fell into bed too exhausted to dream, and that was never a bad thing. Besides, he was used to it, more at home on the grill than in his own bed. But Lenny? He was *tired*. Even if he wouldn't admit it.

So why won't he stop? Nero stared into Lenny's bloodshot eyes, and something clicked in his brain. *Busy. Distraction.* How many times had Lenny told him he had nothing better to do? *He won't stop because he can't.*

Nero relinquished the tongs. "Fill yer boots, mate."

He strode away without another word and went straight to the office, thankful to find it empty. Cass's mobile went to voice mail, so he called the big old house in Berkhamsted.

Tom answered. Nero sighed, irritated. "You never answer this phone."

"Nice to hear from you too," Tom said dryly. "Everything okay?"

"Yup. Cass there?"

"He's asleep."

"Asleep?" Nero checked the time. Half past six? Seriously? "What's the matter with him?"

"Nothing, as far as I know. He nodded off earlier, so I left him to it. Is it important? I can wake him up if—"

"Nah, it's fine."

"Is this about Lenny?"

Nero paused. Cass hadn't asked him to keep Lenny from Tom, but that didn't mean much. He might've assumed Nero and Tom wouldn't cross paths—

"Stop fretting, Nero. It's fine. Jake and I know all about him. It was Jake's idea to send him to you."

"It was?"

"Yes. He seemed to think you'd be good for each other."

Nero scowled. "In what way?"

"I have no idea, just like I have no idea why we're having this conversation. Care to enlighten me?"

"I don't know what to do with him."

"In the kitchen?"

Nero spun around in his chair. "I s'pose. I mean, he's smashing it, considering he ain't trained, but it's not enough for him. If he's gonna be with me—er, here for a while, he's gotta have something else to do."

Tom hummed thoughtfully. "I honestly don't know how long he's going to need refuge. I spoke to the police today, but they weren't very cooperative."

Coppers? Fuck's sake. Nero didn't need that shit, but held his tongue, hoping Tom would answer the questions Nero had spared Lenny.

"And I don't blame Lenny for wanting to keep his head down," Tom went on. "Being in his situation, with no support, must be terrifying. Perhaps a distraction . . . an occupation would be helpful . . ."

Tom trailed off, clearly speculating. Nero waited, his brain whirring at a thousand miles an hour. Tom seemed to think Nero knew it all, but it was fast becoming obvious that he knew nothing about the vibrant, frightened man sleeping on his couch. He pictured Lenny on the fire escape a few weeks ago, smoking, drinking, laughing . . . and too afraid to let the moonlight touch his face. Anger surged in Nero's dark heart, and then the unique pain that came with sadness. Whatever had happened—was still happening—to Lenny, there was no doubt in Nero's soul that he didn't deserve it.

Not like you.

"Nero?"

Nero blinked. He'd forgotten about Tom pontificating in the background. "What?"

"I said, what about getting him to work on the art for the Vauxhall project? Cass wants it to be pretty urban and grungy, and I know Lenny's handy with a spray paint can."

"Oh yeah? How'd'ya know that?"

"Because I'm not a bloody idiot. Do you honestly think someone sprays pink paint all over one of my restaurants without me knowing about it?"

Nero didn't have an answer to that. "What are you doing with the walls at Vauxhall? Leaving them bare brick?"

"I'm not sure about the kitchen, but certainly in the dining areas, though they'll need brightening up, which hopefully Lenny can help us with. I like the work he did at Misfits, and I'm interested to see what he can do for us in Vauxhall, if he wants to, at least. You may find he's not feeling particularly creative right now. Keep me posted."

Tom said his good-byes and hung up, leaving Nero to ponder his proposal as he drifted back to the kitchen and floated through service while his thoughts remained elsewhere. It was ten o'clock when Lenny left the grill and came to his side.

"Did I fuck it up?"

"Hmm?" Nero glanced up from drizzling herb oil around a plate of paprika-hot mackerel. "Fuck what up?"

"I don't know, everything? You haven't spoken to me all night."

"What do you want me to say?"

"I don't care, but don't ever say nothing, Nero. Silence is too loud."

Nero's hand wobbled, and shiny green oil dripped over the plate's rim. *Fuck this shit.* He passed Lenny the plate. "Finish that for me, will you?"

Lenny obeyed and called for service, sending the final table of the night while Nero stood with his tongue tied to the roof of his mouth. What was it about Lenny that rendered him so fucking mute?

Lenny wiped his hands on his jacket—an unforgivable habit in anyone else. "Look, I'm sorry, okay? You must be sick of the sight of me. I'll try and stay out of your way a bit more."

"What?"

Lenny shrugged, chewing on his lip. "I'm under your feet all the time, at home, at work. Must be driving you up the wall, especially with me taking over your living room. Got nowhere to go without me in your face, have you?"

Nero couldn't remember ever having so much company, but his usual cravings for peace and quiet had been oddly absent recently. On the rare occasions he and Lenny had been apart, he'd found himself missing the inevitable warmth Lenny stirred in his belly. "Mate, I'm not fed up with you, I'm worried about you."

"Why?"

"A few weeks ago because Cass asked me to be. Now 'cause I give a shit."

"I meant what am I doing to worry you?"

"Oh." *Daft twat.* Nero turned away, gathering trays and utensils to take to the pot wash.

Lenny grabbed his arm, his slender fingers wrapping around Nero's wrist like molten silkworms. "I'm worried about me too. I've never felt like this . . . so out of control. I swear, you're the only thing keeping me sane."

Nero's heart skipped a beat, though the irony of Lenny's statement hit him like a truck. He might be good for Lenny's sanity, but what about his own? What about the bolts of electricity shooting up his arm, charged by Lenny's touch? Or the gut-wrenching desire to take Lenny in his arms and shelter him from every fear that stood between them? "I can't fix what I don't understand."

"Nero—"

"Mate, I'm not asking you to tell me. I just— I want to help, okay? But you can't kill yourself in here twenty-four-seven. It ain't right."

Lenny's teeth dug harder into his bottom lip. "So what do I do? I can't sit up in the flat by myself— I'll go mad."

"I know. I've got some ideas. I can tell you about them later, if you fancy helping me test the sourdoughs?"

Lenny's expression brightened. Over the last few weeks, he'd appeared to become fascinated by the bubbly doughs Nero was brewing for the Vauxhall project, and had taken on the gluten-free starters as his own. "Is the spelt one ready for pizza yet?"

"Maybe. Get cleaned down and we'll take a look."

Midnight found them knocking the air out of huge bowls of spelt dough and rolling it into small, pizza-sized balls.

Lenny groaned as he covered the trays with damp tea towels. "You're such a tease. Do we really have to leave them another twenty-four hours?"

"Yup. That tray over there is gonna go forty-eight. We're fermenting it, remember?"

"Yeah, yeah, letting the natural yeast work and all that crap. It had better be fucking epic when it finally turns into a pizza."

"First one was, wasn't it?"

"Exactly. What makes you think leaving it out for two days is gonna make that heaven on a plate better?"

"You'll see."

Nero didn't have the energy to explain the magic of sourdough to Lenny again. The dough would have to do the talking. He wiped up some stray flour, then pulled his damp bandana from his head. "Beer?"

Of course they had beer. It had become their nightly ritual to round off their workday with a few beers and a smoke. It meant neither one of them was sleeping more than a few hours a night, but Nero's growing fatigue seemed a small price to pay for those quiet moments with Lenny.

They went to the fire escape. Nero rolled up while Lenny cracked open bottles of Estrella and a packet of Fruit Pastilles.

"Where do you get all that sugary shit?" Nero wondered aloud, because it wasn't like Lenny was going out and buying it.

"Steph gets them for me."

"Steph?"

"Yeah, it's only you she hates. She's quite nice really."

"Steph doesn't hate me."

"No? Why are you so horrible to each other, then?"

"Why do you think?"

"Oh." Lenny frowned. "She's your ex?"

Nero snorted. "If shagging her once makes her that important."

"Don't be a cunt. It doesn't suit you."

"No?"

"No." Lenny's troubled frown deepened. "I've gotta say, though, I'm shocked. Steph's pretty fit and all that, but I'd kind of assumed . . ."

"What? What did you assume?"

"I thought you were gay."

"Oh." It was Nero's turn to fall silent as he opened his mouth. Shut it again. "Why did you think that?"

Lenny shrugged. "I don't know. Probably because you're so close to Cass, and you're so unfazed by having me around. Shit, I'm sorry. I feel like a bit of a dick now. That'll teach me to assume, eh?"

"You're not entirely wrong, if it's any consolation."

"You're bi?"

"I s'pose so." Nero had never thought much past the fact that he wished he had Cass's balls when it came to telling the world he liked a bit of cock. "I like both. Women, mainly, I guess. I've never really acted on fancying blokes."

"Never?"

"Well . . ."

Lenny smirked. "It's Cass, isn't it?"

"That obvious?"

"No, it's just the way you talk about him."

Nero nodded slowly. "He's always been with Tom, but years ago, before Jake came along, they weren't . . . what's the word? Monogamous? Yeah, that's it. They loved each other, but still went with other people."

"And Cass went with you?"

"Not exactly." Nero lit the joint, hoping the smoke would hide the heat in his cheeks. "We went out one night, and he finally noticed I could hardly think straight around him. He kissed me—*really* kissed me—then he opened a bottle of whiskey and educated me."

"You didn't fuck him?"

"No! Don't think I'd have had the guts, even if he'd let it get that far. But I'm glad he didn't. He's my best friend. I need him more than I need his dick."

Lenny chewed his lip again, but he didn't seem anxious anymore. "That's cool. It's hard for bi blokes, isn't it? My mate once said it was like choosing between meat and potatoes on your roast dinner."

Nero laughed. "You're veggie."

"So? Wasn't born that way. I choose not to eat meat. You can't choose between men and women, can you?"

"I've never thought about it that hard."

"Then you're lucky. I know bi people who've torn themselves up trying to find their place."

Nero coughed out a lungful of smoke. "If there's one thing I ain't, mate, it's lucky."

Lenny's gaze fell on Nero's damaged hand. His eyes glittered before he averted his gaze. "There's so much about each other we don't know."

"If you say so."

"Back to that, are we?"

"To what?"

Lenny shook his head. "Never mind. You be obtuse if it suits you."

"I don't know what that means."

"Yeah, you do. You're just too used to pushing people away. For what it's worth, though, I'm jealous of Cass."

"Of Cass? Why? 'Cause he's got it all?"

"No, because he got to kiss you."

Words failed Nero. The heat of the humid night air seeped into him, melding with the heady weed smoke, and his legs moved of their own volition until he was right in front of Lenny, gazing down at him, their faces inches apart. "Do you wear makeup every day?"

"Why? Does it freak you out?"

"Not at all. It's . . ."

"What?"

Lenny's stare hardened slightly, like he was steeling himself for rejection, but pushing Lenny away was the last thing on Nero's mind. An invisible cord drew him closer, and he cupped Lenny's soft cheek in his palm. "It's beautiful."

"Yeah?"

"Yeah." Nero sucked in a breath and time seemed to slow as Lenny's lips came up to meet his in a light kiss that was no more than a brush of feathers. His eyes fell closed. What the hell was he doing? As Lenny-centric as his world had become, never once had he pictured them together like this. Why would he have, when Cass had asked him to keep Lenny safe, teach him, and train him?

Not ply him with weed and snog him on the fire escape. But Nero didn't pull back. Couldn't. Because even as the thought crossed his mind, Lenny's arms slid around his waist, tight and strong, holding him in place as Lenny stretched up to claim Nero's lips once more, this time in a brave, searching kiss, the kind of kiss that couldn't be denied.

Or ignored.

Nero backed Lenny into the flat, stumbling, and pushed him into the kitchen counter. He kissed Lenny again, harder than before—harder than he'd kissed Cass all those years ago—and rubbed his cheek against Lenny's, absorbing the sensation of skin that was softer than his own, but rougher than any woman's he'd held in his arms like this.

No. Not like this. He'd never held anyone like this, never breathed someone in so entirely that he didn't know where they ended and he began. This wasn't just a kiss. It couldn't be. Nero shoved his hands into Lenny's silky hair to ground himself. Lenny gasped and dug his nails into Nero's flesh. The sharp pain brought reality crashing down and finally—finally—Nero saw sense and let Lenny go.

You're not what he needs. Nero wheeled backwards, covering his mouth with his hands, like he could push the kiss back in, cage it, lock it up, and throw away the key. *Nothing stays locked up forever*—but Nero blocked that thought too and collided with the fridge, tripping over his feet, like he'd drunk twenty bottles of beer instead of two.

"Nero?"

Nero shook his head. *Don't. Don't say a fuckin' word.* And Lenny didn't. He stood silent and still as Nero stumbled away from him, the darkness descending like an iron curtain and more of a barrier than his bedroom door would ever be, even as he clumsily slammed it and slid down the smooth wood, burying his face in his bent knees.

Fucking idiot.

CHAPTER SEVEN

"**N**ero . . . *Nero*. Wake up? Please?"

Nero woke with a jump, heart racing, his throbbing hand curled into a fist so tight his knuckles screamed with a new pain. But then gentle fingers touched him, prying his hand open to lay a warm palm in his, a palm that carried a current strong enough to clear his blurred vision and reveal Lenny sitting on his bed. His seraphic face was full of apprehensive concern, and set off by a glittering nose stud that had definitely not been there the day before. Unless, of course, Nero was still dreaming and Lenny was about to evaporate into a puff of smoke, leaving in his place the grim, set features that were carved into the darkest part of Nero's soul.

Fuck you.

Nero wrenched his hand from Lenny's and laid it over his stampeding heart. "What are you doing in here?"

"Apologising."

"What for?"

"For jumping you last night. Don't know what got into me."

"What?"

Lenny groaned softly. "Aw, don't make me say it again. I'm embarrassed enough."

He's embarrassed? Nero searched his jumbled mind for any reason that emotion didn't belong to him alone, but found none. "Don't apologise. It was my fault."

"Was it?"

"Yes."

Lenny pursed his lips, marring their beautiful shape. Nero's hand reached out, unbidden, and cupped his chin, his thumb swiping across Lenny's mouth. "Don't do that."

"Do what?"

"Let my shit get to you. I ain't worth it."

"Thanks for the warning, but I haven't got many choices left, so I'm going to hold on to that one if it's all the same to you." Lenny's gaze remained serious for a long moment, then the mischievous gleam returned to his eyes and he poked his tongue out, pushing Nero's thumb away.

The childish gesture broke through the heavy air. Nero reclaimed his hand and scrubbed his face, wondering if he'd woken to a different world, even with the disquiet of some seriously disturbed sleep lingering in his chest. "What time is it?"

"Early. It's still dark."

"Yeah? Why are you up, then?"

"Couldn't sleep." Lenny bounced on the edge of the bed. "Too much sugar."

Nero knew a white lie when he heard one, but let it slide. Lenny's demons were his own. "What are you doing today?"

"Working?"

"No chance." Nero picked up his phone. "You're banned from the kitchen for twenty-four hours."

"But I want to work."

"I know, but I can't let you. It's not safe, especially if you've been up all night." Nero's phone lit up with a reminder that he was due in Vauxhall that morning, and his heart sank. *Really? Today?* "I'm not working downstairs either. I've got shit to do south of the river. You could come with me, if you want?"

Stupid question. Nero didn't want to leave Lenny, but Lenny's expression told him there was zero chance of him leaving the perceived safety of Pippa's. "Will you be okay by yourself?"

Lenny yawned. "Haven't got much choice if you won't let me go downstairs."

"I'm not saying you can't go downstairs. You can go anywhere you want."

"But not to work?"

"Not in the kitchen, no."

"No point me going downstairs, then, is there?"

Nero sighed. He couldn't think of a sensible reason for Lenny to hang around Pippa's kitchen, but the thought of him pacing the flat all day, climbing the walls while his mind got the better of him . . . nah, that wasn't right either. "How about you do something for me?"

"For you?" Lenny's glum expression brightened. "What do you need?"

"Well, it's not me really, it's the business. Tom asked me if you might be interested in helping them design the Vauxhall project."

"The bakery?"

"And the restaurant. He wants it kinda urban, like Misfits?"

Lenny nodded sagely, like people spouted that crap at him all the time. "They won't want it totally like Misfits, though, will they? You guys never open the same restaurant twice. How about a cross between the hipster-concept thing and a proper old-school pizzeria?"

"Er . . . yeah?"

Lenny laughed just as the first strains of sunlight filtered through the curtains. "What does Tom want me to do?"

"No idea. He did mention that mural you sprayed all over Misfits, though."

"Oh." Lenny winced. "Was he hacked off?"

"Not that I could tell." Nero looked around the room for the jeans he'd discarded the night before. "I'm going down Vauxhall this morning. I can take some photos?"

Lenny hummed thoughtfully. "Yeah, that would be good. Even if I sketch something that Tom hates, it'll give me something to do."

"Don't bank on Tom hating stuff. Me and Cass got arseholed once and decided we wanted a falafel cart. I spent all that summer frying chickpeas outside Fabric in Shoreditch."

"Seriously?"

"Yup. Made a fucking fortune too."

"I'll bet. I used to get pumpkin shawarmas from a cart at Euston Square. Couldn't beat it after a night on the lash."

"Anyway . . ." Nero clutched the duvet to himself and swung his legs out of bed.

Lenny blinked. "What?"

Nero shrugged awkwardly. "If I'm going anywhere, you're gonna have to fuck off a minute, 'cause I'm kinda nekkid under here."

"Oh."

Oh. It was a word Lenny uttered a lot, but the blush that accompanied it this time, combined with the bare hint of a smirk, was too much for Nero. Heat coursed through his veins, sudden and violent, and the memory of shoving Lenny into the kitchen invaded his mind. His attraction to men had been dormant so long he'd half convinced himself it had been all about Cass—that no other would do—but his brief, heady encounter with Lenny had blown that theory out of the water. Kissing Lenny, holding him—shit. Lenny needed to leave, *now*, before Nero made a twat of himself again.

Perhaps sensing Nero's impending implosion, Lenny slid from the bed and edged his way to the door, his cheeks flushed. He opened his mouth as though he had something to say, but he turned and fled without another word.

With him gone, Nero flopped back on the bed and stared at the ceiling. Having Lenny in his room was almost as unnerving as kissing him the night before, and Nero couldn't remember the last time anyone had sat on his bed. Still, he was running out of time to chew his own face off about it. London was calling his name.

He dragged himself up and retrieved the clothes he'd tossed around the room the night before. His T-shirt was out of the game, but the jeans would do. He took a quick shower, trimmed his dark beard, and got dressed. Then he ventured out of his room to find Lenny asleep on his feet in the kitchen, mechanically spooning sugar into a mug of tea. The sight stirred something new in Nero, an ache in his heart that overcame the lingering simmer in his blood. "You can sleep in my bed if you want?"

"Hmm?" Lenny glanced up, his eyes red-rimmed and bloodshot.

"While I'm out," Nero said. "Get in my bed and have a kip."

"But you've been nekkid in it."

"Don't bother me, mate. Just offering you a go on my proper pillows." Though Nero couldn't help imagining how he'd feel sliding back into a bed he knew Lenny had slept in. "Might do you some good to get a few hours' shut-eye. Don't know about you, but insomnia sends me mental."

"What about your dreams? Do they bring you back to earth?"

"No, they send me to Hell, but my dreams ain't yours."

"Aren't they?"

"No, so get some sleep. I gotta roll. See you later."

Nero left the flat without looking back, trying not to contemplate just how many conversations with Lenny were destined to end with one of them doing a runner halfway through. He drifted to the underground, which was oddly quiet. He checked his phone: 5:37 a.m. Damn. No wonder it was nearly deserted. It was too early even for the psychotic commuters he usually tried to avoid. Still, it didn't really matter. Nero had keys to the Vauxhall site and needed nothing but himself and a camera to get his shit done.

On-site, he let himself into the warehouse. Work had already begun gutting the place and installing utilities. Nero's job today was to finalise the floor plan for the kitchen, a task that was far easier without anyone hovering over his shoulder.

He moved methodically around the site, closing his eyes from time to time, picturing the kitchen and bakery, and imagining how it would feel with three industrial and two wood-fired ovens blasting heat into the place. Working kitchens were always hot and dangerous, but this one would be something else. Fire, heat, smoke—

Damn it. Nero's mind took a wrong turn, dragging him back to the dream Lenny's touch had chased away. *Shut it down.* Nero tried, but it was no good. Some devils couldn't be tamed.

With shaky hands, he made the last few notes on the kitchen plans, then moved on to the dining floor, an area that usually held little interest for him. But today wasn't just about him. He pulled out his phone and snapped a few pictures for Lenny, being sure to include all the nooks and crannies that would say more about the building than any fancy design ever could. With the interior of the warehouse documented, he drifted outside and studied the tangled mess of rusting metal that was the patio garden. Eventually, it would become some kind of terrace showing off the best of the river, but for now it was a dumping ground for the builders and— *What the fuck is that?*

Nero stomped his way through the small patch of weeds to where a dilapidated vehicle had been abandoned. At first glance, it looked like a miniature bin lorry, but closer inspection revealed it to be a rusty minibus—a 1956 Albion Nimbus, the same model Nero's long-dead maternal grandfather had driven in the sixties. The bus was battered, the interior utterly ruined, but it still had four wheels, which was a bonus as far as discarded vehicles in London went.

Pizzas forgotten, Nero forced the underfloor panel open, taking note that, albeit eroded as fuck, the engine was mostly intact. Some TLC would get it running, if anyone cared enough to bother. He checked underneath and found more rust, but instead of the lost cause a saner person would see, he saw potential, and a faint lick of excitement tickled his belly. He hadn't had his hands on a good engine since he'd restored a few bits on the vintage fire engine that had pride of place in Misfits, and that had been a year ago.

Nero snapped a few pictures and then reluctantly tore himself away. Time was getting on and an itch in his soul he couldn't quite describe was calling him back to Shepherd's Bush.

He left the warehouse behind, noting that it had filled up with builders and tradesman while he'd been engrossed in the abandoned bus. Not that the workman seemed to be up to much. Most of them were eating bacon butties from the dodgy stall across the road. The sight—and smell—of it took Nero back to the conversation he'd had with Lenny about late-night street food. The Vauxhall project needed an extra layer, and if the minibus could be saved, the harebrained scheme percolating in Nero's mind—

His phone rang in his hand. He looked at the screen. It was Cass's number, but that meant nothing these days.

Sure enough, it was Jake. "Hey. How's tricks?"

"Can't complain. Who'd fuckin' listen?"

Jake chuckled. "You're even more cockney than Cass."

"I try. What can I do for you?"

A rumble of thunder shook the air as Jake rattled off a series of tics. Nero squinted suspiciously at the sky. He'd heard rumours of an impending summer storm, and he didn't fancy getting dicked on by the duke of Spain.

"Anyway," Jake said, "I was calling to see how you got on. Sorry we've left you to it with the kitchen plans. It's been crazy busy at this end. We've hired a master baker, though, if it's any consolation."

Nero grunted. "Good. I ain't working twenty-four-seven, even for you."

"As if we'd ever ask you to. Besides, we know you're a night owl, so we figured you'd be happier running the restaurant."

Running anything got on Nero's tits, but he couldn't deny he was enjoying developing the pizza menu. Bread, fresh vegetables, and artisan cheese; it was the kind of peasant cooking he enjoyed most. "Who's the baker dude? Do we know him?"

"It's a woman, actually, a mate of Gloria's from Bristol. You'll meet her soon enough. Try not to shag her and piss her off straightaway, will ya?"

"Fuck off." Nero glared at no one in particular and lit up a smoke just as the first fat drops of rain began to fall. "I don't do that."

"Steph says different."

Nero sighed. "Fuck Steph."

"Yeah, yeah—" Jake abruptly hung up before Nero could tell him about the bus. Nero waited a moment—Jake's Tourette's often made him do weird shit with his phone—but he didn't call back, so Nero pocketed his own phone and ducked his way to the Tube station just as the heavens opened in earnest.

He'd made it to Earl's Court when an electrical fault closed the line. *Brilliant.* Nero trudged above ground to meet the rain again. The buses were packed and running late, and after stopping at the shops to buy something to make the fridge less bare, it was gone noon by the time he let himself into the flat. And it felt like midnight. *That's what you get for three hours' sleep, dickhead.*

Nero shut the front door behind him and went to the kitchen. He loaded the fridge with eggs, cheese, and green vegetables, and chucked a loaf of bread on the counter, noting that there was no sign that Lenny had bothered to feed himself. *Fucking typical.* The bloke didn't need a bodyguard; he needed a mother. *Not yours, though, right?*

Fuck no. Swallowing the bitter taste in his mouth, Nero went to the bedroom, passing through the living room on his way, but despite the empty couch and his parting words to Lenny that morning, the sight of Lenny stretched out, fast asleep, on the very edge of his bed stopped him short. With the storm still darkening the sky outside, a shadow was cast over Lenny's face, and Nero had never seen anything so hauntingly beautiful.

He sucked in a shaky breath and took a step forward, Lenny's kiss suddenly back on his lips like it had never been gone, but he froze before he could take a second step. Lenny was so tired . . . vulnerable, and frightened of something Nero couldn't see. Drunken kissing be damned, Nero wasn't what Lenny needed right now.

Like he'd heard the conflict in Nero's frazzled brain, Lenny stirred, his arms reaching out. "Nero?"

Nero crossed the room in two strides and grasped Lenny's outstretched hands. "I'm here."

Lenny's eyes flew open. For a brief, heart-stopping moment, they were so full of fear Nero couldn't breathe, but then Lenny focused, smiled, and the sun came out. "Is it my turn to be all sleepy and cute?"

"Cute?"

Lenny's hazy grin widened. "You're adorable when you wake up."

Nero scowled. "I'm not cute."

"Not often, but not never."

"You do talk some cobblers, mate. Sorry for waking you up, though. Didn't mean to."

"It's okay." Lenny released Nero's hands and yawned. "'Bout time I got up, eh?"

"If you say so." Nero mourned the loss of Lenny's fingers around his, and he got the feeling he'd miss Lenny's presence in his bed even more. "Do you need anything? Cuppa? Breakie?"

"Nah, just give me something to do, man."

"Suit yourself." Nero left the room briefly and fetched his folder of paperwork for the Vauxhall project. "I got the photos too."

He passed Lenny his phone, and watched, fascinated, as Lenny drank it all in, muttering to himself, and doodling over Nero's carefully scrawled notes. "This place has potential to be really fucking cool."

Nero rolled his eyes. How many times had he heard a variant of that sentence over the years? *Too many.* "The big bosses are pretty open-minded when it comes to tarting these places up. Don't be shy."

"I'm not shy, mate. Trust me." Lenny shot Nero a devilish grin, then went back to his scribbling and muttering.

Nero took that, and the heat in his cheeks, as his cue to piss off. He stood and turned away.

Lenny's hand around his wrist stayed him. "Where are you going?"

"Er, downstairs?"

"Thought you were off today?"

"I am, mostly. I've got some admin to do—food orders and stock checks."

Lenny let go. "Fair enough. Guess I'll get on with this, then."

Wondering what Lenny would've had in mind otherwise was enough to drive Nero from the room without further comment. He went to the office and got on with his work. Admin was a part of his job he detested, but today he welcomed the distraction of the flashy computer he'd often threatened to smash to bits with his meat mallet. Even the spreadsheets failed to irritate him as much as they normally did.

"Shit, sorry. Didn't know you were in here."

"No?" Nero glanced over his shoulder at Steph. Somehow he'd missed her opening the office door. "My ugly mug not give it away?"

"Can't see through walls, can I? Besides, I can usually hear you growling from upstairs if you're on the computer."

She had him there. He went back to his work as she opened and shut filing cabinets, until the silence—which he normally relished—got under his skin. "So, you all right, then?"

"What?"

Nero closed the stock spreadsheet and turned around. "What's the matter with you?"

Steph stared at Nero like he'd crapped in her handbag and sung her a lullaby. "What's the matter with *me*? You're the one being weird."

"Whatever." Nero spun back to the computer screen.

Steph said nothing for a while until she appeared at Nero's side with a coffee and perched on the desk. "Where's Lenny?"

Nero accepted the coffee and took a sip. "Lenny?"

"Yeah. You two are joined at the hip. It's kinda freaky to see you without him."

"Piss off. He's only been here a few weeks."

"Uh-huh, and you're thick as thieves."

"So?" Nero carefully scanned his food order one more time before he sent it off. "What do you care who I hang out with?"

Steph snorted. "I'm just making conversation. You know, that thing you've not bothered to do for the last six months?"

"Has it been that long?"

"Do you have to be such a wanker?" Steph slid off the desk. "Lenny keeps telling me how nice you are to him. If only he knew."

"I'm not a wanker to you. I just can't be arsed with you getting on my case all the time."

"Getting on your case about what? Do you think I'm in love with you or something? Jesus, Nero. It was one shag. I don't want to bloody marry you."

"What the fuck are you talking about?"

Rant apparently over, Steph flushed. "Never mind. Can't we forget that night happened and go back to being friends?"

Nero couldn't remember him and Steph ever truly being friends, even before they'd drunk a bottle of tequila and shared a clumsy shag, but for once turning away from someone—away from Steph—didn't feel like the right thing to do. He held out his fist. "Deal. Now . . . tell me what else Lenny said about me."

A few hours later, Nero grabbed a carton of posh hipster fruit juice from the bar and headed upstairs. Lenny was still on the bed, but he'd migrated from the edge to sprawling out in the centre, Nero's precious notes spread out around him, along with a healthy pile of balled-up paper.

"That had better not be my shit you've screwed up."

Lenny spared him an absent glance, apparently engrossed in whatever he was doing with a sketch pad and pencil. "It's not. I wouldn't screw up anything of yours. You have gorgeous handwriting."

"My chicken scratch?" Nero leaned on the doorframe. "Can't say anyone's ever said that to me before."

"Well, they should've done. Come here."

Nero pushed himself upright and ventured farther into the room. Lenny tapped his finger on a page of Nero's notes. "Your letters are small, but you space out your words. That means you're meticulous and focused, but you like your own space . . . being crowded freaks you out."

"I ain't scared of crowds, mate."

"That's not what I said. Crowded and crowds aren't the same thing. I've seen you in the kitchen. You're cool as fuck until someone steps into your zone."

"My zone? Where do you come up with this crap?"

"I'm not done yet." Lenny drew a light circle around a sentence Nero had written about gas-pipe placement. "See these big capital letters? That means you're generous, but the grooves you've carved into the page means you're a little uptight, that your emotions are pent up inside you. What's your signature like? I bet it's illegible."

Nero scowled. "You're the fucking doctor."

"No, I'm not, and if you look at my handwriting, you'll see why." Lenny held up his own page of notes, all printed in perfectly formed—and legible—cursive script.

"You write pretty."

Lenny laughed. "I dance pretty too."

Nero tried to smile, but humour was hard to find when Lenny hadn't left Pippa's since he'd arrived, let alone danced his beautiful heart out. "I'm going to make some dinner. You hungry?"

"Not really."

"Tough. You're eating."

Nero left Lenny to his witchcraft and went to the kitchen. His hand itched for his cleaver, craving the satisfaction of bashing the crap out of a big joint of meat, but he picked a small paring knife instead and set about chopping the mountain of vitamins he was planning on force-feeding to Lenny. Making another omelette felt like a cop-out, so he whizzed up some soup and made cheese toasties to have on the side.

Nero took supper into the living room, then went to the bedroom and scooped up Lenny, pencil and all, from the bed before he could protest.

"What the—" Lenny smacked Nero halfheartedly on the back. "Nero! Put me down."

"Okay." Nero deposited Lenny on the couch and handed him a bowl of soup. "Eat."

Lenny took it with a resigned sigh. "Do I at least get a spoon?"

"I reckon I can stretch to that."

Nero fetched spoons from the kitchen. Lenny took his and patted the sofa beside him. "I want company too."

As if Nero had any intention of being elsewhere for the rest of the night. He claimed the spot next to Lenny and his own bowl of soup. "How's the design work going?"

"No idea. You dragged me away from it, remember?" Lenny glared briefly before he took a spoonful of his dinner and his expression brightened. "How do you do that?"

"What?"

"Make a bowl of swamp shit taste so amazing?"

"It ain't hard to boil vegetables, mate."

"Speak for yourself." Lenny had another bite. "Anyway, I've got some ideas for the dining area. How do the bigwigs feel about street art?"

Nero shrugged. "Do hipsters like it?"

"Hipster, millennials . . . anyone trying to be cooler than they really are."

"That'll do. What you got in mind?"

"Colour, mainly, lots of it, but I haven't come up with anything distinct yet. Urban Soul implies by its very name that the business has an emotional, and tangible, connection to something besides the food. I need to find that connection and paint it."

Nero didn't know quite what to say to that. Besides, his recent run of late nights and too much beer had caught up with him, and if Lenny didn't mind sharing the living room for a while, Nero didn't plan on moving—or thinking—for the rest of the evening.

Shame Lenny had other ideas; he'd disappeared while Nero had been lost in thought. He was back quick enough, though, clutching a pile of sketches. "Your silence is scaring me. I think you need to see it. I haven't come up with the main element yet, but I've got some basic ideas for the dining room."

Nero sighed. "Pass 'em over."

Lenny bit his lip and relinquished the sketches. Nero flipped through them, growing steadily more impressed with each one. "I like this. I kinda figured you'd go for the obvious urban-warehouse theme and try to make it Mediterranean with some shit tablecloths."

"Seriously?" Lenny pouted. "You think I'm that shortsighted?"

"Er, no?"

Lenny punched Nero's arm—*hard*—and attempted to prise the sketches from Nero. "That faux-warehouse shit with all the exposed pipework has been done to death, and if you must know, I thought trying to paint Vauxhall, of all places, as Little bloody Italy would be totally fucking ridiculous, especially as you've yet to mention anyone involved who's actually Italian."

It was the most Nero had ever heard Lenny say in one breath. "They have pizza in Spain too, you know, and Turkey. It ain't just an Italian thing."

"Whatever. They still shouldn't try and make it something it clearly isn't."

With convictions like that, it was hard to believe Lenny hadn't been working for Urban Soul from the beginning. Nero probably should've said as much, but didn't, because a breath of wind from the open window fluttered through Lenny's bundle of sketches and revealed the last few. "Jesus. Is that the bus?"

"Yup. You don't strike me as someone who takes pictures of stuff for fun, so I assumed you wanted me to draw it."

Lenny was more right than he knew, and the fact that he had coloured the dilapidated minibus in bright, Ninja Turtle green made Nero's day.

"You're doing that thing again."

Nero studied Lenny's last sketch. "What thing?"

"The thing where you grin like a maniac, and I can't work out if you're about to strangle me."

Lenny's tone was uncertain enough to tear Nero's stare from the minibus, but the emotion he found in Lenny's eyes wasn't one he'd seen before, and it masked the impact of Lenny's unwitting hammer blow. "You think I'd hurt you?"

"Anyone can hurt you, Nero."

Ain't that the truth. But Nero's own bitter cynicism was likely the last thing Lenny needed to hear. He turned back to the bus sketches. "You know, Tom hates green. He never allows it in a restaurant, but if we can put a pizza oven in this bus and make it pay, he might just let us get away with it."

"A pizza oven?" Lenny leaned forward, his unnerving frown all but gone. "I just played around with the outside, thought they could maybe sell it. I didn't think of turning it into one of those food trucks. Do you really think they can?"

"Maybe." Nero tapped the sketch. "I can probably fix up the engine if the bosses spot a bit of dosh, but they'll do the rest—the design, the name, the concept. I'm crap at that stuff."

"No, you're not."

"Yes, I am."

Lenny scowled. "You're so down on yourself."

"Nah, I know my limits."

Lenny looked as though he wanted to say more, but Nero yawned hard enough to crack his jaw, and Lenny took it as his cue to snatch his sketches back. "Enough work. You're knackered."

Nero couldn't deny it, but before they shut business talk down completely, a reckless thought overcame him, spilling out before he could check it. "Do you want to see the site? And the bus? We could get a cab, and Cass could come too. We wouldn't let anything happen to you, I promise. We could even go at night—"

"Nero, I can't."

Of course he couldn't. How could he, when he'd been terrified of the outside world for as long as Nero had known him? *And you thought a trip to a shitty building site would change that?* Guilt and stupidity boiled in Nero's blood, obliterating the inevitable warmth he carried when Lenny was around. *I'm sorry.* But he didn't say it aloud. Couldn't. The shame in Lenny's eyes was too much.

Nero gathered the dirty bowls and plates and retreated to the kitchen. The urge to roll a joint and smoke himself into oblivion was strong, but he settled for a fag instead and stood on the fire escape, watching the last strains of red sunlight as they melted away. Steph had told him earlier that he'd been different since Lenny had arrived—calmer, mellower. Was that true? As Nero's skin itched and his heart pounded, he doubted it. And what the fuck did Steph know? It wasn't like she could see the precipice of madness Nero walked along each day.

Nausea churned in Nero's belly. He took a deep drag on his smoke and leaned on the railing, bowing his head as night swallowed the city.

Despite the bright streetlights, the darkness was all-consuming, and Nero wondered if it would ever end, or if he'd one day have to help it along.

"Nero?"

He didn't look up. Couldn't take the sight of Lenny hovering in the doorway. "Yeah?"

"Have you got Netflix?"

"No, I haven't got fucking Netflix. Have you?"

"What do you think?"

Nero sighed and briefly closed his eyes, and then he raised his head and saw that Lenny hadn't even made it as far as the open door. "Come outside."

"Nero—"

"Come outside."

"*No.*"

"Fuck this." Nero pushed off the railing and strode inside. He grasped Lenny's arms and yanked him to the door. "Look around. No one can see us unless they're in a helicopter or some shit. There ain't nothing to be scared of up here."

Lenny squirmed, fighting Nero's hold on him, his strength belying his slender frame. "Let me go."

"No."

"*Nero.*"

The panic in Lenny's eyes tore Nero in two, but he held firm. "I'm not going to force you outside, but I want you to try, just once, and soon, before these four walls send you too far round the bend to come back."

Nero released Lenny and returned to the railing. The rational minority in his brain was mortified, but he couldn't bring himself to turn and see the fears he'd made his own so long ago staring back at him. He lit another smoke and took a drag harsh enough to make another man choke, but not Nero. A sky of thick, suffocating smoke had set him free, even if he'd had to wait five years to truly know what that meant. Old ghosts could haunt him all they liked, they were still fucking dead, right?

Warm fingers closed around Nero's wrist. Despite his certainty that it couldn't be Lenny, his heart drove him to lean into the touch, and then, as Lenny trembled, to open his arms and hold Lenny tight against him like he should've done weeks ago.

Shivering, Lenny pressed his face against Nero's chest. He mumbled something. Nero held him closer, absorbing the sweet smell of Lenny's hair. "What's that?"

Lenny shook his head, so Nero let him be and gazed out over London. For a while, he was lost in the heady combination of Shepherd's Bush bustling below and the heat of Lenny's terrified embrace. It was some time before he realised Lenny's grip on him had slackened and they were watching the city together. "It's safe up here, I promise."

"Yeah, I see that now." Lenny turned so his cheek rested over Nero's beating heart. "It's just . . . it's hard, you know? I believed you when you said it, I just couldn't bring myself to risk it. I've been wrong so many times."

"I've been wrong a lot too. Sometimes it's easier to accept it, eh? Let the shit wash over you?"

"Something like that."

Nero hummed a lazy reply. Having Lenny in his arms was incredible, but he already dreaded how he'd feel when he had to let go.

Perhaps sensing his thoughts, Lenny sighed. "I wish we could stay up here forever."

Me too. "Bloody starve, though, wouldn't we?"

Lenny chuckled. "You would. I don't think you've ever let anyone go hungry."

"Very funny." Though Lenny's words reminded Nero of the custard tarts he'd stashed in the fridge. "I reckon Cass might've left one of those Fire Stick whatsits in the bedroom if you wanna go inside now?"

Lenny nodded slowly, but he didn't move. "Nero?"

"Yeah?"

"Before we go in, can I tell you why I'm here?"

CHAPTER EIGHT

ero dashed inside and grabbed the custard tarts from the fridge. Leaving Lenny, even for a moment, felt like the end of the world, but if Lenny's drooping eyes meant he was anywhere near as tired as Nero, they both needed some sugar.

Back on the fire escape, Lenny hadn't moved from where Nero had left him, his gaze still trained on the horizon. Nero handed him a custard tart. Lenny frowned. "What's this?"

"Custard tart. It's good for your soul."

"Not my pancreas though, I'll bet, or my belly with all that scrummy pastry."

"Maybe. I don't know shit about stuff like that."

"Tell me something interesting about custard tarts, then. You always know where your food comes from."

Nero rolled his eyes. Was it his fault his nana had never let him eat a bite without lecturing him about the old country? "Custard tarts used to be made by nuns because winemakers gave them the egg yolks for free."

"Why?"

"Because they used the whites to clarify their red wine and sherry."

Lenny smirked around a mouthful of pastry. "You never disappoint."

"Give it time."

Lenny's humour faded. Nero pointed at the wall. "Wanna sit?"

"Why not?" Lenny let Nero guide him to the wall, and they slid down, their backs against the warm concrete, legs stretched out. "Got any more of those tarts?"

Nero relinquished the bakery bag. Lenny snagged one. "Don't let me eat them all. My poor guts can't handle the wheat."

"You stalling?"

Lenny shrugged. "A little, though I don't know why. Cass has told you everything anyway, right?"

"Nope."

"Really? You're his best friend."

"So? Don't mean we tell each other shit."

A faint smile threatened the downward turn of Lenny's lips. "You're such a bloke."

"If you say so."

"You say that a lot. It's like you don't have an opinion of yourself."

Nero grunted. "This what you wanna do? Dissect my personality?"

Lenny sighed. "I guess not. Okay. So . . . what did Cass tell you about me if he didn't tell you everything?"

"He told me you needed help."

"And?"

Nero shrugged. "That was about it. He said you needed a bolt-hole and job, then Tom mentioned the coppers were being dick bags. I don't know how important the details are, but if you being scared as shit of the outside world is anything to go by, I'd say you were hiding from something or someone, like you said before."

"When did I say that?"

"When you took up residence in the fridge."

"Oh."

Oh, indeed. Nero sucked in a breath. "Are you in trouble with the old bill?"

"The police?" Lenny laughed humourlessly. "I wish they were that interested."

Nero's lip curled up before he caught the instinctive snarl in its tracks. This wasn't about him. "Who you running from, then?"

"I don't know."

"You don't know?"

Lenny shook his head. "I can picture every line and blemish on his face, smell him, feel his eyes on me, but I've got no idea who he is."

It took a moment for the words to sink in, for Nero's mind to piece it all together. *Hitman?* Nah, too far-fetched, but the alternative idea rattling his brain felt just as bad, perhaps worse. "Are we talking about a fucking stalker or some shit?"

Lenny blanched, and with a dose of stomach-churning horror, Nero knew it was true.

"Fuck." He swallowed and imagined the terror he'd seen so often in Lenny's hypnotic gaze. "How bad?"

"Bad enough to drive me from Croydon to Camden, to squatting on your couch like a sparkly hobo." Again, there was no humour in Lenny's bleak tone. He looked down at his hands and twisted his fingers in a cruel tangle. "He's everywhere, Nero. He'll find me soon enough. He always does."

"How long?"

"What?"

"How long has this been going on?"

"A year, give or take. The worst of it started last summer when I was working at Shades in Brent Cross."

Nero nodded. The gay dance club was—thanks to some rowdy staff parties—one he knew reasonably well. "I've been there a few times. You worked the bar?"

"Nah, I was a podium dancer."

Nero pictured the colourful dancers who lit up that particular club with their wild routines and flamboyant clothes—or lack of clothes, depending on the dancer—and tried to marry them with the Lenny who had pushed himself so hard against the brick wall behind him that he had to be scraping skin off his spine. It was tough, but Nero's gut told him there was far more to Lenny than he'd seen so far. "Keep talking."

Lenny crumbled a half-eaten custard tart between his fingers, showering the fire escape with pastry flakes. "I don't know where to start, really. I guess it should be the first time I saw him, but that feels weird because it was a while after that before I realised something was wrong."

"Has he hurt you?" Nero's palms itched, his heart, as ever, making a bid to escape through his broken hands.

Lenny shook his head. "He's never touched me, never got close enough, but that makes it worse. I can't explain it, but I'd honestly rather he kicked the shit out of me than lurked in the shadows."

The logic made an odd kind of sense to Nero. How often had he wished his finger was still attached to its stump so he could twist it off all over again? "So he harassed you at the club?"

"Yeah, in the beginning... little things like buying me drinks and waiting outside for me after work. It was nothing I couldn't handle, but then I started seeing him other places too, like the shop by my flat, the pub, even the lobby of my building. I thought that we just lived in the same place, but then the letters came."

"Letters?"

Lenny nodded. "Yup, full-on clichéd newspaper clippings at first, like some dodgy remake of *The Bodyguard*, then he got bolder and used his own hand, which was worse, you know? It felt more personal and invasive, and it didn't matter what he'd written."

Nero brushed the pastry crumbs from Lenny's hands. Conscious, rational thought told him to leave it at that, but he wove his fingers between Lenny's, twining them together. "What did he write?"

"All the things you'd expect . . . that he loved me and he wanted to be with me, and then later, when I started dodging him, that he wanted to cook me and eat my bones."

"Jesus." Nero swallowed. "And the coppers did nothing?"

Lenny shrugged. "They said they couldn't, and I didn't even go to them until just before I came here. I figured if I moved around enough, it would go away on its own. Stupid, eh?"

"Dunno about that. I gotta penchant for sticking my head in the sand."

Lenny said nothing, his gaze fixed on his fingers so tightly tangled with Nero's. He curled his ring finger around the stump. "Does this hurt?"

"No."

"Really? I read a study on amputations that said the site of a missing limb or appendage can give lifelong pain."

"It wasn't amputated."

More silence. Lenny sucked in a shaky breath, but didn't release Nero's hand. "I'm sorry."

"What for?"

"My shitty diplomacy."

Nero forced himself to pull his hands away from Lenny. "I ain't that diplomatic myself. So are you gonna finish your tale of woe or what?"

Lenny's eyes glittered darkly. "Are you making fun of me?"

"Would it help?"

"Maybe. I can't cry over it anymore, so we may as well laugh, but there isn't much to add to my 'tale of woe' as you called it, nothing tangible, at least."

"Go on, then," Nero prompted. "How did you end up here?"

Lenny shrugged. "I sofa surfed until I wound up in Camden, and it stopped for a while. Then a couple of dubious profiles followed me on Twitter and Facebook, so I deleted my accounts. A few weeks later he started showing up outside Misfits, and in the block of flats opposite mine, staring through my bedroom window, leaving bags of chips on my doorstep, all kinds of weird shit. One time it was a dead rat, so I freaked out, decided to go the police on my day off, but the fucker must've read my mind because the very next morning the letters he'd sent me disappeared."

"Disappeared?"

"Yeah. I used to leave my door open when I took the rubbish down to the bin. He must've slipped in and taken them."

"Did you tell the coppers that?"

"I tried."

Nero frowned. The old bill were his nemesis, but Lenny was the innocent here, the victim. Surely there was something—

Lenny tapped Nero's temple. "Don't frown like that. You'll give yourself a migraine."

"Don't give a shit."

"Suit yourself. Where was I?"

"At the part where that creep got into your flat."

Lenny nodded slowly. "That fucked me up, more than him telling everyone at the club he was my boyfriend. I could quit the club and move on, and I did, but knowing he'd been in my place made my skin crawl. I went to the police, even though I had no evidence, but they pretty much gave me some leaflets and—"

"Told you to jog on?"

Lenny's lips twitched. "I wasn't going to be so polite, but yeah. It was harsh, and I lost my shit, especially when he turned up at Misfits the same day. I saw him out back and then the barman handed me an envelope with my own fucking toenail clipping inside. I was so done, I swear. If Cass hadn't turned up . . ."

Nero didn't need the end of that sentence to understand. "Cass is good like that, eh? Saved me from a meltdown or two."

"Yeah?" Lenny cocked his head to one side. "You don't strike me as the hysterical type."

"Define *hysteria*. I break stuff. Hurt people. Cass finds me a reason not to."

Lenny said nothing, and Nero had nothing left either. He tipped his head back and stared up at the sky as he lit a fag. Lenny's story made him sick to his stomach, but merged with the horror came relief. Lenny's terrors and fears were real, but knowing where they came from meant the source could be chased down and obliterated. "Do you know his name?"

"He told a couple of people it was Gareth. Don't know if it's his real name, though."

"Has he been here?"

"Not that I know of. Cass brought me here because the signs don't have the Urban Soul logos on. Reckoned it would take longer to track me down if I stayed indoors enough. I don't know what my long-term plans are, though. I can't kip on your couch forever."

"It ain't my couch." Nero stubbed out his smoke and fought the urge to light another, unwilling to admit, even to himself—especially to himself—how much he would miss Lenny if he left. "But you can stay as long as you like. Told you already: ain't no one gonna hurt you here."

"I believe you, but I *can't* stay indoors forever, Nero. I'm losing my mind."

The anguish in Lenny's voice didn't get easier to bear. Nero slipped his arm around Lenny with little conscious thought and pulled him close. In return, Lenny tipped his head and rested it on Nero's shoulder, and for a protracted moment that was equal parts bleak and blissful, silence enveloped them, dulling the city below to a low roar. Nero had no answers for Lenny, no comfort or wisdom, and Lenny didn't seem to want any. Perhaps sharing his secret was enough, at least for now.

"Nero?"

"Yeah?"

"Are you going to kiss me again?"

It was the last thing Nero had expected Lenny to say, but he went with it, stretched his legs out in front of him, and lit another fag. "Ask me tomorrow."

CHAPTER NINE

"**W**hen did you last take a Sunday off?"

Nero cast an irritated glance over his shoulder. "What?"

"Sundays," Steph repeated. "Cass told me not to let you work every hour under the sun."

"Yeah? Well he didn't tell me shit." Nero wiped the rim of the three millionth plate of roast beef to cross his path that day and banged the counter for service. "And it ain't your concern anyway. Kitchen rotas are mine."

"I know. I'm just reminding you to take a break. You and Lenny have worked every day this week, which is great for Lenny because he's paid by the hour, but you're basically working for free right now."

"So?" Nero turned away from Lenny's questioning stare beside him. It had been a week or so since he'd learned the reason Lenny had wound up camped in his living room, and Nero had yet to come to terms with it. He clenched his fists, picturing the terror in Lenny's eyes every time the outside world edged a little too close, feeling it, breathing it in like it was his own. A fucking stalker? Damn. Nero had seen some nasty shit, but this was brand-new.

"Nero . . ."

Fucking Steph. Nero supressed a sigh. His Urban Soul contract had the same forty-eight-hour clause as everyone else's, but it wasn't unusual for him to pull half as much again in a normal week. Never had been. "Is there a point to this?"

"Not really. I want you out of here by five, though, or I'm calling Cass."

Steph disappeared back into the chaos of Sunday service. Perplexed, Nero watched her go but, with orders crawling out of his arse, had no time to dwell on her words until five o'clock rolled around and she came back with a face even Nero knew not to mess with.

"Out."

Nero downed tools and pointed at Lenny. "I'm taking him too."

Steph smirked. Nero spared her a glare before handing the kitchen to Debs. With that done, he went to the office, resisting the urge to follow Lenny, who'd gone straight to the staff room to change.

He sat at the computer and logged in to the company hub, clocking his hours and recording his wastage notes from the busy lunch service. Sunday evenings were typically the quietest shift of the weekend, but the less admin he left for Debs, the better.

It was gone six when he made it upstairs, and by then, Lenny was already stretched out on the couch, looking for all the world like he was out for the count.

Nero left him to it and took a shower, washing the day's sweat and grime away, but he didn't linger long, and on his way to the bedroom, couldn't fight the compulsion to check Lenny was still safe on the couch.

He threw a pair of ratty trackies on and went to the window, scanning the building opposite and street below for anything untoward—spying eyes, strange faces—but nothing stood out. With a heavy sigh, he dropped the blinds, shutting out the evening sun. It left the bedroom dark and gloomy, but Nero didn't mind; it suited his mood. A rare Sunday night off usually meant a solitary trip to a pub in Bethnal Green, the only place near his old stomping ground he could bear to go, but the call home was absent tonight, replaced by the restless need to watch over Lenny.

With little conscious thought, he drifted to the living room. Lenny's eyes were closed, but he clearly wasn't asleep—he was too still, his breathing too even. Besides, the slight frown pulling his groomed brows together gave him away. Nero slouched on the arm of the couch and shook Lenny's foot. "Are you hungry?"

Lenny opened his eyes, his frown deepening to a scowl that made him look like a stroppy teenager. "No, I'm not bloody hungry. I'm sick of food. If I see one more roast potato today, I'll fucking shoot myself."

Nero laughed, even though Lenny's obvious exhaustion troubled him. "Wait till you've worked every Sunday for a year, then tell me you're sick of roast spuds."

"Yeah, yeah. Just pass me a tabard and I'll off myself right now."

"A tabard?"

"And a hairnet. I've felt like a glorified dinner lady all day."

"Not tomorrow, though, eh? Ain't neither of us working."

"Brilliant." Lenny sat up and swiped his fags from the coffee table. Nero followed him to the fire escape, stepped around him, and lit his own smoke before regarding Lenny, who had stopped in the doorway to glance over the city in much the same way Nero had in the bedroom. *I wish I knew who he was looking for . . .*

Nero left the thought unfinished as Lenny finally stepped outside. *No one* was getting to Lenny through him, but Nero couldn't always be around. Sooner or later, Lenny needed a new plan—a plan that didn't involve counting on the fire escape for his vitamin D.

They smoked in silence. Lenny seemed lost in thought, and Nero was content to let him be. It had been a long day, and as much as it pained him to admit it, Steph had done him a favour by calling time on his working week. Distraction had its limits, and right now Nero could contemplate little more than guarding Lenny and stumbling into his bed. Shame he couldn't think of a way to do both.

"You're fucking impossible, you know that?"

Nero blinked. "Where did that come from?"

"Where do you think? You're so bloody inscrutable I can't think straight." Lenny stubbed his cigarette out on the wall like it had killed his dog, and stormed back inside, slamming the door behind him.

Nero would've been less confused if Lenny had punched him in the face. He stared after him, piecing together the last few hours they'd spent together, searching for anything he might've done to piss Lenny off. But he found nothing in a day that had been spent mostly in a haze of Yorkshire puddings and fatigue. *And what the fuck does* inscrutable *mean anyway?*

Pride kept him from googling it. He finished his smoke and flicked the butt into the ashtray. Common sense told him to give Lenny some space to cool down, but the masochist in him opened the door and followed Lenny to the bathroom.

Lenny was perched on the edge of the bath, painting his toenails a startling shade of pink. He didn't look up, even when Nero turned the light on.

"Can't do that in the dark, eh?"

"Says who?" Lenny swapped feet. "Been doing it since I was twelve."

Nero stored that snippet of information away for later. "Are you going to tell me what I've done to piss you off so much?"

"Nope."

"Why not?"

"'Cause you don't get it."

"Don't mean you shouldn't tell me. I might surprise you."

Lenny snorted. "You *do* surprise me, every day. Doesn't mean Clapham Junction exploding in my tiny brain will make any sense to you— *Shit*."

Pink polish stained Lenny's big toe. He swiped at it with cotton wool, hands trembling. Nero stepped forward and pried the brush from his stiff fingers. "You done with this foot?"

"It all needs a second coat."

Nero sat on the closed toilet. "Give me your other foot."

Lenny deposited his other foot into Nero's lap with a heavy sigh. "Are you always this evasive?"

"You're the one who won't tell me what the problem is."

"I did tell you what the problem was—a fucking week ago. You've hardly spoken to me since."

Nero applied a dubious layer of nail polish to Lenny's toe. "Bollocks. We talk every day."

"Not about anything that matters. First thing you said to me this morning was about bloody fish."

"What did you want me to say?" Nero painted the next nail. "You're gonna have to help me here. I ain't much of a talker at the best of times. Let alone when I got someone jumping in my face about shit."

"That's what you think I'm doing?"

"I don't know what you're doing, or what you want from me. I just know I can't handle you being so pissed off."

"Why?"

"'Cause I like your smile," Nero said almost absently.

"Fuck's sake!" Lenny wrenched his foot away with a groan. "This is why I bloody hate you. How can you say stuff like that when you won't let me see a fraction of what's really going on?"

"I haven't got a fucking clue what you're on about."

"And that's the problem, isn't it?" Lenny stood and hobbled to the door on his heels. "You kiss me, you let me sleep in your bed, you pry my darkest secrets from me, but you won't talk to me. What the actual fuck, Nero? Don't you think I'm crazy enough without you screwing with me?"

"Screwing with you?" Nero stood too, though the slightly crazed glint in Lenny's eyes warned him to stay still. "It ain't me stalking you, mate."

"This isn't about that! *I'm* not about that, goddamn it." Lenny's shout rang out in the quiet flat.

His anger reverberated through Nero's bones, but he welcomed it, though it was slowly dawning on him what Lenny was asking him for. "I know what brought you here doesn't define you. Apart from wanting to deck the bloke, it don't mean nothing to me."

"Doesn't it?"

"No. You mean something to me. Not the cunt who's been chasing you around London."

Lenny shook his head. For a terrifying moment his eyes shone too bright for Nero to bear, then he sucked in a deep breath and seemed to steel himself. "You probably think I'm a fucking lunatic, but can I ask you one thing before I stick my head under a cushion and pretend this day never happened?"

Nero shrugged, knowing Lenny would ask him anyway.

"Do you know who I am?"

"What?"

"Consider it, Nero. Put aside the fact that I haven't seen daylight for a month, and really think about it. Do you know who I am?"

By Lenny's expression, Nero reckoned any response would likely be wrong, but he nodded anyway. He had much to learn, but the frighteningly beautiful man in front of him was far from a stranger. He had to be, or Nero's heart was as crippled as his soul. "I know who you are."

"Yeah?" Lenny cast a pointed glance to Nero's left hand. "So why won't you tell me who *you* are?"

Apparently certain that no answer was forthcoming, Lenny walked away. After a split second, Nero followed him, his bare feet unnaturally loud in the eerily quiet flat, keeping time with the tattoo in his chest—a slow, London thunder that felt like ominous desperation. *Please don't make me do this.*

He found Lenny huddled on the sofa, gazing blankly at the muted TV.

"Forget something?" Lenny said.

"You."

"Excuse me?"

Nero ventured farther into the room and held out his hand. "Look, I can't bare my fucking soul to you, but—"

"But what, Nero? You think you can have everything I am while I only get a fraction of you?"

"No." That wasn't right, or was it? Lenny had shared his darkest secret, but what had Nero given him in return? An omelette and a plate of hollow bullshit? Defeated, Nero dropped his hand and turned away. "Lenny, mate, this is all I got. I'm sorry it ain't enough."

Nero rolled over, chest tight, arms flailing, suffocating in the murky blackness of the dank cellar, his brain vibrating to the stampeding beat of his heart. He cried out, though for who he didn't know, because no one ever came.

Gasping awake, he curled instinctively into the foetal position, but his knees hit a warm mass.

What the fuck?

Nero's eyes flew open, but the paralysing fear he so often woke with was absent, held at bay by the sight of the pale, slender man stretched out fast asleep beside him.

Lenny's shock of white-blond hair gleamed in the dark like a halo. Nero reached out to touch it before he remembered why it was here. He combed lightly through the silky strands, and trailed his fingertips down Lenny's face, tracing his cheekbone, ghosting down his jaw.

Part of him craved the heat of Lenny's fierce gaze, and as the stolen moment tunnelled through the haze of complication between them, Nero found himself willing time to stop so they could always be like this.

Inevitably, though, reality made itself known. Lenny stirred, like he'd sensed the disquiet in Nero's fragmented mind. He opened his eyes, but they were vacant and unseeing, and a split second later they fluttered closed again, leaving Nero to wonder if he'd imagined it.

But there was no make-believe in how it felt to have Lenny in his bed, the warmth of him, and the sound of his soft, even breaths. Nero rarely had shared a bed—to sleep, at least—and as hard as he tried, he couldn't remember the last time he'd woken to someone sleeping beside him. And Lenny's quiet presence was like a drug. Nero's eyes grew heavy, his heart slowed, and he slipped into the kind of sleep he'd been chasing for years.

Insistent banging on the front door roused Nero sometime the next morning. He sat up, grumbling; it would be some idiot from downstairs who couldn't find a teaspoon. *So much for a lie in*—not that he'd truly anticipated one. He woke most days before the sun, unless—

A trembling hand closed around Nero's wrist. "Who is it?"

Nero blinked. *So it wasn't a dream.* But before his brain could implode at the thought of what that meant, the sight of Lenny huddled at the headboard, his knees drawn tight to his chest, his eyes wide with fear, took over. "Len—"

"*Who's* at the door?"

"I don't know, but it won't be anyone we don't know. It's—" Nero checked his phone "—half seven. Debs is downstairs counting stock with Spanks. They wouldn't dare let anyone up here, so it's gonna be one of them, I promise."

Lenny looked far from convinced. "You can't be sure."

Nero's phone vibrated. He tossed it down the bed without glancing at it. "Yes, I can. In all the time I've lived here, no one outside of Urban Soul staff has ever knocked on that door. Some days, Cass don't even bother knocking. Fucker just lets himself in and sticks the kettle on when he remembers his key."

Lenny savaged his bottom lip, digging his teeth in so hard he drew blood. Nero scrambled up on his knees and took Lenny's face in his hands. "Lenny, mate. You gotta calm down. I can hear your heart juddering from here, and I'm telling you, it ain't worth it for Debs's ugly mug."

For a long moment, Lenny said nothing, just trembled, his breath caught in his throat, and his face so pale Nero half expected to see bone. Then he let out a shaky breath and brought his hands to Nero's. "You sure it's Debs?"

"It might be Spanks."

"No one else, though?"

"No one else." Nero brushed a light kiss to Lenny's lips, surprising himself as much as he clearly surprised Lenny. "I'm gonna answer it before Spanks takes a piss though the letterbox. Chill out, yeah? Go back to sleep."

He got up, knowing all too well that his attempts at comfort had done little to ease Lenny's fears. And who could blame him when he'd spent so long with that creep following him around?

Fuck's sake. Rage rumbled in Nero's veins. He pulled on the trackies he'd discarded the night before, trying not to think about the fact that he was stomping around in his pants in front of Lenny, or to imagine his hawkish gaze on the faint scars he'd likely noticed on the backs of Nero's thighs. God knew, Nero had enough bullshit spinning his head without having to dodge Lenny's inevitable questions about that.

Out in the hall, he wrenched the front door open. "All right, all right. Stop fucking with my door—"

The words died on his lips. *Coppers. Fuck.* Nero's blood ran cold, his skin prickled, and every fight-or-flight instinct he'd ever had roared to life.

"Mr. Fierro?"

The first policeman stepped forward. Nero blocked the door. "What's it to you?"

"We're looking for Lenny Mitchell. Your employees downstairs said he was staying with you."

"They're not my employees. I just work here."

"Mr. Fearnes told us you were in charge."

Tom. Something clicked in Nero's chaotic mind, but he widened his stance. *They're coppers. Don't trust 'em.* "What do you want Lenny for?"

"Could we come in?"

It was the younger policeman this time. He braved another step forward, but Nero continued to bar his path. "I didn't say he was here."

The first copper frowned, and Nero watched as bluster crept through him, enhancing his slight paunch and squaring his shoulders. "Is there a problem here, Mr. Fierro?"

"I never said I was him either, so sorry, lads, you ain't coming in."

Nero started to shut the door, closing his ears to the older PC's indignant protests. *Fuck 'em.* If they wanted Lenny, they'd have to go through him—

"Nero." Lenny caught the door and stepped in front of Nero. "Easy. It's okay, Nero. Tom sent them."

Tom. Again. Nero fought Lenny's grip on the door as his phone rang in the bedroom, blaring out Cass's ringtone. So what if Mr. Perfect had seen fit to send the old bill to Nero's door? So what if they were all smiles and "Good morning, Mr. Mitchell . . ." right now? In Nero's world, that didn't mean shit.

"*Nero*, let go of the door."

Nero blinked. Lenny was in his face, staring at him with a mixture of exasperation and concern, the door halfway closed, shielding them from the copper's view. He pressed his forehead to Nero's. "It's okay, I promise. They just want to talk to me, and I *want* to talk to them. Let them in . . . please?"

"No."

"Please. Don't make me talk to them in the bloody bar."

Nero released the door. His step back felt like a stumble as his legs wobbled, but the wall behind him kept him upright. He leaned heavily on it, watching through narrowed eyes as the two policemen walked into his home. *Fuck this.* He eyed the still-open front door, but with every nerve he had stretched to the breaking point, nothing could make him leave Lenny.

He slammed the front door and stormed to the fire escape, grabbing Lenny's fags from the kitchen table. Outside he did a cursory scan for weed paraphernalia, but there was none, save a few dubious butts in the ashtray. Besides, if they searched the place, they'd only find a ten bag. What were they going to do? Lock him up for a couple of joints?

Belligerence surged through Nero, but faded as suddenly as it had arrived. His tiny weed habit was barely a criminal offence anymore, but it didn't take a genius to know that Tom wouldn't stand for shit like that going on at Pippa's. *You really wanna lose your job? Dude, it's all you got.*

Nero silenced the optimistic moral compass on his shoulder and lit a smoke, leaning on the railing and gazing, unseeing, out over the city. He was *tired*, damn it, despite sleeping better than he had in years, and he couldn't shake the discomfort of knowing there were coppers at his back, sitting on his couch, making themselves at home in the only place his adult self had ever truly felt at home.

The urge to go inside and put himself between them and Lenny was strong—too strong. Nero lit another fag from the butt of the first and closed his eyes, hanging his head. His missing finger tingled. Lenny wanted to know who he was, but if he couldn't figure it out by the different way those coppers looked at each of them, then what was the point? With some distance between them, Nero could see it now: those men had wanted to help Lenny, not fuck him over, because Lenny wasn't a criminal, a known name from a place where only bad faces rose and knew no better.

They wanted to help Lenny, because Lenny was good, so why did Nero still feel like there was a mountain at the gates?

CHAPTER TEN

onday. Midday. The coppers were finally gone. Nero had heard the front door close and watched as they appeared in the car park below, got into their car, and drove away. He waited for relief, and then Lenny, but neither was forthcoming, and it took four more cigarettes before he found the inclination to search either out.

Inside, Lenny was in the living room, folding up his bedding. "What did they want?"

"If you'd stuck around, you'd know."

"Don't fuck with me."

Lenny flinched. "Don't talk to me like that. If you want a conversation, go put the kettle on and come back with a cuppa and a face that doesn't look like a serial killer's."

It was the second time Lenny had thrown that insult at Nero, and it didn't sting any less. Nero turned on his heel and went back to the kitchen. Autopilot took him to the kettle and filled it with water, but he didn't flick the switch. Instead, he braced himself on the counter and tried to get a hold on his speeding mind—it wouldn't be long before he couldn't, before he went into meltdown and there was no way back.

Lenny's light touch startled him. "I don't know what the fuck's going on in that convoluted brain of yours, but if you're worried about me, you can stop. It's over. Everything's okay."

"What?"

"That's why they came. Make the tea and I'll tell you all about it."

Lenny left the room as suddenly as he'd appeared, leaving Nero to boil the kettle and mechanically make tea. He threw some sugar in Lenny's and carried them into the living room. "Tea. Now talk."

"Sit, then." Lenny accepted his mug and patted the sofa beside him. "And don't go all ragey and silent on me. It scares me when you do that."

"I scare myself."

The words were out before Nero could stop them, but Lenny just smiled. "I'll bet. We can talk about that after, if you want?"

Nero shook his head. "I'm here to listen."

Lenny let it go. "The police think they know who's been stalking me."

"Who is it?"

"They didn't say, only that they'd picked someone up for another offence last week and found evidence in his home that he'd been harassing me and a couple of other people."

Nero whistled. "So you weren't the only one?"

"Apparently not. The bloke was staying at an HMO in Tottenham when they found him, but they reckon he'd moved around a lot, depending on who he was targeting at the time."

"Sounds like a whack job."

"Or a sadistic wanker. Anyway, it doesn't matter now. They've got him."

"Banged him up?"

Lenny nodded. "The liaison officer is going to stay in touch with me—when I reactivate my phone—but they don't think he'll get bail, and even if he did, there's a court order in place stopping him from coming near anyone on the list of victims."

Victims. *Targets.* It sounded too good to be true, but as the first real smile he'd ever seen from Lenny warmed him from the inside out, Nero didn't have the heart to say it just yet. "Do you feel better?"

Lenny nodded. "I do, actually. Much better. I can get on with my life now."

Nero didn't have it in him to be as optimistic He took a surreptitious deep breath and hid his frown behind his tea mug. "Who died and made the old bill so helpful? Thought they'd fobbed you off?"

"They did, but when I lost my shit at Misfits I told Cass everything. He told Tom, and I guess they took him more seriously than they did me."

"You never told me Tom was helping you."

Lenny shrugged. "Not on purpose, mate. In case you haven't noticed, I've been off my head these last few weeks, and not in the good way."

Again, Nero's lungs cried out for the burn of a weed pipe, but he ignored it. "I know. I'm sorry, and I'm sorry if I'm a dick about Tom too. He's a good bloke."

"Sounds it. I still haven't met him in person, and it's been ages since Cass made me Skype him from the office. I can't even picture him."

"Tall, blond, posh."

"That's all there is to him?"

Nero chuckled. "I doubt it if he's been with Cass this long, 'cause he's a fucking handful. Jake too."

Lenny said nothing. He drained his tea mug and ditched it on the coffee table with a dull thud. Suddenly Nero noticed the neatly folded bedding and zipped-up bag of clothes. "Are you leaving?"

"Um . . ." Lenny shrugged. "I don't know. Cass said I could stay here as long as I needed to get this shit sorted out. Now it is, I should probably find somewhere—"

"Why?"

Lenny blinked. "Because I'm bodging around your kitchen, hogging your couch, and generally fucking up your life."

"You're not fucking up my life."

"No? Then why are we creeping around each other? Or screaming at each other in the middle of the night? Tell me, Nero, 'cause I've got no bloody idea."

"I don't want you to go." Nero knew bugger all else, but of that he was certain. "I like having you—I like you being here."

"Why?"

"For fuck's sake, I don't know!" Nero's frustration boiled over, sudden and violent. He stood and drove his fist into the wall. The brutal impact with the plaster was instantly calming, the pain washing over him like an old friend. "I don't know anything, okay? So you can ask me any question you like, just—"

Nero's voice cracked, ragged and broken, like it belonged to someone else. Lenny came to him and claimed his clenched fist, prying it open so he could press their palms tight together. "Finish the sentence. That's all I'm asking."

"I can't," Nero whispered. "Just don't go . . . please? 'Cause I want you to stay, and I don't know what the fuck to do about it."

Nero woke for a third time that day as the sun was beginning to sink behind the building opposite. He yawned and stretched his arms above his head, absorbing the heat of the body pressed tight against his, as the events of the last twenty-four hours drifted back to him—shouting, screaming, the coppers. More shouting, and then peace, as Lenny had slipped his arms around Nero and whispered softly in his ear. *"I'm not going anywhere."*

What that meant in reality, Nero wasn't quite sure, since the conversation had descended into a kiss that had taken them to bed, rolling them again and again until they'd both passed out. Now, it was—*shit, 7 p.m.* . . . and the day was nearly gone. Nero scrolled through his phone, taking care not to jolt Lenny, who was still fast asleep. Five missed calls from Cass, two from Debs. Three voice mails, and a series of text messages that provided all the warning he could've hoped for about coppers banging on his door, if only he'd picked up his phone.

Idiot. Not that it mattered now. Nero ditched his phone and looked back in time to see Lenny's eyes flutter open, hazy at first, but then bright and anxious as they settled on Nero.

And then Lenny moved fast, sitting up and covering Nero with his body. His kiss was hesitant, perhaps testing himself—and Nero—until Nero responded, wrapping his arms tight around him and crushing him to his chest. They kissed over and over, like they had before they'd fallen asleep, but it felt different now, as though an invisible barrier had faded away.

Nero flipped them, pinning Lenny to the mattress as his hands roamed Lenny's upper body. Lenny wrapped his legs around Nero's waist, and then Nero felt it—a dick that wasn't his own, or Cass's, digging into him, hot and hard. His heart skipped, and his already tempestuous blood roared in his ears. Lenny's dick felt *big*, and solid, and strong, and all the things Nero had dreamed about when his imagination cut him a break. He gripped Lenny's hips and pressed against him tighter, absorbing Lenny's desperate moan, but inside he was flailing, lost on a path untrodden. *I need to touch him.*

Lenny squirmed in Nero's bruising hold and pulled his T-shirt over his head, revealing his slender chest. Nero stared. He'd seen Lenny shirtless more times than he could count, but Lenny seemed paler now, smoother, like iridescent porcelain. He laid his palm on the dark stamp of ink over Lenny's heart. *What does this mean?* But he didn't ask, couldn't, because as Lenny shoved Nero's sweatpants down his hips, coherent thought abandoned him.

Nero made short work of yanking Lenny's pyjama bottoms down his legs. He tossed them over his shoulder and shivered as Lenny's bare legs wrapped once again around his waist. With just a thin barrier of underwear between them, Nero kissed Lenny fiercely and ground down on him, searching out the friction he'd craved ever since that first electric kiss, a clumsy fumble that seemed a lifetime ago now.

Heat surged through Nero, his cock harder than it had ever been. He drove against Lenny again and again, a coil of pressure growing in his belly as Lenny's teeth grazed his lips, then moved to his neck, nipping and biting, savaging the tender flesh at the juncture of his collarbone.

Nero gasped. Lenny took advantage of his distraction and toppled him over, hooking his arm under Nero's knee and raising his leg to his chest. The challenge in Lenny's eyes was clear—daring Nero to fight him and roll them again—but Nero didn't. Why would he, when having Lenny bearing down on him, dry-fucking him, was the best feeling in the world?

He threw his head back, arching his hips into Lenny, their cocks grinding together, scraping and rubbing. The sensation was dizzying and addictive, and Nero couldn't imagine how he'd ever stop. He brought his arms around Lenny, caging him, searching out his mouth, and swallowing his cries.

Groaning, Lenny kissed him back and rocked forward, and Nero reared up like a starving man. He pulled his lips from Lenny's and sank his teeth into Lenny's neck. It felt almost wrong to be so rough with Lenny's delicate flesh, but as Lenny's thrusts got sharper, his moans deeper, Nero realised there was nothing delicate about the man who was making his head spin . . . and his cock weep.

God, I'm gonna come.

Nero tore his mouth from Lenny's neck. "Lenny—"

But his choked exclamation was cut off as Lenny scrambled back and shoved Nero's boxers away, freeing his cock. He wriggled out of his own, then spit on his hand and closed his fist around both of them. Nero watched their cocks glide together, mesmerised, but there was no time to enjoy it. Orgasm crept up on him, and then it rushed him, tearing out of him so sweetly it almost hurt, and he came with a low cry, spilling over Lenny's hand.

"*Fuck.*" Lenny thrust hard against Nero's still throbbing cock, once more . . . twice, and then he came too, his moan so carnal Nero almost climaxed again.

It went on forever. Nero trembled and shook, chasing breaths that didn't seem to be there, all the while clutching at Lenny like a life raft.

Lenny responded in kind, smearing the sticky mess of sweat and come between them, his slim shoulders heaving. "Oh God, you have no idea how much I wanted to fuck you then."

Nero chuckled hoarsely, his throat dry and raw. "Ditto."

"Yeah, yeah. Don't tease me, mate. Let me have my fantasies."

"I'm not teasing you."

Lenny abruptly sat up, his hair a wild mess like Nero had never seen. "What does that mean?"

"Erm . . . I don't know? What are you asking me?"

"Whatever you're trying to tell me."

"Oh man, don't do that." Nero scrubbed a hand through his damp hair. "You know I'm shit at this. Just ask me? I'll answer, I promise."

Lenny fell silent, trailing a fingertip along Nero's still-twitching dick, grinning at Nero's shiver. "You're giving me the impression that you want to bottom, but my brain's telling me that's too good to be true."

"Your brain's wrong." Every sexual thought Nero had ever had replayed in his mind at hyperspeed, confirming what his heart already knew. "I wasn't sure I'd get as far as shagging a fella, but whenever I've imagined it, I've always kinda been on the bottom."

"'On the bottom.'" Lenny repeated the words like he'd dreamt them. "Jesus."

Nero shifted, suddenly aware of how much he'd exposed himself. "Is that a bad thing?"

Lenny's head snapped up. "What? No! God, no, I'm just . . . shocked, I suppose, that you're so cool about it."

"About what? Liking dick or getting fucked?"

"Both?"

Nero snorted. "I've had plenty of time to get used to liking dick, mate. And as for getting fucked, I dunno. I guess it just feels right."

Lenny frowned, apparently still nonplussed.

Nero touched his face. "What is it? You don't top?"

"Fuck, no. I top, trust me—Jesus, I top. It's more, I don't know . . . I had it in my head that you'd be kind of uptight about fucking. I mean, I'm not being rude, mate, but you're uptight about everything else." A faint hint of Lenny's impish grin lightened the mood.

Nero rolled his eyes. "Am not."

"Yeah, you are, so I figured you'd be some kind of power top, fucking my brains out to ease your frustration."

The idea had legs. Nero pictured it and bit his lip, but he couldn't escape the craving deep in his gut to have a man—to have *Lenny*—buried inside him, fucking him, owning him, making him come, and then—

"Oh man. I'm in so much trouble."

Lenny's heady whisper broke through Nero's dirty daydreams. He refocused and pulled Lenny onto his lap, flexing instinctively as Lenny's thighs squeezed tight around him. "I coulda told you that way before we ever did this."

"Hmm." Lenny's hum was drowsy. "I can believe that. What we gotta do now is work out what to do about it."

"Do?"

"Yeah, because I want to fuck you, Nero, more than anything, but you aren't ready for that, and neither am I. I've spent the last god-knows how many years hooking up with blokes who were hardly more than strangers. I don't want to do that anymore, and I don't want it to be like that with you."

"It won't be," Nero said, though he couldn't deny he'd spent as long as he could remember falling into bed—and other places—with near enough anyone willing. "We know each other just fine."

"We're getting there." Lenny kissed Nero's cheek. "But we're not there yet."

Nero's dick protested, but his heart knew Lenny was right. Something was brewing between them, something neither one of them could control, and fucking like rabbits would likely implode them before they'd even got started.

"Besides," Lenny said when Nero failed to respond. "First things first. In the morning, I'm gonna need you to take me out."

"Out? Out where?"

Lenny shrugged. "Anywhere. I don't care. Just get me out of this place, please? Then we can come home and do this shit all over again."

LENNY

CHAPTER ELEVEN

L enny gripped Nero's hands like they were the only anchor tying him down to the world. If he'd been clutching anyone else, the wobble in his legs would've been humiliating, but not with Nero. With his dark eyes blazing a path to his soul, Lenny felt nothing but heat . . .

And blind panic. Who knew the streets of Shepherd's Bush could be so terrifying?

Nero leaned down, his lips brushing Lenny's ear, his aniseed-laced breath warming the line of silver hoops Lenny had worn for the occasion. "You know we could just get a cab, right? There ain't no need for you to walk nowhere."

"Yeah, but what about tomorrow? Longer I leave it, the harder it'll be."

Nero's only response was a grunt, and Lenny couldn't tell if he agreed or not. *Standard.* Lenny had assumed that time would make his inscrutable companion easier to read. It hadn't, and it seemed Nero Fierro was destined to remain a beautiful enigma.

And fuck, he *was* beautiful. Lenny took the last step out of Pippa's back door and lost himself in all that was Nero—his molten eyes and broad shoulders. His strong neck and cropped dark hair. If he closed his eyes, he'd see the intricate tattoo on Nero's chest—the tiger lurking behind the butterfly, or was it the other way around? Lenny saw Nero shirtless every day, and he still wasn't sure, and thinking about that kept him preoccupied as they ventured farther and farther along the bustling streets of Shepherd's Bush.

"There ya go. Weren't so hard, was it?"

Nero's rough cockney brogue brought Lenny back to the present. He blinked, surprised. Somehow, while he'd been lost in his

Nero-themed daydreams, they'd made it all the way to the underground. "I can't remember the last time I went on the Tube."

"Why? That cunt follow you on that too?"

"No, actually." Lenny squeezed Nero's hand like he could stem the dark anger that simmered in Nero's life-hardened gaze every time *he* was mentioned. "I just didn't need to because I lived and worked in Camden."

As though he'd read Lenny's mind, Nero guided them onto the right train, then turned to Lenny with a quizzical frown. "You don't make no sense."

"Excuse me?"

Nero shrugged. "You're scared of your own shadow, but you get this weird sympathy in your eyes when we talk about that lunatic."

"I can't be angry with someone so sadistic. It would make me no better than him."

"You're soft in the head."

Nero's frown remained, but his tone wasn't unkind, so Lenny chanced a smile, hoping it would soothe the anxiety attack still threatening his fragile calm. "I'm trying to be positive, mate. Help me out?"

"If you say so."

It seemed to be Nero's baseline answer when he wanted to be as infuriating as possible. Lenny resisted the urge—*ha, craving*—to bang his head against Nero's strong chest, and let the subject drop, hoping Nero would do the same. After all this time, Lenny was done thinking about the bullshit that had kept him a virtual prisoner in Nero's living room.

Vauxhall came around far quicker than Lenny anticipated. He'd forgotten how deceptive the slow rumble of the underground trains were. "I feel like I just blinked."

Nero grinned a little in that maddening way of his. "You pretty much did. Thought you were asleep on me."

Lenny was fast learning how amazing it was to do just that, but he poked his tongue out anyway. "Piss off. I was resting my eyes."

"Yeah, yeah. Come on. Off with yer."

Nero took Lenny's arm and guided him off the train. Lenny hopped onto the platform, bouncing on the balls of his feet. "I'm excited."

"Thought you were terrified?"

"Positive, remember?"

"Sorry." Nero peered over Lenny's shoulder, clearly and instantly distracted. "Look at that over there. Vegan chocolate cake. Gluten-free and everything."

Despite the nerves churning Lenny's stomach, he followed Nero's gaze to the pop-up food stall at the station's entrance. The wheeled wooden cart was painted bright pink and was surrounded by an orderly throng of lunchtime commuters. "Cake for lunch? I could live with that."

Nero snorted. "You'd eat Haribo for lunch if I let you."

"You don't, though, do you? Can't remember that last time I didn't get my five-a-day." Not that Lenny was complaining. Living with Nero had given him the best skin he'd ever had, despite the long nights he'd lain on the couch, counting the cracks in the ceiling, listening for the shuffle of grubby trainers that never came. *And won't come. It's over, remember?*

"Earth to Lenny?" Nero waved his hand in front of Lenny's face. "Fine, come on. You can have some cake."

Lenny let Nero drag him to the cake stall. Moments later, all thoughts of creeps in the night were gone, banished by a dark, decadent wodge of sinfully good cake. "Oh. My. God. You have to try this. It's so good."

Nero leaned back on the bench they'd drifted to while Lenny had been in cake heaven. "Nah, you're all right. Chocolate and avocado ain't my thing."

"You don't know what you're missing. Here . . . try it." Lenny held a chocolate-smeared finger to Nero's lips, half-expecting Nero to bat him away like he often did when Lenny "tickled the fucking bricks." But he didn't. He held Lenny's gaze and parted his lips, letting Lenny's finger slip slowly into his mouth.

Jesus fucking Christ. Lenny had succumbed to the sensation of Nero's tongue before—namely when it had been wrapped around his own—but this was something else . . . something that Lenny couldn't overtly respond to because they were on a bench outside the Vauxhall tube station, *Goddamn it.*

Nero smirked, like he was immune to the inferno brewing between them, but Lenny remembered his face when he'd come, shooting his load all over Lenny's hands. *He feels it.*

Lenny reluctantly reclaimed his finger and finished his lunch. "What about you? I can't stuff my face while you go hungry."

"I'm not hungry. I had breakfast while you were snoring this morning."

Lenny smiled as the warm normalcy of Nero's teasing washed over him. Christ, they'd only slept together a couple of times, but it was like they'd been doing it all along, and Lenny didn't relish the idea of going back to the lonely couch. *You'll have to, though, won't you? Unless he asks you to stay—*

"Fuck's sake, you're off with the fairies today." Nero snatched the paper napkin from Lenny's hands and tossed it into a nearby bin. "You taking a nap, or you gonna wake your arse up and come to the site with me?"

"Fuck you. I'm coming."

Nero flushed. Lenny smirked, though it was tempered by a dose of nerves. The real world wasn't half as scary as he'd imagined, but he'd be fucked if he let Nero out of his sight.

Thankfully, Nero seemed to concur. He held out his hands and yanked Lenny to his feet. "Don't worry. I've got you."

They left the station and joined the crowds on the bustling pavements. Despite having pored over the plans most nights before he went to sleep, Lenny couldn't picture the disused warehouse, and so he was surprised when Nero stopped again just a few minutes later. "This is it."

There was no mistaking the subtle pride in Nero as he pointed at a building that, to Lenny's layman's eyes, looked nothing like a warehouse at all. Lenny squeezed Nero's hand, taking in the double set of ground-to-ceiling glass doors, albeit still in their protective casings, and the pile of reject timber that had been cut into firewood and shaped into an abstract sculpture, ready for use in the winter. The place, even half-finished, was incredible. "Fuck."

"That a good fuck?"

"I'm always a good fuck, Nero, but . . . wow, yeah. It's a good fuck. This is amazing. It's not what I imagined."

"Never is. I'm always knocked sideways by how these things end up. Not so much this time, though, 'cause I've watched most of it happen."

Lenny nodded, still awed by the subtle slickness the Urban Soul designers had managed to weave into the rustically utilitarian building. "I love the windows. They didn't look so big in the plans."

"They weren't. Some of the brickwork was rotten, so they knocked it out. It's good to have more light, right?"

Lenny shrugged. Nero had likely forgotten more about restaurants than Lenny would ever know. "Can we go inside?"

Nero pointed to the side of the building. "Entrance is round the back for now. Come on."

They ventured around the back of the building, where they found a hive of activity that had barely been detectable from the front.

"They usually try and hide the construction once they've got the new frontage on. Makes it intriguing, or some shit."

It was a good theory, and it worked for Lenny. "Do they know what they're going to call it yet?"

For the second time that day, heat crept into Nero's cheeks, and he looked away. "They want me to name it."

"You? Why?"

"Dunno. Weren't really listening."

Lenny didn't believe that. Nero was a man who missed nothing. "Perhaps it's because you've done all the work?"

"If you say so."

Lenny rolled his eyes. "Whatever. You gonna give me the grand tour, or what?"

Nero took Lenny around the site, pointing out the newly installed kitchen—complete with the biggest ovens Lenny had ever seen—and the dining area that was in the middle of having a dark hardwood floor put down. With its super-high ceilings and huge windows, the restaurant itself was a work of art, but Lenny found himself drawn back to the kitchen, half of which would be the artisan bakery. "I thought it would feel disjointed in here."

"Disjointed?"

"Yeah." Lenny spun in a slow circle. "I guess I figured there'd be some kind of divide between the pizza kitchen and the bakery."

"Why? It's all cooking."

"Yeah, but you're going to run one side and that lady—what's her name . . . Efe—will run the other. I couldn't see how it would fit together."

"But you can now?" Nero looked amused, though it was often hard to tell for sure.

Lenny considered his question. "I think so. It'll make sense when it's up and running."

It suddenly struck Lenny that life would be very different once the Vauxhall project was complete. Nero hadn't outright said he'd taken the job there, but him moving on to run the pizzeria would effectively put an end to a summer that had so far been spent in each other's pockets. *Perhaps he'll be glad of the space*—who the hell knew? But for Lenny, the idea of seeing Nero for no more than a cuppa in the morning, and a quick beer at night, was so depressing the sticky cake in his belly turned to ash. *And that's if Pippa's still wants you without Nero around to carry your arse.*

What was left of Lenny's good mood evaporated. He'd never imagined he'd enjoy slogging his days away in a windowless kitchen, but he'd grown to quite like his job at Pippa's, even if much of his contentment stemmed from Nero's gruff company. He didn't *want* to leave, damn it.

Nero gently punched Lenny's arm. "What are you sulking about now?"

"Sulking? What makes you think I'm sulking?"

"You're gnawing on your bottom lip like your belly thinks your throat's been cut, and I know you ain't hungry. What's up? You wanna go home?"

"What? No. *Fuck*, no. It's not that."

"Then what?" Nero was suddenly in front of Lenny, up in his personal space in a way that, somehow, wasn't invasive. "You gonna tell me? Or do I have to guess?"

Lenny scowled. "Didn't know you cared."

"No?" For a short moment, Nero's dark gaze was hurt, but the emotion was gone too fast for Lenny to feel bad, replaced by the vague irritation that seemed to be his constant companion. "Fuck this."

"Wha—" Lenny's feet left the floor as Nero lifted him by his collar. The half-finished restaurant blurred, and his back collided with the bare brick wall behind him. "Nero!"

"What?" Nero demanded. "You think you can act like a fucking brat and I'll put up with it because I like you so much?"

The confirmation that Nero did actually like him was enough to stifle any retort Lenny may have made. "You like me?"

Nero stared like Lenny had four heads. "What do you think?"

"Thinking is all I've got. You're not much of a talker, remember?"

Being slapped with his own words seemed to briefly amuse Nero, then he let Lenny slide down the wall, and ducked his head, claiming a kiss that stole every ounce of breath from Lenny's lungs.

A firebolt of heat hit Lenny's groin. He groaned as Nero pulled away, and pictured him naked, and then with the only person he knew Nero had slept with—Steph. Lenny had never been sexually attracted to women, but Steph was beautiful—all hips and curves. Throw Nero into the mix and—

Wow. Combined with the fact that Nero wanted to bottom, it was a hell of a picture. Lenny swallowed. In all the excitement of leaving the flat, he'd forgotten the earth-shattering moment that had kept him awake most of the night: *Nero wants to bottom.* As thrilling as the idea of that was, Lenny just couldn't see it. Nero Fierro was the man in charge, not the guy who bent over and begged for it.

Nero tilted his head to one side, like he'd felt the party going on in Lenny's jeans. "Not enough, eh? You're still not going to tell me?"

"*Tell you what*— Oh." Lenny came back to earth with a bump. Nero had only kissed him to get his attention, not to ravish him against the brick wall Lenny supposed to be bringing to life with the paint kit he'd abandoned in Camden. *And he wants to know why you're sulking, dickhead.* "I don't want you to leave Pippa's."

There. He'd said it, and out loud it sounded even more pathetic than it had in his head.

"Leave Pippa's?" Nero frowned, apparently mystified. "You mean when this place opens?"

"Well, duh," Lenny said, before he remembered he was trying to curb the sassy brat Nero had no patience for. "And you'll be leaving before that, won't you? To set up the kitchen and train the team?"

"I haven't said I'll do it yet."

The echo of Lenny's own thoughts did nothing to calm the panic-laced strop building inside. "But you will. I think Cass set this up especially for you—to give you a place of your own. Why wouldn't you take it?"

Nero said nothing. For the first time since they'd met, Lenny could truly see the cogs turning in his usually inscrutable mind. "Cass wouldn't set this up for me. He's a good fella, but they like me roaming around the other kitchens too much. Saves them the trouble."

"Not true. We only don't see them because they don't need to come when you're there. It's you that won't settle."

"That right? What makes you the expert?"

Lenny shrugged. "I've had a lot of time to brood over you recently. And I hear things. Everyone knows how tight you and Cass are. If you don't believe he'd set a business up just for you, you're bloody dense. Admit it . . . you *love* all the Mediterranean food you've been doing for this project, don't you?"

"What's that got to do with anything?"

That Nero didn't deny it gave Lenny a boldness that was, perhaps, foolish while he was caged in Nero's strong arms. "Cass told me that every Urban Soul business was dedicated to someone, whether they knew it or not. *Bites* is for the old ladies who raised him. *Misfits* is Jake's. I reckon this one is for you."

"You're fucking mad." Nero pulled back with a shrug. "And daft, 'cause, Lenny, mate, there ain't nothing stopping you from coming to work here too."

Nero walked away then, leaving Lenny with a painful boner and little option but to suck it up and trail after him like a lost puppy. A stupid lost puppy, because why the hell hadn't he thought of that? There was no reason for him to stay at Pippa's without Nero, or indeed, at all. *He* was gone now, and he'd taken with him a cage that had been far less pleasant than Nero's arms.

Lenny caught up with Nero by the back door. "You want me to work in the pizza kitchen with you?"

"If you like. You're a good enough chef."

"Gee, thanks."

Nero chuckled, warming the room with a humour that was far too rare. "I meant that it would be entirely up to you what you did here. I could use the help with the food styling when we pull the basic menu together, but that don't mean you have to work in the kitchen. I hear things too, and word is you were the best server Misfits had. They were gonna offer you a step up before shit hit the fan."

That was one way of describing the clusterfuck Lenny's life had become, and he couldn't deny the buzz being out on the restaurant floor gave him. The kitchen had an adrenaline-laced energy all of its own, but he craved interaction, damn it, even if working at Nero's side was an addiction he'd struggle to quit.

"Do you think the big bosses would go for it?"

"For you working here?" Nero nodded. "I'm pretty sure they'll give you a job wherever you want, as long as there's room, which there is here, 'cause as far as I know, ain't no one works here yet 'cept me and Efe."

"So you have taken the job?"

"Piss off. Here, stop your stirring and come look at the garden." Nero opened the back door and shoved Lenny outside. "I'll buy you dinner after if you can behave yourself long enough."

Lenny glanced around the bizarre hipster café. "I can't believe you talked me into coming back here."

"Thought you said you hadn't been here before?"

"I meant Camden in general."

"Oh." Nero poked suspiciously at the chocolate-marshmallow sundae he'd bought Lenny for his dinner. "I thought you were too hyped up from your sugar rush to care."

He had a point. Months ago, Lenny had watched the Cereal Killer Café set up with eager anticipation, but life had moved him on before it had opened, and he'd forgotten all about it until Nero had gently coerced him off the Tube in Camden. "This is lush. Sure you don't want to try it?"

"I'm good. There's a tapas place round the corner. I'll get something there."

"Works for me."

They left the cereal bar behind, bought Nero some spicy potatoes that seemed to cheer him up to no end, and drifted to a nearby park. They ate in companionable silence until Lenny noticed Nero's scowl return. "What's up? Still fretting about that bus?"

Outside the warehouse, they'd made plans for Nero to work on the abandoned bus while Lenny painted the walls, but he hadn't seemed hopeful that he could get it running without having it towed. "A bit," Nero admitted. "It's going to take a lot of money to make it into something that pays for itself."

"You don't think the bosses will pay?"

"I don't know if I want them to. I kinda . . . I think I want to do it by myself, maybe."

"Okaaay." Lenny scraped the last of his cereal-studded ice cream into his mouth. Urban Soul paid well above average wages, and Nero was about as senior as it got outside the holy trinity of men in charge. Add in the fact that rent on the flat above Pippa's was minimal, and it wasn't inconceivable that Nero had cash to throw at a derelict minibus. "So what's stopping you?"

Nero shrugged. "I'm crap at making decisions. I'd probably fuck it up."

The logic made no sense to Lenny. Nero never fucked anything up. He ran the kitchen with an iron fist, managed Lenny's impromptu chef career, ran a million errands for Urban Soul every week, and—

Ah. "You mean you're shit at making decisions for *yourself* . . . because you spend your whole life running around after everyone else."

"I like it that way. Keeps me out of bother."

"How much bother could you get into with that old bus? It doesn't even start."

Nero shrugged again, and his nonanswer didn't matter, because the bus was hardly the point. Beneath it all, Lenny was fairly sure Nero's reluctance to take the project on alone stemmed from the fact that he didn't believe he deserved the rewards it would bring.

"I think you should do it," Lenny said. "Say it does go tits up, how bad could it be? You've lived through worse, right?"

"Lenny, mate, you won't ever know what I've lived through."

CHAPTER TWELVE

The sun always seemed to shine brighter in Shepherd's Bush than it had in Camden, and this morning was no exception. Warm rays filtered through the half-closed curtains as Lenny dragged his teeth along Nero's collarbone, absorbing the answering low moan that turned his bones to molten heat. Mornings weren't Lenny's best time of day, but he'd woken with Nero's dick in his hand and there was nothing bad about that.

He worked his way to Nero's chest, tracing the dark ink with his tongue. Nero shivered and arched into the touch, then rolled them over, baring his own teeth against Lenny's neck.

Lenny's eyes fluttered, though Nero's bite was gentle. He'd noticed that this morning—that Nero seemed more careful than he had the first time they'd done this a week ago, more aware of who he was with, whose lips he was bruising, whose body he was pressing so hard into the mattress. And he kept his eyes open too, like he didn't want to miss a moment.

Lenny fumbled with Nero's shorts, shoving them down his hips, a gesture that, in recent days, had become Nero's cue to flip them again. But this morning, it seemed, Nero had other ideas. He freed Lenny from his underwear, letting his dick spring back and slap his stomach. For a protracted moment, he gazed down at it, apparently fascinated, then he sat up, his leanly muscled legs straddling Lenny's waist.

"*Jesus.*" Lenny threw his head back and thrust up, his cock seeking out whatever Nero was prepared to give him. "Don't do shit like that if you don't mean it."

Nero chuckled darkly and met Lenny in the middle. Then he dropped his chest to Lenny's and pressed their foreheads together. "What makes you think I don't mean it?"

Lenny groaned again. "You don't seem the riding type."

"No? My thighs not strong enough?"

As if. Even half-addled by the urge to drive his dick deep inside Nero, the tight, unyielding grip of Nero's thighs around his waist was unmistakable. *He's gonna be the death of me.* "Just . . . keep going."

Nero obliged, grinding down on him again and again, and it wasn't long before they rang in another heady summer morning with the kind of release Lenny had often dreamed of when he'd had only his hand for company.

"*Fuck.*" Lenny dropped back on the bed, chest heaving, and his belly a sticky mess of his and Nero's come. "What the hell are we doing?"

Nero lay down beside Lenny, wearing his sheen of sweat considerably better. "Literally? Or is this one of them trick questions you already got the answer to?"

Lenny loved the way Nero's caustic cockney accent wrapped around the wrong words, making his grammatical imperfection utterly perfect. "I don't know what I mean."

"Fair enough. You hungry?"

Lenny groaned. "Food? Really? Already?"

"Morning, ain't it? That's breakfast time in these parts."

"I'm a Londoner too, you know."

"Yeah, but you're posh."

"I am not posh."

"Posher than me." Nero rolled onto his back and stared at the ceiling. "Though I s'pose you ain't a toff like Tom."

"Thanks."

"Hey, I'm trying to be nice."

"No, you're not. You're deflecting the question, but that's fine. I'm not sure I want you to answer."

Nero shot Lenny a frown. Lenny turned his back on him and sat up. His heart burned for Nero, and though Nero's every touch told him the feeling was reciprocated, he wasn't in the mood for Nero's reticence. Not today, when he had to do something he'd never done before: work a shift in the kitchen without him. Fears of hawkish eyes and creepy hands had faded since Lenny had identified *him* for the police on a photograph they'd brought to Pippa's, but that didn't make working the grill without Nero's watchful guidance any less daunting—like one fear had replaced another.

Great.

"You won't be on your own today," Nero said. "Cass is in."

"That makes it worse," Lenny snapped. "I don't want to fuck up in front of him after all he's done for me."

"So don't. Get in there and do it the same as you always do."

"As *you* always do. I'm just the passenger."

Nero's arms came around Lenny from behind, drawing his back to Nero's chest. "Yeah? And how do you think I feel every time we go to bed? I ain't got a clue what to do with you."

Lenny snorted. "It doesn't show."

"So? Don't mean I ain't fucking terrified when you get your dick out."

The comparison was fairly ludicrous, but for some reason it made more sense than Lenny could say. He slid off the bed and dropped between Nero's legs, taking his still half-hard cock in hand. "If that's the case, I should probably teach you the way you taught me."

Nero swallowed. "How's that?"

"By making you watch."

A little later than planned, Lenny left Nero in bed—*when has that ever happened?*—and drifted downstairs with Nero's gravelly moans lingering in his mind. *Fuck, he's hot when he comes.* Well, all men were, really, but Nero was in another league—captivating, enthralling, and the fourteen hours Lenny had to spend without him now felt like a year.

Lenny got changed and went to the kitchen. He pushed the door open and the haunting strains of Morrissey vocals reached his ears. *The Smiths? What the fuck?* Then he remembered Cass, the only man who'd dare breach Nero's unwritten code of fevered silence in the kitchen.

"Morning, kid."

Speak of the devil. Lenny turned to face him. "I'm not a kid, you know. I just dress like one."

"Nah, with that blond hair you look like that lad from the Milkybar advert. Anyway, come here. I haven't seen you for ages."

Cass enveloped Lenny in the kind of hug that would've turned him to mush had he not had Nero's embrace to compare it to. Lenny laid his cheek on Cass's chest. It was firm and warm, but he felt nothing close to the inferno Nero's arms often wrapped around him. "Your heart skips," he said absently.

"Yeah?" Cass released Lenny, still grinning. "Must be giddy with excitement."

"If you say so," Lenny deadpanned, channelling Nero before he caught himself. "They're called ectopic beats. Not stressed out, are you?"

"Nope. Was pissed as a fart last night, though, if that makes any difference."

"That could do it."

"If *you* say so." Cass cocked an eyebrow, clearly amused. "Anyway, that's enough of that nerdy bollocks for one day. Nothing wrong with me that not getting arseholed won't fix. You ready to roll?"

As he'd ever be. Lenny trailed Cass to the main-line section and went to work setting up the kitchen according to Cass's rules, which turned out to be vastly different from the regimented order Nero demanded. Gone were the neat lists, penned in Nero's gorgeous handwriting, and in their place came the radio, lots of bad singing by the team of chefs who arrived throughout the morning, and a million cups of builder's tea. And then, as Cass got ready to fire up the chargrill, a power cut stopped the whole kitchen in its tracks, plunging it into darkness before the dim emergency lights came on.

Cass fruitlessly jiggled the ignition switch on the grill. "Fuck's sake, the gas too? How does that even happen?"

Lenny had no idea. He guzzled the last of his most recent mug of tea and carried on slicing cod into neat fillets Nero would've been proud of.

Cass disappeared, presumably to investigate. Lenny took advantage of his absence to allow his mind to drift back to his early morning encounter with Nero. Blowing him had been incredible, but he couldn't help wondering how it would feel to slide his own dick into Nero's mouth. Nero seemed more at peace with touching Lenny than his comments about stage fright implied, but as hard—*ha*—as Lenny tried, he still couldn't picture Nero as a submissive lover. Would he let Lenny fuck his mouth?

"Ah, Nero said you were a dreamer."

Lenny jumped a mile and, for the second time that morning, spun around to find Cass grinning at him like a friendly snake. "Am not."

The retort was out before he remembered Cass was his boss, not the man who'd trained him, cared for him, and ultimately shared his bed with him, but Cass's grin merely widened, and Lenny realised that he lacked the irritable edge Nero wore like a second skin.

Lenny finished chopping the tomatoes for the fish stew Cass was planning to make with the cod. "Did you fix the power?"

"Nope. Got the generator going, but we're fucked for gas."

As he spoke, the lights came back on and the extractor fans whirred to life. Lenny glanced around the kitchen, trying to remember which appliances required gas. "So what do we do with no grill or burners?"

"Fry shit. Bake shit. Make salads. At a push I can dig the portable hob out of the cellar, but it'll only do one of us." Cass banged on the counter and called the chefs close. His plan was simple. "Old-school fish and chips with the cod. Debs, take your peas and whizz 'em up for mushies. Jolen, roast up that chicken and make a Caesar salad. I'll do some steak tartare shit with that filet. Still need a veggie option. Lenny?"

Lenny blinked. "Huh?"

Grinning, Cass ruffled Lenny's hair. "Can you fudge a veggie main for me? And fast? We haven't got long to put this together."

"Erm . . . okay?"

"Good. Get to work and find me when you've got it sorted. Sooner the better, so we can get the menus printed."

"Come on, come on. Pick up." Lenny twisted the phone cord around his finger as he counted the rings. "What the fuck is he doing?"

No answer was forthcoming. An automated voice mail kicked in, but Lenny hung up, since Nero rarely checked his messages. If he saw the missed calls from Pippa's, he'd likely come downstairs—except he wasn't in the building today. He'd gone to Vauxhall with Tom to meet his new kitchen team.

Excitement and panic warred in Lenny. The Vauxhall project had come to life in the past week, but with Cass's deadline for menu options looming, the prospect of a new start there seemed far away. *What the fuck am I going to cook?*

Lenny picked up the list he'd made of available ingredients. None jumped out at him, especially without the option of bunging something on the grill and hoping for the best. *Ha. Maybe you are a carnivore after all.* Lenny shuddered. Fuck that. He'd spent weeks grilling all kinds of meat to a perfect medium-rare and filleting more fish than he'd ever heard of, but the temptation to eat them just wasn't there—

The office phone rang. Lenny eyed it, assuming Steph would pick it up in the bar, but it rang and rang until he couldn't take its noise a second longer. He snatched the receiver. "Hello, Pippa's?"

"You almost sound like Steph."

Warmth flooded through Lenny as Nero's gravelly voice reached his ears. "I sound like a girl?"

"No, you sound like you give a shit."

Lenny snorted. "Won't matter if I give a shit if you don't help me."

"Why?" Nero's tone sharpened. "What's the matter?"

"The gas is fucked. We're running a limited menu, and Cass asked me to come up with the veggie dish."

Nero laughed. "That all? Thought you was gonna say something was proper fucked up."

"It is proper fucked up," Lenny grumbled, though he knew all too well what Nero had likely been imagining. "There's nothing in the fridge but beetroot and rabbit."

"Ah, now, that ain't true. There's a whole case of summer squash, and a load of pea shoots."

"I literally have no idea what you're talking about."

"Fuck's sake. What kind of veggie are you?"

Lenny glanced at the clock. *Shit.* He didn't have *time* to pry sense out of Nero. "You know what kind of veggie I am—one that lives on chips and ice cream when you're not around to feed me."

"I'm always around."

"Not here now, are you?" Silence. Lenny tapped his fingers on the desk, for the millionth time that morning, feeling Nero's absence like a missing limb. "What would you cook?"

More silence, then Nero sighed. "I'm not gonna tell you what to cook. You've been in the kitchen long enough to know how to put together a dish with whatever we have, and if you don't . . . well, I'm wasting my fucking time, ain't I?"

Nero hung up. Lenny stared at the phone and wondered if he'd imagined the weary disappointment in Nero's voice, or the anxious resolve that notion ignited in his bones. Nero seemed to expect bad shit to happen, and the only time it apparently surprised him was when Lenny fucked up something simple in the kitchen. *"Come on, mate. You know this, don't you?"*

Did he?

Lenny thought back over the many long days he'd spent shadowing Nero in the kitchen, pictured the methodical way Nero worked through the fridges and dry stores, using every ingredient available so nothing went to waste. For a man who claimed he couldn't make decisions, he was pretty fucking efficient. *"Start with your star element and work through the dish from there."* Lenny still wasn't altogether sure what that meant, but the fridge seemed as good a place to figure it out as any.

He slipped back into the kitchen, dodging Cass's questioning glance. In the fridge, he claimed the summer squash—which looked like something from a Ladybird book—a bunch of sage, some lemons, and a healthy amount of butter. From the dry store, he took pine nuts and scoured the shelves for pasta. Among the regular stuff, he was surprised to find a case of corn pappardelle. *Result.* Lenny was far from a professional chef, but gluten-free pasta was one thing he knew how to handle.

He added it to his box of tricks and returned to his bench. Cass appeared at his shoulder and peered curiously at the ingredients he'd laid out.

"So that's why Nero ordered this crap. Thought he'd gone fucking mad."

Lenny clanged a giant pot onto the counter. "No one's using that hob, right?"

"Right. I'll get it for you." Cass vanished briefly, returning with a portable electric hob that seemed more suited to a Delia Smith TV show. "Did you ask Nero to order this?"

"What?" Lenny glanced up to meet Cass's quizzical stare. "What's Nero got to do with pasta?"

Cass shrugged, the beginnings of a knowing smirk twisting his lips. "He's done every order here for the past two months, and as long as I've known him, he's thought this gluten-free shite was bollocks."

"So?"

"So . . . I happen to know a certain baby-faced waiter-turned-chef that don't like wheat."

Lenny poked his tongue out. "I'm not baby-faced, so I don't know who the fuck you're talking about."

"Yeah, yeah." Cass pushed off the counter and started to turn away. "Just get yourself together and have a sample dish to me by eleven thirty."

Cass left Lenny to his pasta, and seemed halfway impressed when Lenny presented him with a bowl of roast squash and lemon-sage scented papardelle a little while later. The dish went on the menu and flew out all through lunchtime service. Lenny had barely had time to blink before Cass was turning the order screens off.

"Clean down, folks," he said. "Lenny, come and find me in the office when you're done."

Lenny knocked on the office door. "You wanted to see me?"

Cass spun around in his chair. "I did . . . I do. Take a seat."

Lenny sat in the spare chair, which was actually a three-legged stool that wobbled a lot. "Sacking me?"

"Far from it. I've been talking to Nero about the Vauxhall project. He said you might want to go with him?"

Lenny nodded slowly. "Maybe. I don't know what I'd do, though. I'm not much of a baker. Nero carries me here. It'd be unfair to expect him to do it over there too."

"So work out front. Run the serving team for us."

"Run it?"

"Why not?"

"Er, 'cause I've never run anything in my life."

"Not true. You ran every shift you worked at Misfits. Couldn't help yourself."

Lenny winced. "Didn't make me any friends."

"That's because you had no authority to boss people about. I'm offering it to you."

"Why?"

"Because you deserve a chance to put your life back together."

It sounded so simple, but to Lenny's jaded ears, even with the memory of Nero's arms still burning a path around his waist, it seemed like a distant dream. A pipe dream. "What if I fuck it up?"

Cass sighed. "Mate, do you honestly think me and Nero ain't sat in this office and fretted about every step forward we've ever took? But we've both done bird and come out the other side. If we can do that, *you*, my friend, can do anything you want."

It took Lenny a moment to translate the East-End slang. "*. . . done bird.*" Nero had been in prison? *Jesus.* What the fuck for? But instinct told him that once Cass realised he'd let slip something that Lenny hadn't known, he'd clam up, and the painful ignorance that surrounded Lenny's infatuation with the man who'd saved his sanity would remain.

Lenny sighed. "You're as dark and mysterious as Nero."

"No, I ain't. That motherfucker's got shades on me." There was laughter in Cass's eyes, but it faded fast enough for Lenny to worry what his own face was doing. "How you two getting on, anyway? Nero's a grumpy sod, but he's salt of the earth, really. I'd trust 'im with my life."

Lenny didn't doubt it. Reticent and obtuse Nero might have been, but his kind, gentle ways had carved a path to Lenny's heart. "We get on great when I'm not being the world's worst agoraphobic veggie, and he's not in one of his growly moods. I just . . ."

"Just what? Wish you knew him better?"

Lenny wondered when he'd become so easy to read. "Yeah, that pretty much sums it up. We're . . . close, but I don't know how long that can last if he won't let me in."

Cass was silent for a long moment, tapping his fingers like an ex-smoker with an itch to scratch, and then his own sigh echoed Lenny's. "I can't tell you shit about Nero, 'cause I don't know the half of it, but be patient with him. He's not used to letting people in."

"He lets you in."

"Yeah, but only so far. I reckon you already know him better than I do."

There was nothing Cass could say to convince Lenny that was true, but the opportunity to debate it was curbed by the appearance of the man himself, leaning tiredly in the doorway and looking anywhere but at Lenny.

"All right, mate?" Cass rose up enough from his chair to punch Nero's arm. "We were just chinwagging about you."

"Why? Got nothin' better to do?"

"Clearly not. Did the tables arrive for the dining area?"

Nero shrugged. "How the fuck would I know? I was too busy trying to figure out what made you hire that band of bellends you're calling a kitchen team."

If Cass was offended by Nero's bad temper, it didn't show. He merely grinned. "Don't matter who I employ, you're never happy until you've got 'em all writing lists in their sleep and scrubbing the walls on a Saturday night."

"So? It's gonna take this lot longer than most." Nero finally looked at Lenny. "How'd the big veggie adventure go?"

"Good—"

"Great, actually," Cass cut in. "He sold out. Who knew that weird corn-pasta shite would be so popular?"

Nero rolled his eyes. "Everyone. Loads of guests ask for a gluten-free option when we have a pasta dish on."

"Must be why I don't cook pasta. Fucking ball ache." Cass slapped Lenny on the back. "Speaking of which, I'm gonna close for the rest of the day while the gas fellas come in and stomp all over everything. Lenny, mate, you might as well chip off now."

"Seriously?" A few weeks ago, Lenny's heart would've sunk, and then clawed its way back to his throat with a tattoo that roared in his ears. Any empty hours in his day had driven him half-mad, but now, with the crippling anxiety he'd brought to Pippa's all but gone, the prospect of a night off was exciting.

I want to go dancing.

The thought came suddenly and unbidden to him, and his foot tapped reflexively. It had been *months* since he'd last hit a club and danced till morning. Did he even remember how?

A weighted silence crept into Lenny's consciousness. Nero was staring at him, his expression one Lenny had seen before, usually when he'd zoned out and missed an important instruction. "Um . . . pardon?"

Nero shook his head. "Never mind. I'm gonna head back to Vauxhall to work on the bus. I'll see you later, yeah?"

And with that he was gone, striding away before Lenny found his tongue.

Lenny stood and drifted to the door, frowning after Nero's retreating back while Cass's shrewd gaze burned a hole in the side of his head. "What's up with him?"

"Fucked if I know," Cass said cheerfully, like Nero stormed out on him all the time—perhaps he did. "Reckon you can probably fix it if you get a wriggle on, though."

"Eh?"

"Get after him, numbnuts. He only came back here looking for you."

Cass's words made no sense, but he didn't have to tell Lenny twice to be wherever Nero was. Lenny dashed out of the office, unbuttoning his chef jacket as he went. If he hurried, there was a chance he'd catch Nero before he got on the Tube.

He barged into the staff room, shoving his trousers down his hips. The prospect of riding the Tube alone was faintly terrifying, but the need to be close to Nero was far stronger. He'd *missed* Nero's quiet presence, his gravelly voice, and deep, throaty chuckle. The heat of his strong, leanly coiled body as he—

Lenny collided with a warm mass that felt remarkably like the one lighting up his imagination. His nose hit a hard shoulder, and his elbow lashed out and caught Nero in the face. "Jesus!"

Nero glared, though he appeared unmoved by the glancing blow to his cheekbone. "Why are you running around like a maniac?"

"Why do you think?" Lenny snapped. "Chasing after you, aren't I?"

"What the fuck for?"

Put like that, Lenny had no idea. He rubbed his nose with the heel of his hand. "I was going to ask you if I could grab my paints and come to Vauxhall with you, but if you'd rather be a dick and go on your own—"

"Ah, I see. So you need me to hold your hand?"

Lenny raised an eyebrow as Nero's ill humour hit home. "Have I done something to piss you off since I saw you this morning?"

"If you'd pissed me off, you'd know about it." Nero turned back to the stacked oven cloths he'd clearly been sorting when Lenny had barged into him. "I'm just tired, mate. Got a lot on."

Lenny didn't buy it, but he'd been around Nero enough to know there was little he could do to ease the set of his jaw. Sighing, he went to his locker and stripped off his chef jacket, and the thin white T-shirt he wore underneath. He usually went into the cubicle to change his trousers, but Nero's glowering presence behind him made him feel reckless.

He dropped his chef trousers and bent to retrieve them from the floor. Nero slammed the washing machine shut. Lenny heard the door close, and disappointment bloomed in his belly. He wasn't quite sure what reaction he'd hoped for, but Nero walking out on him was like a kick to the chest. *Loser. What the fuck did you expect? That he'd fall for your great seduction and—*

"Fuck this."

Lenny's chest hit the lockers, his nipple ring clanging against the cool metal. He snatched a breath, but Nero stole whatever words he might've had by yanking his head back, claiming his mouth in a searing kiss. *Jesus.* Lenny's pulse jumped, and his dick hardened. He deepened the kiss, dragging his teeth over Nero's lips, and tried to turn, but Nero held firm, kissing him over and over until Lenny's head spun from lack of oxygen.

Nero broke away, holding Lenny's fist against his chest. He glared down at Lenny, his eyes a perfect storm of lava and ice, then seized Lenny again, shoving him in the direction of the cubicle.

Inside, he kicked the door shut. Locked it. Lenny swallowed. Something was brewing in Nero's chaotic gaze, but the danger was hard to gauge. Did Nero need Lenny to match his fire with an inferno of his own? Or was he on a precipice he desperately needed Lenny to pull him back from?

"Nero—"

"Don't." Nero shook his head. "I don't *want* to fucking talk."

Of course he didn't, but that didn't mean he didn't *need* to. Or did it? As Lenny stared at Nero, losing himself in his molten eyes, he had no idea. *I never know what he needs.*

The realisation stung. Nero had fast become Lenny's best friend—his only *real* friend—but what had Lenny done for him?

Fuck all, except inconvenience him and eat him out of house and home.

The guilt in Lenny's veins burned, but, like he'd read Lenny's mind, Nero shook his head, his message clear. *I don't want to talk.*

Well, fine. There were other ways of communicating. Lenny wrenched himself from Nero's grip and shoved him square in the chest, walking Nero backward until their positions were reversed. Nero tensed, like he was bracing himself for the same bruising kiss he'd claimed from Lenny, but Lenny's hands on his face were gentle, his lips light, and the slide of his tongue easy, like the summer drizzle glittering the windows.

Nero's tall frame melted slack against the wall behind him. Lenny moved closer, wrapped his fingers around the base of Nero's skull, and kneaded the last of the tension away. "There you go," he whispered. "You don't have to fight me for it. It's yours, whenever you want."

"It is, or you are?"

"I am, Nero. What do you want? What do you need?"

The fire in Nero's eyes reignited. He licked his lips, and lowered them to Lenny's ear. "I want to suck your dick."

Lenny had expected silence. He shivered and breathed deeply, inhaling Nero's warm, spicy scent. "You wanna get on your knees for me? Now? In here?"

"That a problem?"

As if. Lenny had dreamed of this ever since Nero had confessed his desire to bottom, and in moments like this, fucking Nero wasn't so hard to imagine. *He wants this.*

Lenny backed away and hooked his thumbs into the waistband of his underwear. He inched them slowly down his hips, giving

Nero time to change his mind. But it didn't happen. Nero's hands replaced his and stripped him bare, and Lenny sucked in a breath that seared his lungs. They'd been naked together before, but in the cramped cubicle Lenny had never felt more exposed.

Nero dropped to his knees and took Lenny's cock in his mouth like he'd done it a thousand times before.

"*Fuck*!" Lenny shoved his fist in his mouth and his knees buckled, his balance saved only by Nero's unyielding grip on his thighs. He gazed down. The sight of Nero kneeling between his legs didn't quite match up with the man who'd shoved him face-first against the lockers, but as Nero took Lenny's dick deep down his throat, Lenny didn't much care. Nero Fierro was a perfect contradiction, he had to be, or Lenny was fucking dreaming, and the premature release rushing mercilessly through his veins belonged to someone else.

He leaned forward, bracing himself on the wall, and fucked Nero's mouth, gently at first, but then harder as Nero opened his throat and tilted his head, submitting in a way that Lenny couldn't quite believe. "Why do you like this so much? What does it give you?"

In answer, Nero took his hands from Lenny's thighs and placed them behind his own back, clasping his fingers together. He pulled his mouth from Lenny's cock. "Like this, with you . . . I feel safe."

Oh, Nero. Lenny cupped his chin, catching a bead of moisture from the corner of his mouth with his thumb. No sensible reply came to him, so he tapped Nero's lips with his cock and slid back in. A heartbeat later, he came hard in Nero's mouth, but he didn't linger in the heated bliss. He withdrew and yanked on Nero's shoulders, tugging him to his feet and throwing himself at him, almost tumbling Nero back to the floor. "You *are* safe with me, Nero. I promise. For as long as you want to be."

Nero's only answer was a crushing embrace. Lenny pressed his face against Nero's chest and tried to count the beats of his racing heart. What the fuck had just happened? Nero was his rock, his port in the storm. How had he not seen that Nero needed sanctuary too?

CHAPTER THIRTEEN

Lenny rolled over for the millionth time, torn between having the warmth of Nero behind him, and the compulsion to stare at him while he slept, rubbing his palm over Nero's short hair, and gently scraping his fingertips through the dark beard. Even the pad of his thumb found entertainment in Nero's beautiful cheekbones.

But the frown marring Nero's face as he slept was hard to take, so Lenny turned his back on it over and over until he gave himself whiplash and settled for lying on his stomach, searching for solace in Nero's hypnotic breathing.

Solace, though, was hard to find at 4 a.m. when there was no reason to be awake apart from the whirling dervish in Lenny's mind, which had been there every night since his encounter with Nero in the staff changing room. With his cock still hard and his tongue in Nero's mouth, it had been easy—too easy—to believe he knew what Nero needed, that he understood the storm in his gaze, the painful strain in his clenched fists, but when the cold light of day had dawned the following morning, Lenny had met Nero's dull half smile and realised he knew nothing at all.

I don't know him.

And it hurt. Lenny was more attracted to Nero than he'd ever been to anyone—consumed, fascinated, and addicted to his quiet company, but it stretched beyond that. Far beyond. Lenny *ached* for Nero, and seeing the torment in him each and every day was tearing Lenny apart.

I need to know him.

But how? Nero wanted Lenny—Lenny didn't know much, but of that he was certain—but his reticence was so deeply entrenched,

Lenny reckoned even Nero couldn't find a way round it. And likely didn't want to. Nero wasn't a talker; he'd made that plain.

I can't force him.

Could he? What if—

"Fuck's sake. How's anyone s'posed to sleep around here with all that huffing and puffing?"

Lenny turned his head to find Nero glaring at him through heavily hooded eyes. "I'm not huffing and puffing, and last time I looked you were sleeping just fine."

"Says who?"

"Says me."

"Yeah? How do I know that you've been drawing them bloody tigers on my stomach all night, then?"

Ah. Nero had him there. Lenny had painted a technicolour tiger on the biggest wall at the Vauxhall site, and stray wild cats had possessed his fingertips ever since. Jake had asked if he could digitally paint a smaller one for the marketing graphics, but Lenny had never been into small art. He liked it *big*, like Nero's cock.

Damn it. And that was the other thing keeping Lenny awake— the raging horn, despite starting off each night with his dick in Nero's mouth. *Or his dick in mine.* Either way, there was no shortage of orgasms. "Sorry I woke you."

"Don't sound it."

"What do you want me to do? Kneel at your feet and weep?"

Confusion flickered in Nero's gaze, then it hardened, throwing up the guard Lenny was tired of butting his head against. How was it that a man could stare at him with such naked hunger and submission, all the while keeping so much of himself hidden?

Lenny turned his eyes to the ceiling, waiting for Nero to sigh and leave the room. And for Lenny to let him, and wonder if it was time he returned to his place on the couch. Because as addictive as the warmth of Nero's embrace had become, what did it mean if his arms were those of a stranger?

Lenny jumped off the Tube in Vauxhall and let the crowd carry him above ground. On the pavement, he lit a cigarette, then turned in the direction of the bakery site and sniffed the air, detecting for the first time the telltale scent of fresh bread. *They've turned the ovens on.*

Excitement skipped in Lenny's veins. The last few weeks had been frenetic, but with the slick Urban Soul machine at full throttle, the Vauxhall project was nearly complete. All it needed was a name, and Lenny was here today to tell the powers that be that he thought he had one.

He shifted his portfolio case to the other hand and followed the happy smell to the site. Inside, he found a full house—Nero, Cass, Jake, and a Bradley Cooper lookalike he knew to be Tom, plus a team of chefs at work in the kitchen, testing the restaurant menu Nero had honed to perfection.

Nero had his back to the door, working the pizza oven. Lenny didn't need to see his face to know his tongue was caught between his teeth, his brows knotted in a concentrated frown that cast a perfect shadow across his chiselled features. Cooking brought Nero to life in a flawless contradiction of inanimate fire.

Lenny left him to it and approached what was clearly the inner circle—Cass, Jake, and Tom all huddled around giant stacks of paperwork. Cass looked bored, Jake intense, and Tom, well . . . despite the authority Lenny had always sensed from the other two—and Nero—it was plain who was in charge.

And it was Tom who noticed him first. He glanced up with a broad smile. "Lenny?"

"It's me."

Tom's grin widened. "I wasn't sure I'd recognise you in the flesh, but Nero said you were on your way, so I've been watching out for you."

"He did?"

Cass chuckled. "Course he did. Reckon he's gonna have a nervous breakdown if you don't go tell him you got here safe. Give me that case. We ain't going nowhere."

Skipping out on Tom so soon after meeting him seemed a little wrong, but Lenny couldn't deny the invisible force that was drawing him to Nero's side. He relinquished his portfolio case. "The stuff for the frontage is all in there. Have a squiz while I'm gone, that way I can piss off home if you hate it."

"Yeah, yeah."

Cass took the case and laid it on the huge wooden table. Lenny cringed and turned away. Late last night while Nero had smoked alone on the fire escape, the concept of the wandering wild cat had made perfect sense, but in the cold light of day, faced with the three men who commanded London's hottest restaurant company, he had to wonder if it was the daftest idea he'd ever conceived.

No, dying your hair rose gold is the stupidest thing you've done recently, dickhead. Lenny moved across the buzzing restaurant, running his fingers self-consciously through his freshly tinted hair. Would Nero even notice? Given the brutal way he was digging pizzas out of the giant wood-fired oven, probably not.

Lenny chanced a hand on Nero's arm, sliding his fingers around his wrist. "Hey."

Nero spun around, pizza shovel raised, his beard dusty with flour, and the relief in his eyes unmistakable. "You made it."

"I did. Were you worried?"

"Yes."

God, I love him and his bluntness. "So was I, if I'm honest. It was weird being outside without you."

"Managed just fine, though, eh? Don't need me at all."

There was humour in Nero's eyes as he spoke, but it felt hollow. Lenny frowned, his fingers digging of their own accord into Nero's arm. "I do need you. I want you."

"Why?"

"Why do you think?"

Nero turned slightly and scraped a pizza out of the oven. "Don't ask me shit like that. I ain't got a clue why someone like you would want a bastard like me."

"You're not a bastard."

"Uh-huh." Nero dumped the pizza at the mouth of the oven. "Feel like one when you stare holes in my soul."

Lenny glanced around. No one was looking their way, not that Nero seemed to care. "I only stare because I want to see."

"I know."

Another dead end. Lenny suppressed a sigh. Part of him wanted to shake Nero into a submission of a different kind than the one that made his bones burn, but aside from the fact that Nero could subdue him with both hands tied behind his back, this was a conversation best had, or not, at home.

Lenny let it go and studied the pizza still sizzling at the mouth of the oven. "That smells amazing. Which one is it?"

"The asparagus and feta. I did the meat ones this morning."

"Good." Lenny wrinkled his nose. "I hate the smell of that sausage one."

Nero snorted. "If you say so."

"Fuck you."

"Later."

Lenny's pulse quickened as Nero's eyes smouldered, then he remembered that *later* was a long time away. It was the Urban Soul staff party that evening—a BBQ and bar crawl in Farringdon—and it would likely be arse o'clock in the morning before they stumbled home together. And before the party even started, Lenny needed to meet Debs in Angel to help her with her hair extensions.

Reluctantly, he released his death grip on Nero's arm. "I'd better get back to the bosses."

"Yeah? Cass said you've designed the frontage."

"I've tried. I'll find out soon enough if they liked it."

"They will. Cass loves that tiger."

"So do I, mate. So do I."

Lenny left Nero to his pizzas and drifted back to the big round table. Only Tom was there, Lenny's scribbles and designs spread out in front of him, his unreadable frown one Nero would be proud of. Lenny bit his lip. "Um . . . hi."

Tom glanced up. "Hi. Thought I'd lost you to the kitchen."

"No, just checking in with the boss."

"The real boss, eh?"

Lenny winced. "Sorry—"

"It's fine." Tom held up a hand. "Nero runs this business on the ground, and he's the face frontline staff see most. I don't have a problem with people calling him boss."

Fair enough. Lenny peered over Tom's shoulder. "You gonna put me out of my misery?"

"Do I need to? Or do you seriously not know how talented you are?"

"Erm ..."

"Why tigers, Lenny?"

He shrugged. "They just fit."

Tom nodded slowly. "I think you're right. They're strong and warm, a little bit mysterious, *and* a little mismatched with the rest of the decor. I like that. It makes me feel like there's a place for everyone here—" He stopped and something seemed to click. When he spoke again, his voice had lost its briskness. "We wanted Nero to do this, but we always knew he wouldn't. This is the next best thing."

"You really like it?"

Tom's gaze flickered to the pizza oven as he traced a finger over the restaurant name Lenny had painted on the draft front sign. "Yes, Lenny, the Stray Tiger ... it's everything we envisioned and more."

Later that night found Lenny and Debs fighting through crowds in one of Farringdon's busiest bars—a gay bar, no less—searching for the Urban Soul crew.

Debs tugged his sleeve. "They'll be by the dancefloor. They always are."

"Thought you said you hadn't been here before."

"I haven't, but they're animals, all of them, and they've been out since eight. If they ain't doing the conga to the YMCA by now, I'll eat my bra."

Charming, though she turned out to be not far off the mark. The dance floor was packed with Urban Soul employees, Cass and Jake right in the middle of it, busting out some dubious moves to an old Alice Cooper track. Lenny itched to join them, but first he wanted—needed—to find Nero. It had been hours since they'd spoken in Vauxhall, and Lenny craved his fix, damn it, even if the nonconversations of recent days had left him a bundle of pent-up nerves.

It wasn't long before Debs abandoned Lenny for the dance floor. Laughing, he scanned the rest of the Urban Soul crew. Tom was at the bar, which seemed the most sensible place to look for Nero too, but there was no sign of him nearby.

The volume of the blasting music went up a notch. Lenny swayed to the beat, absorbing it, letting it seep into his bones and melt away the tension in his muscles and joints. *Think about it. Where would he be in a club like this?*

Truthfully, Lenny had no idea, as every night he'd spent with Nero outside of the kitchen had been a party for two, but logic pulled him to the smoking area on the club's terrace, and sure enough, there was Nero, sitting on a wall with Jolen, drinking what looked like rum.

"Hey." Nero's dark eyes glittered over his glass. "Debs with you?"

"She was. I left her with Cass."

Nero snorted. "Disco twats."

"You don't dance?"

"No."

"Shame."

Nero tipped his glass back, draining it. "Is it?"

Lenny shot a pointed glance at Nero's slim hips and shrugged. "I reckon so."

Jolen cleared his throat and slid down from the wall. He socked Nero's arm and disappeared into the crowds, sparing Lenny a knowing wink. Lenny watched him go, then turned back to Nero. "I don't think I've ever heard him speak."

"I know. That's why I like him."

"Bollocks. You like noisy people 'cause it keeps the attention off you."

"If you—" Nero caught himself. "Even if that's true, it don't explain why I like you, 'cause you flit from one to the other like fucking whiplash."

"Do I?"

Nero reached for a second glass of rum Lenny hadn't noticed. "Yeah."

With no further explanation forthcoming, Lenny left it at that and plucked Nero's glass from his fingers. "How many of these have you had?"

"A few."

"A few, eh?" Lenny chugged half and passed the rum back. "By the flush in your cheeks I'd say you'd had a few too many."

"Nah, that's just you making me hot."

Lenny stepped between Nero's legs and laid a hand on Nero's forehead. It felt more heated than usual, but it was a warm night, and the club was packed and sticky. Add in the rum, and the palpable current lacing Lenny's own blood and—

Nero's kiss cut Lenny's thoughts in half, though why he was surprised, he couldn't say. And he didn't try. He wrapped his arms around Nero's neck and pulled him closer, deepening the kiss, losing himself in it, in *Nero*, until the need for air won out.

He sucked in a breath and dove back in, despite the fact that they had never done this in public, and that he had no idea if Nero's bisexuality was common knowledge to anyone but Cass. Lenny let his self-control slip free, because everything about Nero drove him insane—his smell, his strength, and the cool way he leaned on the wall and turned Lenny inside out all at the same time. Nero still claimed to be bad at making decisions, but as he took what he wanted from Lenny with devil-hot strokes of his velvet tongue, he was anything but.

He wants me. And he could have Lenny, anytime, anywhere.

Here.

Now.

Lenny pulled away with a gasp that bled out into a breathless groan. "How long do we have to stay here?"

"Long enough to rinse Tom's credit card. It's behind the bar until midnight."

"Free drinks?" The prospect didn't calm the heat throbbing in Lenny's groin, but if Nero wanted to stay, Lenny was damn well gonna get drunk. "Why didn't you say?"

Nero grinned and kissed Lenny's nose. "You were too busy harping on about dancing. Come on. I could do with a refill."

Lenny let Nero take his hand and lead him back inside. There was a crowd at the bar, but, like magic, Tom appeared with more rum for Nero and a questioning grin for Lenny.

"What are you drinking?" he asked.

Lenny peered over the bar, scanning the dozens of novelty flavoured vodkas. "Bubblegum voddie and lemonade, please."

"Fair enough."

Tom disappeared, leaving Lenny at the mercy of Nero's obvious amusement.

"Bubblegum vodka? Is it gonna turn your tongue blue?"

"Pink, actually. To match my hair."

"Or that neon shit you've got on your eyes."

So he had noticed. Lenny couldn't deny that he'd had Nero in mind as he'd rummaged through the bag of tricks he kept in the bathroom, because despite spending the past few months fighting to be invisible, Lenny *needed* Nero to see him, now more than ever.

Because maybe then he'd let Lenny see him.

Tom returned with two glasses of Lenny's pink vodka. He hovered a moment, as though he wanted to linger, but Cass bounced up and dragged him away. Lenny watched them go, watched them reach Jake's side and envelop him between them, Cass kissing first him, and then Tom, like his soul burned for them both. Lenny's heart ached with a heady mix of awe and envy. Nero cared for him, wanted him, but he'd never loved as freely as the three men Lenny couldn't stop staring at.

"You never look happy."

Lenny fought to keep his gaze from Nero's. "What does that mean?"

Nero stepped into Lenny's space, claiming what was left of it as his own. "It means, you've got the best smile, but you don't let me see it enough."

"You're drunk."

"Uh-huh. Who gives a fuck?"

Nero had a point. Perhaps Lenny's sudden black mood was down to his sobriety. He downed lurid pink vodka until both glasses were dry and held them out to Nero. "I'm gonna dance. Who knows? Might cheer myself up."

He wriggled from Nero's loose embrace and stomped away without waiting for a response, if there had been one. Nero habitually left conversations unfinished, his only answer a dull stare that drove Lenny insane. Still, dancing was the best cure for all kinds of frustration, and for the first time in months, a packed dancefloor and a kicking beat were right in front of him.

Lenny lost himself to the sea of sweaty bodies and throbbing bass. He closed his eyes and raised his arms above his head, let his body move of its own accord, and ignored every shout and grasping hand that came his way, even the ones he knew, not that there were many. His ex-coworkers from Misfits had barely acknowledged him, and Pippa's crew had migrated to the bar, apparently intent on catching the last of Tom's generosity. Lenny didn't look long enough to see if Nero was among them. He danced to the other side of the floor and stayed there, hugging the speaker, until his mind was devoid of everything except the pounding beat.

He could've stayed there all night. Perhaps he did. It felt like hours and hours had passed by the time strong arms hauled him away.

"Come on," Nero growled. "I wanna go home."

Dazed, Lenny let Nero hustle him outside. Took the bottle of gin he offered and swallowed a healthy swig. "Where's everyone else?"

"Don't give a fuck."

Fair enough. Lenny drank more gin and gazed at Nero through eyes that felt brand-new. His ears were ringing, but his mind was clear. Dancing. Yeah, baby. Worked every time. "Do I look happy now?"

Nero lit a cigarette. "Wouldn't know."

"Liar."

"Am I?"

"Yup. You know me better than you think."

"How'd you know what I think?"

Lenny stepped closer and plucked Nero's smoke from his fingers. "I'm guessing, 'cause that's all I've got. Humour me?"

Nero cupped Lenny's face in his heated palm. "Okay . . . so, I think I know you, but then you change, and I have to start again. I can't figure out if you're the cleverest person I've ever known, or a brat who just won't let me be."

"Maybe I'm both."

"Maybe." Nero dragged his thumb under Lenny's eyes, smearing the makeup that was bound to have smudged by now. "I love this, though. You're beautiful without it, but I couldn't stop staring at you tonight. You ain't no wallflower, mate. You're like . . . a pink dandelion."

"Are you comparing me to a weed?"

"It's an East End thing. My nana said dandelions were healing and they meant happiness. Good job really, 'cause we could never afford to buy her posh flowers."

"My dad bought my mum flowers from Harrods every Friday—expensive ones to make up for the fact that he'd spent all week with his mistress in Hampstead. Frankly, I'd rather have the dandelions."

"Me too, but that's a cockney thing."

Lenny stared at Nero, but too soon, a commotion up the road broke the loaded moment—a fight, by the sound of it. Nero took Lenny's arm and guided him in the opposite direction. Lenny let his pensive silence hang and drank more gin. By the time they reached the underground, he could hardly put one foot in front of the other.

Nero lifted him onto a train and deposited him on an empty seat.

"How can you be so gentle when you're as drunk as me?" Lenny asked crossly.

"Imagine how gentle I'd be if I was sober." Nero dropped into the neighbouring seat and tipped his head back, stretching his long, elegant neck. "Besides, I'll never be drunk enough to hurt you. I'd kill myself first."

Nero's eyes were closed, but his dark words still hit Lenny like a train. He sat up and climbed into Nero's lap, paying the half-empty carriage no heed. "You scare me when you say stuff like that."

"I've never said that before."

"I mean your tone. It's like you've got a shadow you can't escape."

"Just the one?"

"Open your eyes, Nero. Please?"

Nero opened his eyes. Bloodshot and drunk-blurred, they were as hard to read as ever, but a flash of resignation in them made Lenny feel reckless. He gripped Nero's hands, stroking his thumb over the stump of his missing finger, and pressed their foreheads together. "Tell me who you are."

"Why?"

"*Nero.*"

"Why?"

The temptation to bang their heads together was strong. Lenny pressed harder into Nero, like he could push Nero's every hurt out the other side. "I want you to be free."

"I am free."

"No, you're not."

Nero shifted Lenny from his lap and stood. "Why are you so convinced you know what's going on in my fucked-up head all the time?"

"I'm not convinced of anything." Lenny spoke quietly even as Nero's words lanced his heart. "Don't you get it? I don't know you at all, and it's fucking with *my* head."

"So? What do you want me to do about it? Tell you my life story so you can sleep at night? 'Cause trust me, Lenny, it don't work like that, 'cause there ain't nothing I can say that'll give you the dreams you deserve."

"What dreams are they?"

"Not mine."

Nero's dark, hard gaze softened, but only briefly. Lenny stood too and fell into him as the train swayed, but Nero pushed him away.

"I know what you're saying, Lenny, 'cause I've heard it before. You're telling me you can't be with me because I'm a closed book and I won't share my feelings, and that makes you think I don't care, right?"

Nero's tone was mocking enough for Lenny to flinch. "I never said you didn't care."

"Yeah, but you've assumed I don't."

"That's not true. I know you care about me, about Cass. You give a shit about the people who give a shit about you."

"If you gave a shit about me, Lenny, you'd leave me alone."

"Leave you alone?"

"Leave this alone. Whatever. You can't fix this. The damage is done, and it ain't going nowhere."

"Nero." Lenny grabbed Nero's arm as the train rumbled to a stop. "I'm not trying to fix you. How naïve do you think I am? I'm just saying we can't go on like this. I want to be with you, in every way, I fucking love you, for God's sake, but—"

"You love me?" Nero's bitter laugh cut Lenny to the bone. "Pull the other one, mate. I don't know jack about whatever picture you're trying to paint, but you don't love me. I'm a stranger, remember? And that ain't going to change."

The train doors opened. Nero wrenched his arm from Lenny's grasp, slipped through the doors, and walked away.

Lenny watched him go, mouth open, heart shattered. His brain hadn't read the mess between them as concisely as Nero's apparently had, but as Nero disappeared into the crowds at Liverpool Street, he knew with a painful certainty that Nero was right. Without trust, they had nothing, and as long as Nero kept his soul under lock and key, nothing was all they'd have.

CHAPTER FOURTEEN

Lenny went home. What else was there to do? Stumbling drunk and missing the chunk of his heart Nero had taken with him, he couldn't think of a sensible alternative.

Not that sensible was a priority. Back at Pippa's, he swiped a bottle of vodka, scrawled a barely legible IOU, and weaved his way upstairs.

In the flat, his hazed mind half expected to find Nero already there, smoking on the fire escape, or sulking on the couch, but the flat was dark and silent. And horrible. For the first time since Nero had shaken him awake at the start of the summer, Nero's cosy home felt like the last place on earth Lenny should be.

Vodka in hand, Lenny roamed the small space, drifting from the living room to the bedroom and back again, before he retreated to the fire escape, taking Nero's customary place at the railing, staring out at the city below. His fingers itched for a cigarette, but they were in Nero's back pocket.

I could roll a joint. But without Nero, that felt wrong too. Which left Lenny nothing but his own thoughts for company, and those led to nowhere but the devastating realisation that he'd pushed Nero too far. *Why couldn't you let him be?* But as guilt scorched painfully though his veins, Lenny's heart knew tonight had been inevitable. The shadows around Nero's soul were thick and vast, and the fear in his eyes had been there long before Lenny had ever known him. He loved Nero—how could he not?—but it wasn't enough. Nero needed more.

He needs a friend.

Lenny set his vodka bottle carefully at his feet and went inside. He hadn't touched his phone in months, not since he'd taken the sim card out and buried it at the bottom of a pile of old clothes, but with his wages building up in the bank, he had plenty of money to load it with credit.

He retrieved it and the iPhone charger Nero kept by his bed, and wandered into the living room. The phone activated a minute or so after he plugged it in, and a series of messages popped up, all from different numbers. The first could've been from anyone, or a wrong number, but the second, and then every one after, confirmed that they were clearly a hangover from the dark days when the buzz of his phone had haunted him.

Lenny deleted them one by one, but his thumb lingered over the last: *Your hair reminds me of the dolls I've burned.*

Ew. Absently, Lenny fingered his newly pinked locks. Previous letters and messages had often mentioned his hair—mainly lamenting the colour, or that Lenny had chosen to wear a hat—but threatening to burn him was new . . . or old, Lenny supposed. The messages were all dated and timed at the moment they'd come through, but they'd likely been stuck in cyberspace for months.

Fuck it. Lenny deleted the last message, and his focus returned to the task at hand. It took a while to find the debit card he'd stored for payment, but after a few tries, it was good to go. With shaking hands, Lenny tapped in Nero's number and saved it. His finger hovered over the Call button, but his nerves failed him. Couldn't handle the humiliation of an unanswered call. *'Cause an unanswered text is so fucking different.*

Lenny silenced the devil in his heart and opened WhatsApp. Nero used it to keep in touch with the staff groups Jake ran for Urban Soul and new messages showed on his lock screen, meaning they were impossible to ignore.

Hey so . . . I'm sorry I fucked up. Again. Please come home. I'll leave if you want me to. Just please . . . come home.

It's Lenny, by the way.

Lenny stared at the screen. *Smooth, man,* but with his only card dealt, there was little he could do but curl up on the couch and stare at the tiny grey tick, waiting for the second one that signalled the message had been delivered. Nothing happened. Lenny wondered if Nero was on the Tube, or perhaps out of battery. The latter option made Lenny feel sick. At least if Nero read his message and chose to ignore it, Lenny would know he was okay.

Ten minutes later, a second grey tick appeared on the screen. Lenny released a shaky breath and sank back into the sofa cushions. He closed the app, made sure the alert-tone volume was turned up high, and set the phone on the arm of the couch. The ball was in Nero's court now. If he chose not to respond, or asked Lenny to follow through on his promise to leave, so be it. Lenny owed Nero that, and so much more.

He closed his eyes. Sleep seemed a distant dream, but the megaton of booze he'd drunk had other ideas. Lenny's body sagged, and his chin dropped to his chest. He fought the inevitable, but the spinning blackness of a vodka-laced coma took hold, and he slipped into a blank doze.

His Years & Years ringtone woke him sometime later. He fumbled for the phone and answered without looking at the screen. "Nero?"

"Yeah."

"Fuck." Lenny searched for words, his sleep-addled brain unprepared for the unlikely possibility that Nero would call him. "Are you okay?"

"Erm . . . dunno. Probably."

Lenny sat up. Nero was clearly as drunk as when they'd parted ways, but beyond that he sounded utterly exhausted. "Where are you?"

Nero didn't answer straightaway. There was a faint clanging, and then the flick of a lighter. "I'm at work."

"Which work?"

"Does it matter?"

Any hope in Lenny evaporated. If Nero didn't want Lenny to know where he was, he likely didn't want to see him. "I just want to know you're okay."

"I've never been okay, mate. Cass coulda told you that."

"So why didn't he?"

"Dunno. Ask him."

"I can't do this, Nero. Just come home, okay? I'll go somewhere else."

Silence, then a sigh so heavy that Lenny's heart broke a little bit more. "I don't want you to leave."

"How can I stay? You won't talk to me, and . . . I—" Lenny pressed his thumbs into his eyes. "I can't live in silence while you tear yourself apart. It's killing me."

Lenny didn't know how true it was until his voice cracked and weeks—months—of pent-up frustration boiled over. Tears coursed down his face, and he fought to keep his wracking sobs inside. "Nero, you gave me my life back, but I need you to live too. Can't you see that?"

The eerie quiet on Nero's end of the line went on so long Lenny feared he'd gone, then another bone-weary sigh reached him, and defeat weighed heavily in the air. Lenny hung his head, the tears still coming, and let the phone slip from his ear. If Nero couldn't hear him now, he never would, and what did that mean for both of them? Lenny couldn't imagine this strange new life without Nero, and even as the walls of the flat closed in on him, knew his heart would never let him leave.

"*Lenny.*"

Lenny sniffed and looked at his phone. Somehow, Nero was still there. He brought it back to his ear. "What?"

"I'm gonna drive the bus home later when I sober up. Go to bed. We'll talk when I get home."

"Talk?"

"Yeah . . . talk. I can't be who you want me to be, Lenny. Maybe by tonight, you'll understand why."

Nero really did hang up this time. Lenny's heart plummeted painfully into his stomach, and the first strains of a blistering hangover brewed as he stared at his phone's blank screen. *He's coming home. He wants to talk.* Ten minutes ago, it had been all Lenny had wanted, but now the prospect filled him with dread. *"I can't be who you want me to be."* Was that Nero shutting them down? Until he came home, Lenny had no idea, and the impending wait felt like the end of the world.

He dropped his phone on the floor and flopped back on the couch. The recent nights when Nero had got up and left him in bed, Lenny had found him in this exact position the following morning, passed out in front of *Storage Hunters*. It wasn't a programme Lenny had ever watched, but it always seemed to be on. He found it and curled up on the sofa with the remote. His brain felt too wired for sleep, but as the sky outside began to lighten, his body gave up. Sleep consumed him. He longed for dreams of Nero, but none came.

Lenny woke at lunchtime to streaming sunlight and an empty flat. He paced around to be sure, but came up blank. Nero wasn't home, and there was no sign he'd come back and gone out again while Lenny had slept.

Despair nearly sent Lenny to his knees. He went to the bedroom and retrieved his phone. The screen was blank—no messages or missed calls. In desperation, he checked WhatsApp, but Nero had been offline since he'd read Lenny's message eight hours ago.

Logic told Lenny that Nero had likely fallen asleep in Vauxhall, stretched out on the couch in the newly refurbished office. With the business mere weeks from launch, there'd been plenty of Urban Soul staff who'd done just that recently. But not Nero. Wherever and however late he'd worked, he'd always come home. Every night. Until now.

Lenny rang Nero's phone, his heart clattering against his diaphragm, but the call went straight to Nero's automated voice mail. Cursing, Lenny hurled the phone across the room, sweat beading his brow. His hands shook and his stomach churned. *Damn you, Nero.* How had they gone from the safest Lenny had ever felt to this . . . insanity?

Fuck this.

Lenny jumped in the shower and rinsed away a night of sweat, booze, and tears. His body ached, and his head thumped a constant reminder that mixing drinks and angst never ended well, but the temptation to curl up and die in the bathtub was outweighed by a primal need to hunt Nero down and put this shit to bed once and for all. He dressed in the first clothes he found, grabbed his Oyster card, and charged downstairs. The side exit would've taken him straight outside without having to face anyone, but habit took him past the office and straight into Steph's path.

"Ow!" Steph recoiled and rubbed her shoulder. "Where are you off to in such a hurry? I hope it's to the bar to pay for the vodka you pinched last night."

Shit. Lenny had forgotten about his IOU. "It's not pinching if I pay for it, is it?"

"Bloody hell, you're as bad as Nero. At least you're not wearing last night's clothes, though."

"What?"

"Nero," Steph repeated, eyeing Lenny like he'd crapped in her handbag. "He crawled in an hour ago, but I've had to send him into the kitchen."

The kitchen? Lenny frowned. Cass had lost the bet to run the kitchen the day after the staff night out, and his misfortune had given Nero the entire day off—a day Lenny had hoped to spend in bed, together, before his tiny world had imploded. "Nero's working?"

"Yep. He looks rough, but that's what you get for staying out all night pissing around with that stupid bus—"

Lenny pushed past Steph and hurried along the corridor. Civvy clothes in the kitchen during service was strictly forbidden—unless you were Cass and did whatever the fuck you wanted—but Lenny didn't care. A wrathful Nero was better than no Nero. Hell, *any* Nero was better than nothing, despite Lenny's ever-present certainty that whatever affection Nero held for him just wasn't enough on its own.

"Whoa, Lenny, man."

For the second time in as many minutes, Lenny charged headlong into a coworker. This time, it was Jolen, who seemed far less bothered than Steph had been. The quiet man simply stepped aside, though Lenny was sure that his grin was the same as the one he'd flashed last night when he'd left Lenny and Nero kissing on the bar's smoking terrace. *Bastard.* Did everyone know Lenny was head over heels in love with Nero? Everyone *except* Nero?

Lenny didn't have time to contemplate a sensible reply. He stumbled into the kitchen in time to catch Nero roaring at an unfortunate waiter.

"I don't give a fuck whose mistake it was! Get it out of my fucking sight!" Nero shoved a plate across the pass so hard it was only the waiter's trembling hands that kept it from flying out the other side and shattering on the floor.

The waiter disappeared, presumably to rectify the error, and Nero turned back to the grill, his expression an alarming combination of his volatile temper and an intense exhaustion Lenny had never seen in him before.

Lenny stepped behind the line and put himself between Nero and the grill. "What are you doing down here? Where's Cass?"

"He had to leave. Something's up with Jake."

"Jake?"

"Yeah, he— Shit. Hang on." Nero reached around Lenny and flipped some meat on the grill. "Damn it. This burner's not fucking working right. Move over, will ya?"

Lenny moved out of the way as Nero jiggled the temperature knobs under the chargrill. His face was lined with fatigue and stress, and it was clear he didn't have time to explain himself to Lenny. Though still, Lenny couldn't help asking, "Do you have to work all day?"

"What?" Nero slammed the heel of his hand against the control panel. "Fucking thing. Yeah, probably. Can't see Cass coming back. You gonna be okay?"

"Are you? I can—"

Nero waved Lenny away. "You ain't getting lumbered with this shite too. I'll be home as soon as I can. I promise, mate. I haven't forgotten."

Their eyes locked, and Lenny's world centred, but the moment was fleeting, broken by a mayday call from another harried waiter, and Lenny knew it was time to go.

Reluctantly, he retreated from the kitchen and went back upstairs. In the flat, the walls seemed too close, but he couldn't bear to go out and leave Nero behind. Instead of pacing, he spread out his work for the Vauxhall project on the living room floor. With Tom's approval in place for the name and basic designs, Lenny had the go-ahead to work on the final art. The Stray Tiger title had originally come to Lenny's mind for the eclectic pizzeria Nero had brought to life alongside the bakery, forgetting that it needed to encompass the *whole* project, but the more Lenny thought about it, the more it seemed to fit. Efe, the master baker charged with running the bakehouse, was much like Nero in temperament—fierce, strong, hardworking—and she'd wound up with Urban Soul after the breakdown of her marriage, a stray, of sorts, as much as the rest of them. The Stray Tiger—artisan bakehouse and pizzeria. *Yeah. I like it.*

Lenny spent most of the day designing the sign that would also become the project's logo. Jake had promised to help him paint it digitally, and when it was done, Lenny found himself itching to see it plastered all over the once-derelict warehouse. He retrieved Jake's business card from his folder and tapped the number into his phone, remembering too late that Jake apparently had other things on his mind today.

Jake answered with a low whistle.

Lenny winced. "Sorry. Did I wake you?"

"Nah, mate, nah. I'm all good."

"Really? You sound fucked."

"I am. Cass gave me a Valium."

"For your tics?" It was none of Lenny's business, but he'd never forgotten some of the case notes he'd read at uni before it had become obvious that he was in the wrong place, and the use of benzodiazepines to treat Tourette's syndrome had been debated in one of his favourite textbooks.

"Yeah. They . . . um, got all nasty and shit. Couldn't stop." Jake's medicated drawl was pronounced enough for Lenny to know he'd called at a bad time, but Jake spoke again before he could bow out. "So . . . what ya got for me? Tom loves the name. I love the art. Wanna see how you've pulled it all together."

"I can send you a picture if you want?"

"Can you send it now?"

"Um . . . if you're sure?"

"I'm sure. Text it over."

Lenny snapped a picture on his phone and sent it to Jake. Then waited, tapping his fingers on the coffee table while Jake studied it, absorbing Jake's Valium-mellowed buzzing tics. "Well? Do you like it?"

Jake popped, then laughed lazily. "I love it—*fly him to the moon*—I'd like you to paint the main sign by hand onto some reclaimed wood we've got, and then we can scan it and tweak it for the branding. Only trouble is we're running out of time. How long do you need for painting?"

Lenny considered the murals he'd already painted on the walls and tabletops. "A few days? I need more paint, though, and somewhere to work now the bakery is up and running."

"Uh-huh . . . um . . . Did Nero bring that rusty bus home yet?"

"I don't know." Lenny drifted to the fire escape and looked out, by now used to Jake's chaotic brand of conversation. "I can't see it outside."

"If it's anywhere, it'll be in Cass's old space by the launderette. There's a shed out there Cass keeps car shit and tools in. Nero has a key . . . Oh and, actually, the wood is in there too. I chucked it in the other day."

Fair enough. Lenny absently checked his wallet for the company credit card he'd been given for expenses. If he shot out now to buy paint, he could get started this afternoon. "Is there anything else I can do for you?"

"Hmm? Oh . . . no. I'm fine, mate. Gonna sleep for a bit. Call me if you need anything, and take care of Nero, yeah? He's working too hard."

Lenny couldn't argue with that. "I do try and look after him, but he's shit at letting me."

"That's because he's Cass's long-lost twin. It's these East End boys. They think no one will ever love them like their nanas did, so they throw everything back in your face like you don't love them to the moon and back. You just gotta keep on keeping on, mate. He'll fall when he's ready."

Lenny wondered if Jake had meant to be so poetic with his advice, but the lump in his throat kept him quiet as Jake said good-bye and hung up, and after a protracted staring contest with the city below, Lenny ditched the flat and went shopping.

At the quirky art shop on the high street he bought paint and some new brushes, and across the road, a New Age shop caught his eye. He went inside and was immediately drawn to a pendant at the back. It was brushed silver, hanging on dark-brown leather, and a clever mix of a sugar skull and a grungy butterfly. Lenny didn't know if Nero would wear it, but he bought it anyway, and the matching bracelet, and carried them home in a paper bag clutched close to his chest.

The rest of the day was spent painting, locked in the shed. The sign was more complex than the murals, intricately layered, and wrapped around the bespoke typography that had seemed so simple when he'd drawn it in pencil—typography that definitely *wasn't* based on Nero's handwriting. *Yeah right.* Lenny lost himself in a cloud of denial, and only stopped working when the fading light forced his hand.

He checked the time—9:45 p.m. Service had just finished, but Nero wouldn't be done for a while. Still, Lenny couldn't stop the invisible cord between them drawing him past the rusty bus that was parked in the yard, and into the kitchen. Eight hours without Nero was long enough, damn it.

But Nero wasn't in the kitchen. Steph was in his place, cleaning down the worktops.

"I sent him up," she said by way of explanation. "He's ready to drop, and I don't think it's a hangover."

Lenny didn't need to hear any more. He hurried upstairs and let himself into the flat to find Nero on the bathroom floor, pale and sweating. Lenny dropped down beside him and felt his forehead. "Whoa. You're burning up."

"Chucking up, actually, though I don't think I can puke again without losing my appendix."

Lenny grinned, though worry gnawed at his heart. "How long have you been feeling ill?"

Nero shrugged. "All day. Thought it was the rum, but I ain't never had a hangover like this."

"It's not a hangover." Lenny felt Nero's swollen glands and counted his rapid heart rate. "It might be an infection—maybe viral. Got a headache?"

"Like a bitch."

"Anything else? Joints? Bones?"

"Yeah." Nero tilted his head back and closed his eyes. "I'm all right, though. Don't go frowning that old-lady frown of yours. I just need some kip."

Lenny wasn't anywhere close to being convinced, but there was little he could do but wait until Nero was ready to move, then help him up and into bed.

Nero fell asleep almost immediately, face down and still dressed in last night's clothes, minus the jeans that he'd dumped by the door. Lenny wrangled his T-shirt over his head, then pushed the duvet aside, searching for his socks. Nero's heated skin scorched his palms, but there was something undeniably sensual about the idea of curving his hands around Nero's strong calf muscles, tangling his fingers in the silky dusting of dark hair. And Nero's feet were gorgeous—clean and perfectly shaped. *How have I not noticed them before?*

Lenny had no idea, and the urge to kiss them, and suck Nero's elegant toes into his mouth, was strong. Only worry for Nero's fast-rising temperature reined him in. That, and the first good look he'd ever had of the pale scars lining the backs of Nero's thighs.

Jesus. Up close, they ran far deeper than Lenny had imagined, and there was no hiding from the fact that they'd been put there by deliberate force. The white lines carved into Nero's flesh were clearly old, and it was heartbreakingly obvious that they were the mark of a belt—or worse.

Lenny swallowed thickly. Nero had made no effort to hide the scars—why would he when his missing finger was there for all to see?—but it had gone unsaid that Nero wouldn't talk about. *Won't or can't?* All this time Lenny had been so sure it was Nero's *choice* to keep himself so hidden, but with the certainty the marks on Nero's body hadn't been caused by accident, came the possibility that Nero *couldn't* articulate what had happened to him. That it was so awful he didn't know how.

And that Lenny's insistence that they had no future without forcing Nero to try was so fucking selfish Lenny could hardly breathe.

Horrified, he covered Nero's legs with the thin summer duvet and left the room, guilt and shame prickling his skin with the worst kind of heat. Nero was running on empty after months spent looking after everyone else—Lenny, Cass, the business—and now he was sick in his bed after a sleepless night that was all Lenny's fault. Add in the strain that had lined Nero's chiselled features even before he'd fallen ill, and Lenny pretty much wanted the ground to swallow him whole.

He paced the living room, periodically checking on Nero, but when it became clear that he wasn't waking up anytime soon, he gave in and lay down beside him. *Rest, baby. I've got you.*

CHAPTER FIFTEEN

A low groan woke Lenny sometime later. He sat up like he'd been burned, then realised he pretty much had been, if the blazing heat from Nero's arm was anything to go by.

Lenny leaned over Nero and felt the back of his neck. *Damn.* "Nero? Can you wake up a sec?"

Nero grunted, his face in the pillow. "Piss off."

The words were muffled, but the sentiment clear. Lenny supressed a sigh and shook him anyway. "Just wake up, will you? I want to check something."

With a sigh of his own, Nero raised his head, squinting in the dark. He sat up slowly, like every muscle was torn, every joint broken, and fixed Lenny with a tired, long-suffering glare. "I'm up. What do you want?"

"To check you're not dying." Lenny took Nero's pulse and examined him as best he could remember from his days as a half-arsed medical student. "Does your neck hurt?"

"Nope."

"Your chest?"

"Nope."

"Do you still feel sick?"

"As in do I wanna puke my guts up?"

"Yes."

"Nope. Can I go back to sleep now?"

"If you tell me what hurts."

Lenny half expected another monosyllabic response, but as they stared at each other, Nero's belligerence seemed to crumble. He grasped Lenny's hand, then raised it to his head. "It's fucking killing me, Len. I need to sleep."

Len. It was a nickname Lenny despised, but uttered by Nero it suddenly held a certain magic. He relinquished his grip on Nero's shoulders and let him lie down. "I'm going to get you some water. You can sleep when you've drunk it."

Nero grumbled, and obediently stayed awake until Lenny had poured a pint of water down him, but he was asleep again by the time Lenny returned from the kitchen a second time. The urge to lie down beside him and snooze away what was left of the night was strong. Even sick, Nero was the best bedmate a man—or woman—could ask for. But it was 5 a.m., which meant Nero was due back in the kitchen in a matter of hours, and if Lenny was going to step into his shoes, he had to start early.

He left Nero sleeping and went downstairs to the kitchen, glad he'd paid attention when Nero had shown him how to set up the kitchen. Thankfully, it was Tuesday, a service he could maybe handle on his own if he did enough prep.

His first port of call was the huge walk-in fridges. Meat products still made him want to hurl, but Nero had taught him well, and he knew just what to do with the trays of steaks, poultry, and chops. Next up, fish. There were scallops, but Lenny despised them. He picked haddock and new potatoes and made a summer fish pie that he could pre-portion and chuck in the oven when the orders came in.

The veggie special was simple—the last few bags of gluten-free pasta, paired with courgettes and pecorino, and with all the ingredients laid out ready for prepping, Lenny allowed himself a cup of tea. He had a few hours to kill before the rest of the team filtered in, and he found himself enjoying the quiet. The only thing missing was Nero.

I miss him. Pain squeezed Lenny's heart as he realised how true his errant thought was. Nero wasn't far away, but Lenny wanted more than anything to lie with him, rub his aching head, and kiss it all away.

He had to settle for peeling courgettes and grating cheese. Pouring seasoned oil over meat and parboiling pasta. He was loading his prepared pies onto trays when a low chuckle startled him.

Lenny whirled around, searching for Nero, though his heart knew it was Cass. "Jesus. You scared me."

"Ditto, mate. Thought we were being burgled." Cass ventured forward and peered at the fruits of Lenny's early start. "This looks good. Bit twatish of Nero to have you in here so early, though. What's he doing? Cleaning some shit like a grumpy old woman?"

"He's in bed, actually. He's sick."

"Sick?" Cass frowned. "What's up with him?"

Lenny shrugged. "I think it's a virus, but he's exhausted too. I'm gonna work for him today."

"You did all this on your own?" Cass's frown faded a touch. "Wow. I'm impressed. You sure you wanna go back to front-of-house?"

"I never agreed to that. I'd rather help Nero, or Jake."

"Jake? Ah, with the branding and shit?"

"I think so." Lenny wrapped the last of his trays in cling film and day-dotted each one. "He said he'd show me how to use the digital studio. If I can help him and work in the TST kitchen at the same time, I might be able to do something useful with my life."

"TST? Oh, you mean the Stray Tiger? Sorry, I'm still half-asleep." Cass rubbed his face. "Lenny, mate. You can do whatever you want, and it will be useful to *us*. All you gotta do is find what makes you *want* to come to work in the morning. Figure out what that is and we'll talk. Now, what do you want to do today? I'm here, so you can have the day off if you want?"

"What about Jake? He's not home alone, is he? He sounded pretty out of it when I spoke to him yesterday."

"Jake's fine. He don't like being mothered by me and Tom. Gets right on his tits, so we've left him to it. He'll call if he needs us. He ain't Nero."

"I should probably stay, then, in case you have to leave again. Is it okay if I go and check on Nero, though? I haven't been up in a while."

"Course, mate. I'll finish this lot. Come back at twelve."

Lenny didn't need telling twice. He explained his menu plans, then left Cass to finish the prep and organise the rest of the kitchen, and dashed upstairs, ditching his chef whites at the door and padding into the bedroom sans trousers.

He sat on the edge of the bed and lightly rubbed Nero's forearm, expecting a disgruntled groan, but Nero shot bolt upright and gripped Lenny's shoulders, nearly sending them both tumbling off the bed.

Lenny steadied them. "Whoa. Easy, mate. What's the matter?"

"Fuck." Nero released Lenny and scrambled unsteadily from the bed. "I'm late for work. Why didn't you wake me? *Bollocks.* I've got shit loads to do today too."

"No, you haven't."

"Yes, I have. Where's my fucking jeans?"

"They're on the chair, but you don't need them. Cass is downstairs."

"Cass is—" Nero abruptly stopped spinning around. "What? Say all that again?"

"Cass is downstairs. He's going to work today."

"What about Jake?"

The echo of his own thoughts warmed Lenny's chest. "Cass says he's fine, but I'm going to work too, so he can leave if he needs to."

It seemed to take Nero a few seconds to compute Lenny's words. He rubbed the puzzled crease in his forehead. "How did Cass know to come in? Did you call him?"

"No, he came in anyway. He didn't say why. Does it matter?"

Nero blinked. "What?"

"Never mind. Look, Cass is here, I'm here. You don't need to work. You don't even need to be awake. Just go back to sleep, or at least rest, okay? The world isn't going to end if you take a day off."

"It ain't my day off."

"It bloody is now!" Lenny exploded. "Jesus. Why are you such an arse when it comes to taking care of yourself?"

Nero's eyebrows shot up, then a faint grin brightened his tired eyes. "Are you shouting at me?"

"No."

"Sure about that? 'Cause I reckon they heard you in Pimlico."

"Fuck off."

"Thought you wanted me to lie down?"

Lenny sighed. "Do one or the other, will you? Before I lose my shit."

"You've already lost your trousers, mate."

Damn. Lenny had forgotten he was enduring this shambles of a conversation in his pants. "Don't change the subject. How are you feeling?"

"All right . . . I think?" Nero finally sat back down. "Reckon I could sleep another week, and I feel like I drank *way* more rum on . . . shit, whatever day it was, than I actually did. But I'll live."

Lenny laid his palm on Nero's bare chest, absently wondering if Nero had made the connection between Lenny's obsession with his tattoo and the technicolour beast TST took its name from. "You don't feel as hot."

"No? Shame."

Lenny rolled his eyes. Nero must still be half-delirious if he was making quips like that. "Sorry I screeched at you."

"Don't be. I'm a dick. What time is it?"

"Nine-ish. Cass doesn't need me till twelve. Are you hungry?"

Nero blanched and shook his head. "Fuck no. Could murder a cuppa, though. Want one?"

"I'll get it." Lenny started to get up.

Nero beat him to it and pushed him back down. "Stay. I want to sit with you before you go back downstairs."

As if Lenny could argue with that. Nero left the room, weaving slightly, and Lenny lay back on the bed, enjoying the cool breeze that filtered through the open windows. He'd thought the flat above Pippa's a little gloomy when Cass had first brought him here, but he enjoyed the relative tranquillity now, craved it, even, and with Nero for company, it felt like home.

Nero returned with tea and a banana for Lenny. "Don't tell me you've eaten," he said. "Cass never gets the brekkie started on time."

Lenny accepted the banana and made short work of it. Forty-eight hours without Nero forcing food on him had left him quickly slipping back into his old habits of binging on Haribo, and his body reacted instantly to the hit of vitamins and energy, while Nero yawned. Lenny sat up and leaned back on the headboard, opening his arms. "Come on. I've got a few hours. Take a nap."

Nero looked briefly like he might protest, but then folded his long body back into bed without another word. He curled against Lenny and laid his head in Lenny's lap. For a long while he lay very still, eyes open and unseeing, apparently mesmerised by Lenny's fingers combing gently through his hair, but eventually his breathing evened out and he fell asleep.

The hours passed in a flash. Cursing his commitment to Cass downstairs, Lenny carefully disentangled himself, wincing as Nero groaned and rolled over. Leaving was gut-wrenching, but Lenny knew Nero would rather suffer alone than have the kitchen neglected. *Bloody workaholic.* Though Lenny was starting to feel like one himself as he made his way back to Cass, half a mind on the unfinished painting outside in the shed. He'd promised Jake he'd get it done fast, but with Nero's shift to cover, he was already a day behind, and there was no *way* he was letting Nero sleep alone while he pulled an all-nighter. Urban Soul had saved his life, but Nero had saved his heart. The painting could wait . . . right?

It turned out not to matter. Lunchtime service was quiet by Pippa's standards, and at tea time, Cass informed Lenny that between them, they'd somehow managed to prep enough food for the whole day and then some.

"Go on. Piss off," Cass said. "I'll be all right even if I get slammed. Got nothing to do except grill some shit."

"You sure?" Lenny hovered. Nero could handle the grill on his own any night of the week, but Nero was the exception to just about every rule, and his ability to man the grill, run the pass, and supervise the entire kitchen single-handed was nothing short of inhuman. "I can—"

"*Go,*" Cass insisted. "Seriously. Nero's never had a sick day in his life, and I'll feel less guilty about that if I know you're with him. You make him smile, kid. Now fuck off, before I get all emo and shit."

Lenny left Cass to the order pad he'd been glaring at for the past hour, went to the staff room, and tried not to think about *that* blowjob in the cubicle as he changed and dumped his chef whites in the laundry bin. Tried and failed, because it was an image that would be on his mind forever, or at least until next time.

Next time. The notion was sobering, because with Nero apparently on the mend, the elephant in the room was hard to ignore. They needed to *talk*, not fuck, and until that happened, no one would be blowing anyone.

Lenny let himself into the flat with a heavy heart, and went straight to the bedroom, but Nero wasn't there. A quick search turned up empty rooms, and a note written in Nero's beautiful handwriting, directing him to the shed where Lenny had intended to end up all along once he'd checked Nero was still in the land of the living.

He found Nero in the yard, his legs poking out from beneath the dilapidated old minibus. Lenny kicked his feet gently. "You'd better be sleeping under there."

Nero chuckled, throaty and low, and wriggled gracefully out from beneath the minibus. "Stop glaring at me. You look like a psychotic chicken."

"Chicken?"

"Mother hen, whatever. I'm okay, I promise. Just got bored. I ain't used to kicking around the flat on my own anymore."

The backhanded compliment almost made up for being compared to angry poultry, but Lenny knew he couldn't take credit for Nero's grin. He'd noticed during the all-nighters they'd pulled in Vauxhall that tinkering with the bus took Nero to his happy place. "I'm glad you feel better. I was worried about you."

"I know, and I was kinda relieved."

"Eh?"

Nero shrugged. "You told me you loved me. I thought I'd dreamed it."

"And my charming bedside manner changed that?"

"No, but it did remind me that I love you too."

Lenny blinked. "You do?"

"You didn't know?"

It wasn't the most romantic declaration, but Lenny couldn't help the shit-eating smile that split his face. "How would I know? You aren't much of a talker, remember?"

"So? Who needs words? Come here . . ." Nero beckoned Lenny to lie down beside him and peer under the bus. "See this?"

Lenny studied that mass of metal and wire. "What exactly am I looking at?"

"All of it. Cass knows engines as well as I do, and he reckoned it was a goner, one for the scrap heap, you know? I didn't see it that way, but Cass's logic made sense to me, perhaps more than my own."

"But you worked on it anyway. Why?"

"Because I wanted it."

"And I wanted you." Lenny couldn't be sure Nero had meant his cryptic words to turn them full circle, but he couldn't deny the engine's mystery was on par with his reticent lover. "I still want you, even if we can't get past this . . . impasse."

"I don't know what that means."

"Deadlock," Lenny said around a heavy sigh. "I can't keep asking you for something you can't give."

"Pass me that spanner."

Lenny crawled to Nero's pile of tools and fetched the spanner, trying not to let the pain of Nero's nonanswer cripple him. Nero had said he loved him too, but what now? And how many times could they recycle this conversation?

"So, where do you want me to start?"

"What?" Lenny turned his head sharply.

Nero kept his eyes on the bolt he was attacking with his spanner. "You stare at my stumpy finger a lot, but I reckon you know it's the missing tip of a fucked-up iceberg. And you're right. I can tell you what happened on that day, but it don't mean nothing without the rest."

"Will you tell me the rest?"

"I'll tell you anything, Lenny. You just gotta listen."

CHAPTER SIXTEEN

It wasn't the way Lenny had envisioned they'd have this conversation—Nero chipping away at the bus engine while Lenny sat cross-legged at his feet, passing him tools—but it somehow felt right. "You were born in London?"

"Uh-huh." Nero pointed to a spanner, then held out his hand. "In my grandparents' front room."

Lenny passed the spanner. "Your mum's parents?"

"No, my dad's. We lived across the road from them in Bethnal Green until I was seven."

"Then what happened?"

Nero did something loud to the engine. "My dad worked in a factory up the road from the estate. One day, he didn't come home. A machine broke down and collapsed on him when he tried to fix it."

"Oh God. I'm so sorry."

Nero sighed. "It was a long time ago. So much has happened in between, I can't really remember it."

"Do you miss him?"

"Sometimes, but I don't know if that's because I'm comparing him to someone else."

Dread churned in Lenny's gut. Nero had rarely spoken of his family, save the occasional mention of his paternal grandparents and the way his lips curled around *someone else* seemed more ominous than Lenny already knew this conversation to be. "I'm sorry you lost your dad. What was his name?"

"Raffa."

"I like that name."

"Yeah?" Nero dropped his spanner and pushed himself out from under the car. He lifted his T-shirt high enough to reveal the bottom of his epic tattoo. "Maybe that's why you seem to like this so much."

Lenny frowned. Nero's ink was etched on his own soul in minute detail—or was it? As he peered closer, he saw a faint, swirling script layered in the tiger's left eye. *Raffa.*

Damn.

The threat of tears heated Lenny's face. He looked away, swallowing hard to contain himself. "I've never noticed that before."

"I know. Otherwise you would've plastered it all over the wall in Vauxhall, right?"

So he *had* made the connection between Lenny's paintings and himself. "Are you pissed off with me?"

"No, I just don't get what it means to you, or the business."

Lenny snorted softly. "That's why it means everything, because you have no idea how much you mean to the people around you."

Nero let his shirt drop and returned to his cave beneath the bus. "Do you want to know what happened to my finger?"

"Is it relevant?"

"I'd imagine so."

"You can tell me . . . if you want to." Lenny's hand hovered over Nero's ankle, but he curled it into a fist and pressed it against his lips. For a long moment, it appeared that Nero was done with the conversation, but then his heavy sigh broke the weighted silence.

"My mum came back after my dad died. She got a flat in Tower Hamlets and took me to live with her."

It hadn't occurred to Lenny that Nero's mother had been absent in his life until that point, but instinct told him that interrupting Nero could end this before it had truly got started. He settled for letting his hand have its way, and squeezed Nero's calf. "What happened next?"

"Nothing, for a while. I don't remember much about life with her until after primary school. Then my mum got a job at the pub down the road and started bringing men home."

"Men? You mean like, um, punters?"

It was Nero's turn to snort. "No, she wasn't hooking."

"She got a boyfriend?"

"Yeah, Malcom. We moved in with him a few months later. He had one of those old houses in Hackney: huge rooms, high ceilings . . . a cellar. I liked running up and down the corridors, hearing the old floorboards echo."

"Sounds nice."

"Does it? Well it wasn't. Turned out my mum's Prince Charming was a bastard. And he didn't like ten-year-old me telling him so."

"Ten-year-old you sounds fierce."

"Not really. Just gobby, and it got me in trouble with Malcom. Nothing I couldn't handle at first, a few clips round the ear here and there, but then my mum started leaving me with him when she went to work."

"Did Malcom have a job?"

"Never. Fuckin' dole scrounger, weren't he? That's why he moved my mum in—to give him extra money for the bookies."

Lenny had a horrible feeling he knew, in part at least, where Nero's tale was going. "Was he a drinker?"

"Yeah, he was all the stereotypes, but he got worse after I turned twelve. I can't remember why . . . but I remember him tying me up in the cellar every night when my mum went to work."

"That's awful."

Nero grunted as he wrestled with a metal pipe. "It weren't fun. I can still smell that place if I don't keep my mind busy."

"Is that what you dream about?"

"Sometimes."

There's more. Nero didn't need to say it. "How often did your mum work?"

"Three nights a week—Tuesday, Friday, Sunday. Funny thing is, if she'd worked all week it would've stopped sooner. My school was already suspicious when it all went tits up."

Tits up for who? Lenny didn't ask. Nero's style of storytelling was beyond frustrating, but he was getting there . . . slowly. Lenny picked a hole in his jeans as Nero continued.

"It was a Friday night, around Christmastime, when it kicked off good and proper. My mum had gone to work, and I was down in the cellar, as usual, but the rope he used to tie me had gone missing. He accused me of hiding it—which I hadn't—and flipped his shit.

He kicked the crap out of me. He, uh, took my clothes, and used a cable to string me up to this old picture hook, and then he turned the TV on loud and went out."

Cold sweat beaded on Lenny's neck. Hearing this kind of horror about any child was bad enough, but this wasn't any child. It was Nero, and the slashed scars on the back of his legs now made a sickening sense. "How long did he leave you there?"

"I don't know, to be honest. I was pretty out of it for the most part, but I woke up when my hands started to slip out of the cable. My finger got caught, so it was holding my bodyweight. The bone snapped and the cable eventually severed it."

"Jesus." Lenny gagged, glad Nero wasn't looking his way. *Some doctor you'd have made.* "I can't imagine how much that hurt. I'm so fucking sorry."

"I'm not." For the first time in what felt like days, Nero slid out from under the bus and met Lenny's eye, letting Lenny truly lose himself in his molten gaze. "I lost my finger, but what I got back in return was worth every fucking limb I had."

"You escaped?"

"And then some. I ran screaming into the street—naked and covered in blood, battered from years of that cunt stamping on me. I never went back to that house . . . not inside, anyway."

Lenny let out a long, shaky breath he hadn't realised he was holding. "Did your mum leave him?"

Nero pushed himself free of the bus and shrugged. "She didn't have much choice when he got sent down for child abuse, but she didn't get me either. Social services decided there was no way she hadn't known what was going on, and gave me to my grandparents— my dad's parents—instead. She didn't bother arguing, just fucked off to Birmingham to shack up with someone else. Never heard from her again."

Despite Nero's matter-of-fact delivery, crippling sadness washed over Lenny. He searched for relief that Nero's tale was over, but found none. Nero absently rubbed the stump on his left hand, and Lenny closed his eyes. "It's not over yet, is it?"

"Can be, if you want it to be. We can leave it right here and forget this conversation ever happened."

Lenny's nerves jangled, and he shook his head, forcing himself to look at Nero again. "Never. Keep talking. I'm good."

"Liar." Nero scrambled to his feet and disappeared briefly into the shed. He returned with yet another bottle of rum. "One day we're gonna have to figure another way of making it through these conversations."

Lenny accepted the bottle and took a deep swig. "The fact that you think we'll have more conversations like this terrifies me."

"Why? I thought you wanted this?"

"I wanted to understand, Nero, not force you back to a place so fucking horrific." Nausea roared again. Lenny clamped his hand over his mouth and counted to ten.

Nero nudged his shoulder. "I'm sorry I'm upsetting you."

"Why? It's my own fault for being a nosy bastard, isn't it?"

"That's not what this is. Do you think I'd have put us both here if it was?"

Lenny shook his head. "I'm so sorry."

"Don't be. Just let me finish? Please?"

Lenny swallowed another gulp of rum and passed the bottle to Nero, nodding for him to continue.

Nero took a healthy swig of his own, then set it aside. "Where was I?"

"Your mum moved to Birmingham."

"And she's still there, as far as I know."

"What about Malcom? Is he still in prison?"

"No. He did three years, then they let him out." Nero's hands twitched, like they were itching to reclaim the bottle. "And that's when it really got messy, because his house was two streets away from my grandparents' flat, so I saw him every day, whether I wanted to or not."

"The police couldn't do anything?"

"You know the answer to that."

The truth hit home, and Lenny shuddered. "Did you ever speak to him?"

"No. I tried to avoid him, but he knew where my school was and the route I took to get there. It was like he wanted to run into me, the sadistic fuck, and that was him all over, and *that* was what I couldn't forgive. He enjoyed it, you see, what he did to me. It was fun for him. His only saving grace was that he didn't try to knob me. I'd have cut his fucking dick off if he had."

It seemed a scantly positive point, but the terrifying conflict in Nero's gaze kept Lenny quiet. He scooted closer and rubbed his cheek on Nero's shoulder. Nero rested his own head briefly on Lenny's and let loose a bone-deep sigh.

"I didn't deal with him very well. I was a little shit at school already, but when I started seeing him on my way there, I just stopped going. Fell in with the wrong crowd, started terrorising the estate . . . fucking stereotypical messed-up kid. Picked up my weed habit too, but I ain't too bothered about that. Most days it's the only thing that stops me becoming that person again, you know?"

"Um, I guess?"

"Anyway . . ." Nero gave in and reached for the rum bottle. "I started to go a bit mental. I saw him everywhere, even when he wasn't there—in my sleep, in every shadow. Drove me round the fucking bend, until one day I woke up and something snapped, you know? I couldn't take it anymore, and some weird compulsion took over, so I got up and went to his house."

Lenny swallowed and closed his eyes. "What did you do?"

"I burned it down."

"You burned it down?"

"Yup, and him with it. But I didn't know it at the time. I thought he'd be at the bookies. I didn't know he was inside. You've got to believe me, Lenny. I was a fucked-up kid, but I didn't want to kill no one."

Lenny took a deep breath and opened his eyes. He waited for shock—revulsion—to wash over him, but none came. How could it, when he looked at Nero and saw nothing but a frightened, traumatised young boy who'd acted out of terror? "I believe you."

"Yeah, well. You're probably the only one. I got done for manslaughter and sent down for twice as long as he did for everything he done to me."

"You went to prison?"

"Young offenders, actually—Feltham, same one as Cass."

"Were you in at the same time?"

"No. He found me when they kicked me out. I was sitting outside with a bag and nowhere to go when he pulled up and offered me a job."

"Couldn't you go back to your grandparents?"

"No. They both died while I was inside." The cool distance in Nero's tone wavered. "My granddad first, then my nana. She didn't last long without him."

"I'm sorry, Nero."

"Me too. I missed their funerals, and I didn't really grieve for them until Cass took me to an ink studio and told me to carve something into myself that brought me to life again."

"Ink?" Fuck. Massive it might've been, but Nero had only one tattoo. "So it's not about you?"

Nero snorted. "Course it ain't. What that word . . . narcissist? Yeah, I ain't one of them, am I?"

Lenny should've known Nero wouldn't have let an interpretation of himself be plastered over the walls of the Vauxhall project. There was still much to learn about him, but he wasn't that man. Fuck no. "I'm sorry. I'd have asked first if I'd known what it meant."

"You did know what it meant, just not what it meant to *me*. And I like that. You don't have to know it all to know what matters."

Lenny absorbed that, and let it flow into the part of his soul that would always belong to Nero. "So your granddad was a bit of a tiger?"

"Not in the slightest—it was the other way around. My nana was the tiger. My granddad was a delicate man, an artist, really. He worked for a funeral director in Hackney, engraving gravestones. The butterfly reminded me of the ones he'd done for stillborn babies. He'd spend weeks on them, and it broke his heart—" Nero's voice cracked. He reached for Lenny's hand and squeezed it so hard Lenny thought his fingers would surely snap. "What I did to that cunt finished him off, I'm sure of it, and that's what I'll never forgive myself for. I don't care that I killed Malcom, and that ain't gonna change."

The raw emotion in Nero's voice turned to defiance, but it was wasted on Lenny. How many times had he wished for his stalker's death, despite only suffering a fraction of the hell Nero had endured? A man had died at Nero's hand, and the notion that he'd deserved no better was easier to accept than Lenny could quite believe.

And the relief came now too. Relief that he'd made some headway into truly knowing the man he loved so much. Relief that Nero's tormentor could hurt him no longer—in person, at least, because there was no doubt that he haunted Nero's dreams. "I don't know what to say."

Nero shook his head sadly. "I know I've hurt you, because I've hurt people before, good people, who really cared about me."

"And you wanted to hurt me."

"What? No, I didn't—"

"Yes, you did. Bad relationships breed bad habits. They're hard to break, even when you find that one soul who loves you more than anyone else ever will."

Nero's gaze faltered. "Do you still love me?"

"You'll have to try harder than that to get rid of me." Lenny spoke to himself as much as to Nero, like his head needed to hear what his heart already knew—that nothing and no one could come between them as long as they both cared enough to fight.

But his thoughts were cut short by Nero's kiss, hard and searching, and his strong hands lifting Lenny up like he weighed nothing.

"I didn't know I needed you until you found me, but I *do* need you, so much, Lenny. Come to bed with me . . . please?"

CHAPTER SEVENTEEN

Lenny's back hit the mattress, driving the air from his lungs in a startled gasp. But shock had no time to register as Nero's heated palms cupped his face, and his lips met Lenny's in another of the bruising kisses that had carried them upstairs, tumbling them through the flat and onto the bed.

Is this really happening?

God yes, and there was no doubt about where it was going. They were going to fuck, and despite how many times Lenny had imagined it, it was clear Nero had his own ideas of how it was going to go down.

Nero claimed Lenny's mouth again and again, making short work of removing his clothes, then he shoved Lenny up the bed, splaying him, so he was prone, and inserted himself into the cradle of Lenny's legs. He dropped a palm on either side of Lenny's head. "I want you."

Lenny drank in the perfect contradiction of Nero's shyly bold smirk. "Any way you want me, I'm yours."

"I know."

Those two little words meant everything. Lenny stretched his neck and pressed his forehead to Nero's, gently rubbing nose to nose. "Then have me."

It was, apparently, all the encouragement Nero needed. His touch grew rougher, braver. His clothes followed Lenny's, littering the floor, and when they were both naked, bare to the last of the balmy summer heat, it was like nothing bad had ever happened to either of them, because there *was* nothing else, only them, now, together, like this.

Nero stared down at Lenny, his pupils blown with desire, his hand around Lenny's cock, and his fingers, God, his fingers probing where Lenny wanted them most. Lenny groaned, arching his back, his breath sharp, rapid, and airless, as Nero's fingers moved with precision, stroking and twisting, rubbing on the bundle of nerves that set him on fire.

"Fuck, are you sure you've never done this before?"

Nero grinned. "I do have my own body to play with, you know."

A bolt of pleasure ripped through Lenny. Damn. He'd never imagined Nero touching himself. "Oh God, I can't handle you."

"Try." Nero withdrew his fingers and walked on his knees up Lenny's body, straddling Lenny's chest. He tapped his cock on Lenny's lips. "I dream about sucking you sometimes. I never thought I'd like it so much."

Lenny believed him. Nero on his knees in that damn fucking cubicle would stay with him forever.

He opened his mouth, granting Nero entrance, and swallowed him until Nero's dick scraped the back of his throat. The urge to gag was intense, but he fought it, and Nero's pleasured half-moan made his eyes roll. He sucked harder, working his tongue along every ridge and vein, committing it all to memory, until Nero pulled away.

Nero sat back on his heels, tugging Lenny up with him. "I've got johnnies, and I think Cass left a family-sized bottle of lube in the bathroom."

"He did," Lenny panted out. "And it's good stuff. Get it."

Nero scrambled off the bed and out of the room, returning in a flash with condoms and lube. He tossed them on the bed beside Lenny and reached for the condoms while Lenny went for the lube. "Ready?"

Lenny nodded, his tongue stuck to the roof of his mouth, his heart jumping with every inch Nero moved closer. He'd long ago lost any fear of bottoming, instead coming to crave the heady-dark burn of being stretched and filled, but this was different—this was *Nero*—and Lenny could hardly breathe for wanting him. He was dizzy with arousal, half-mad with it. His body tightened, anticipating Nero's sheathed cock breaching him, but at the pivotal moment, Nero's rough hands gripped his hips and flipped him over.

"On your knees."

Nero left enough space between them for Lenny to wriggle free, but *fuck that*. Lenny didn't want space between them, he wanted— *yearned*—the sensation of Nero pressed against him. He reared back, seeking Nero's chest. Nero found him and wrapped his arms tight around him, one at his waist, one at his throat, like Nero couldn't get close enough to him without climbing inside his skin. "Is this what you want?"

"Yes—shit, *Nero*. Do you want me to beg you to fuck me?"

"You might have to beg me to stop."

It was a world away from the scene he'd planned—all those nights Lenny had lain awake, picturing the moment he'd lay Nero down and fuck him—but whatever had turned their dreams upside down made such perfect, illogical sense, that Lenny could barely stand it.

He dropped his head and closed his eyes, steeling himself for the stab of discomfort that could only be seconds away. Nero handled him with strength and grace, but he'd never done this before, never eased his dick inside another man in the seamless slide that took practice to get right.

"*Oh!*" Lenny's fingers curled around the sheets as Nero's dick eased home, but instead of stinging pain came the intense rush he'd dreamed about in that distant other world before Nero, the world where he'd had no idea what it meant to want someone so absolutely as he did Nero. As pleasure sent him soaring, he truly understood for the first time in his life that who put what where meant nothing. "Damn, Nero."

Nero's arm tightened around Lenny's throat, and he cupped Lenny's face in his hand, jerking it back for a kiss that was no more than a breathless brush of lips. Then he rocked his hips, driving his cock in and out until coherent thought left Lenny. That first, long, piercing stroke had been mind-blowing, but this? Fuck, it was *insane*. "Harder, God . . . oh, harder."

"Yeah?" Nero gripped Lenny's hips and fucked him deeper, faster, pushing him down until his chest hit the mattress and his face mushed into the duvet. "Oh God . . . I didn't know it could feel this good. This ain't gonna last long."

Any disappointment in Lenny's brain was quickly overwhelmed by an imminent orgasm that would wait for no one. *Fuck. Already?* But the need to come was unbearable. Lenny bit his lip hard enough to draw blood and fumbled for his cock, praying he wouldn't fall apart before Nero blew inside him. God, he needed him to come, needed to hear him, feel him. *I need him to come for me.*

Nero's rhythm faltered and his breaths grew ragged. He dug his blunt nails into Lenny's hips. "Lenny—"

Whatever he'd been about to say was cut off with a strangled moan. His dick swelled and pulsed inside Lenny, and Lenny's vision turned white. The world stopped. Nero drove deep and came with a yell, and Lenny tumbled over the precipice he'd been teetering on ever since they'd first kissed all those weeks ago. He shuddered and cried out, cursing, trembling, and then screaming Nero's name as he spilled on his hand and the sheets below him.

He opened his eyes to find they had toppled to the side and landed in an ungainly heap of tangled, sweaty limbs. "Jesus."

Nero's only response was a low hum. Lenny reached for him and found his chest. He laid his palm over Nero's thudding heart and counted the beats, absently this time, without the worry of recent days, when the heat beneath Nero's skin had made him so anxious. "You weren't supposed to be so good at that."

"Eh?" Nero cracked open a lazy eye.

Lenny shrugged. "I thought you wanted me to fuck you?"

"I do, not because I didn't know how to fuck *you*, though. I ain't a one-trick pony, am I?"

Clearly not, if the haze still clouding Lenny's vision was anything to go by. "Why do you want to bottom, then? If it's because you're craving pain, you'll be disappointed, 'cause I'm not going to hurt you."

"I don't want you to hurt me." Nero's gaze focused on something Lenny couldn't see before he looked at Lenny. "You fucking me is just what I see when I close my eyes."

"What about tonight?"

"Tonight? Lenny, mate, I didn't stop to think about it, what I wanted, what you wanted, even. It happened, and isn't that how it's supposed to be? I don't want to spend the rest of my life organising who puts their dick where."

Put like that, Lenny could hardly argue, and the notion of spending the rest of his life with his dick anywhere near Nero warmed his chest. He took Nero's hand. "Still, are you sure you've never done that before?"

"I've never done it with a bloke."

"Oh." *Oh*, indeed. Again, the thought of Nero with a woman was oddly thrilling, despite having no desire to be with one himself.

Nero sat up and stroked Lenny's sweat-dampened hair back from his face. "I keep forgetting to tell you how much I like this."

"The colour?"

"Yeah. It suits you. Cass told me you had pink hair when he met you. I was jealous, 'cause I missed it."

"All this time you've had me worried I'm too flamboyant for you."

"Why would you think that?"

Lenny shrugged and fingered the bangles he wore on his left arm, the silver glinting in tandem with the metallic paint splatters on his hands. "Because I'm a muppet."

"If you say so." There was mirth in Nero's voice. He grinned warm and wide, before swooping in for a kiss. "What time is it?"

"Ugh, I have no idea." Lenny forced himself to sit up and looked around for his jeans. They were hanging from the bedroom door, the skinny legs crumpled and bent at unnatural angles. "Does it even matter?"

"Not really. Bed?"

Lenny didn't need asking twice. He scrambled under the covers, seeking Nero out the instant they were both safely under the duvet. Their lips met in a kiss that was warm and languid, gently stoking the embers of the inferno that had gone before. Lenny breathed Nero in, and then pulled back, searching him for any sign of distress or regret. "Are you okay?"

Nero nodded. "I'm good, mate. Better than good. I feel kinda free. Is that weird?"

"No weirder than I am."

Nero chuckled. "Ain't that the truth. Did you finish your painting?"

"Not yet. Might get it done tomorrow if you're okay to get back in the kitchen."

"I was okay to be in the kitchen today."

"Liar."

Nero's grumbling reply faded away. For a while Lenny thought him asleep until he sighed softly and opened his eyes. "Everything's about to change."

"I know." Disquiet threatened the tranquil calm that always came with being in Nero's arms. "I've been in a bit of a bubble here, but it won't be like that commuting to Vauxhall, will it?"

"Depends what role you decide to take on, but it can't be worse than schlepping into Covent Garden every day like I did when I was at Pink's. Twatty businessmen everywhere. Dick bags."

Lenny laughed. Nero seemed to enjoy early mornings, but his ingrained dislike of the general population was something else. "You hate everyone."

"Do not. And it won't matter anyway if we move to Vauxhall."

"'We'?"

Nero raised an eyebrow. "You think I'm going without you?"

"Erm, no?"

Nero's scowl was terrifying and heart-warming all at once.

Tears stung Lenny's eyes. He blinked them away and tried to focus on the other source of his uncertainty. "Work-wise, I think I'd like to help Jake, if he'll have me. I like waiting tables, but I kinda promised myself when I quit uni that I'd do something with my art."

"So why didn't you?"

"Couldn't, I guess. I shut it down when . . . *he* was around. I wanted to be invisible, and it was like all facets of my self-expression stopped working. I had different-coloured hair every week before all that shit . . . makeup, bright clothes. My old workmates at the club used to call me a chameleon and sing Boy George at me every time I came into work."

"If you want serenading, you'll have to ask Cass. I ain't no singer."

"And you like the quiet too much. But that's been good for me. I lived my life at a million miles an hour before I came here, and it blurred by so fast I missed it all."

Nero combed his fingers through Lenny's hair again. "I get that, 'cause I feel the same in reverse, I s'pose. I'd forgotten how to see colour before you came along and trashed my living room. You even brightened up my food."

Lenny knew Nero well enough to know how much the last statement meant. "Does this mean you've come around to building sculptures out of pea shoots?"

"Fuck no, but I can't imagine a world without watching *you* do it."

It was as close to a compromise as Nero ever got when it came to cooking, and in a week or so it wouldn't matter. Nero would be manning the pizza oven at TST and Lenny would be . . . well, who knew? Their days of bickering over the chargrill at Pippa's were numbered, and though it had been the last thing Lenny had imagined himself doing when Cass had offered him the lifeline, lying in bed with Nero now, he couldn't have been more thankful.

Because being with Nero was all there was, and all there would ever be.

CHAPTER EIGHTEEN

The following week passed in a blur of dashing between the old kitchen and the new as Nero prepared to hand Pippa's back to Jimbo and take his place at TST. And in the first week of September, Lenny said good-bye to working at Pippa's too, and took on his new job as Jake's assistant. Commuting from the flat, his new role exhausted and excited him in equal measure, and the renewed spark in his hypnotic eyes kept Nero's head above water as the launch night for TST fast approached.

God, I'm tired. But they all were, even Tom, usually so unflappable and cool. "How are you going to prepare the calzones if the grate trays don't arrive in time?"

Nero shrugged. "Have to buy some from the wholesalers up the road, won't we?"

Tom's jaw twitched. "Why didn't we do that in the first place? I don't understand how we've ended up panic-ordering equipment two days before opening."

"Because we didn't know the ovens would be too hot to cook calzones on the stone. They take longer than pizzas so they're burning on the bottom, and it ain't like we can turn the stone down, is it?"

"Are you trying to piss me off?"

"No, but you told us not to buy stuff from the cowboys up the road, so what do you want me to do?"

"Nero—"

"*Tom.*" Cass stepped in, perhaps knowing Nero's short fuse well enough to be cautious, except he was wrong this time. Lenny had obliterated Nero's fiery temper to the point where now, Nero simply turned away from Tom's irritation and scooped another pizza out of the oven. Who cared if they couldn't serve calzones on opening night? They had plenty of other good shit to sell.

He tuned the conversation out, letting Cass uncharacteristically play the role of pacifier, and his thoughts drifted to the pinky-blond bombshell he'd kissed good-bye at Shepherd's Bush tube station at the arse crack of dawn that morning. Lenny wasn't, and would never be, a morning person, but his sleep-addled smile had been on Nero's mind ever since. That, and the toe-curling fuck they'd managed to squeeze in before work. Nero had never been much into anal sex with women, and the yearning to have Lenny inside him still made his head spin—even if it conversely terrified him enough for Lenny to be scared of it too—but fucking Lenny was something else; the way he moved, the sounds he made, the way his body clamped so tight around Nero's dick it felt like he'd never let go.

And Nero didn't want him to let go. Falling in love with Lenny had taken him by surprise, though he'd known it long before he'd said it aloud, but he was lost in him now, and could hardly imagine the time when running from him had seemed the safer option.

"You're different," Cass had said to him just a few days ago. And he was right. Happy wasn't a place Nero believed was for him, but with Lenny sharing the load of his demons, he was as close as he'd ever been. He felt alive instead of lost in the constant search for oblivion.

Didn't stop him worrying that Lenny saw him as some kind of psycho, though. And if he did, was he wrong? Most days, Nero didn't think so, and despite his good mood and temper, four hours of grafting over a hot pizza oven was beginning to fray his tired nerves, like the heat penetrated his soul with every scrape of metal on stone. Baring his soul to Lenny, it seemed, wasn't a miracle cure.

He handed the reins to his newly appointed sous chef and went outside for a smoke. His craving for peace and quiet was almost as strong as the one for nicotine, and he was in his own world when Tom made him jump a little while later.

"Sorry for being ornery," Tom said. "I'm just a bit fraught. I've never known so many stupid things to go wrong on a project. It's usually the people I have to worry about, not a shortage of teaspoons."

"You're complaining about *not* having to fret about some lunatic band of idiots wrecking your baby?"

"Pretty much. I left the employment to Cass this time around, and he's somehow managed to pull together the tightest new team we've ever had."

In spite of his initial misplaced pessimism, Nero couldn't argue with that. If the TST kitchen team lived up to his expectations, his new role would be a piece of piss, which felt slightly too good to be true.

Like he'd heard Nero's thoughts, Tom leaned on the railing and gazed out over the waterside dining area. "I suppose I'm just waiting for the real hammer to fall."

"Why? Don't worry about shit till it happens, mate. Makes you old."

Tom sighed. "I suppose you're right. Have you heard from Lenny today? Jake hasn't checked in for a while."

It was Nero's habit to fob Tom off any chance he got, but the infinitesimal edge to the question made him look up. "He messaged me a while ago. Said they were still in Stockwell sorting the glass delivery. Why? Something wrong?"

"No."

"Really? 'Cause you look like a bulldog chewing a wasp."

"And you sound like Cass when he's not getting any." Tom's frown turned droll. "Seriously, though. I like that Jake has Lenny with him. All the running around he does gets on top of him sometimes. It's hard not to worry that we won't be there when he needs us most."

Nero's habitual sarcasm died a death as Tom's words hit home. Tom and Cass adored Jake as much as they did each other, but Jake wasn't like them. His TS left him vulnerable in a way Nero would never truly understand, and he could hardly bear to imagine how tough it was for Cass and Tom who loved him so much. Pain lanced Nero's chest as he recalled the day Lenny had finally forced himself to leave the flat, and then every day after for weeks and weeks when he'd jumped at every little sound. It seemed to be all behind him now, but Nero couldn't forget the terror in his eyes. Wouldn't ever forget it. He pulled his phone from his pocket and waved it at Tom. "Save me getting my knickers in a twist too, eh?"

He called Lenny, trying not to melt under Tom's watchful gaze as Lenny answered with a giggle. "Where you at?"

"Just got off the Tube. Be there in five."

"Hurry up," Nero said. "Tom's twitching for Jake, and . . . I miss you."

"Me? Or the twenty fags I've got in my pocket, 'cause I know you'll have smoked yours by now."

"You're all heart."

"Not really, but what I have is yours."

Nero turned away from Tom as heat flooded his cheeks. Would he ever get used to the certainty in Lenny's voice when he said shit like that? He hoped not, because all the rum in the world didn't carry a buzz quite like the one that came with loving Lenny. "Just get your arse here."

He hung up and faced the music. Tom was grinning a grin that would've looked more at home on Cass. "All these years, I had no idea."

"No idea about what?"

"That you swung a little our way. Cass kept it from me until recently—for your sake, I think. And he was right. You weren't ready for Lenny before now."

"You read that on the back of a cereal box?"

Tom chuckled. "Maybe. Regardless, I'm pleased for you, Nero. You deserve to be happy, even if you think you don't."

Nero had never been sure how much Tom knew of his history, but in that moment it was obvious he knew it all. "You don't get to decide what I deserve."

"No, Nero, I don't, which is a shame, because I reckon it's a hell of a lot more than you'll ever give yourself. Now, shall we end this conversation before you lamp me one? I have enough to do without getting decked."

Nero was saved from having to formulate a response by sinuous arms winding around him from behind. Tom forgotten, Nero spun and lifted Lenny clean from the ground in a crushing bear hug. "Don't ever leave me again."

"Are you being serious, or dying for a smoke?"

Lenny's voice was muffled against Nero's chest. Nero loosened his grip a little and let him breathe. "I don't give a fuck about your packet of fags. Got me own earlier."

"You're serious, then?"

"Deadly."

Lenny's answering smile was dazzling. "I had great day, if it's any consolation. Jake's taught me loads of cool digital-art stuff. He's going to help me finish all of the menus and marketing stuff later so we can get an overnight order to the printers. It's going to be tight, but if I get it done we'll be laughing."

The spark in Lenny's half-manic gaze was infectious. In projects gone by, any enthusiasm Nero might have had at the beginning was long gone by this stage, eclipsed by exhaustion. But Lenny had changed all that—changed Nero—and the imminent opening truly felt like the fresh start they both needed, perhaps even deserved. "Are you coming home tonight?"

"Are you?"

Nero eyed the chaos of the restaurant's section of the kitchen and considered if he had time to hoof it back to Pippa's. "Doubt it. Efe's coming in early to talk me through the changes she's made to the bread menu, but I don't think I'll be ready for her until gone midnight. Too much to do."

Lenny's face fell. Despite starting the week with a bang— literally—they'd only made it home to the same bed two nights since—Lenny kipping with Jake at the Hampstead flat Urban Soul had finally bought last year, and Nero forgoing any sleep at all as he and Cass worked through the night to get the kitchen properly set up. "You'll be home in the morning, though, right? You need to sleep, or you'll make yourself sick again."

Nero refrained from rolling his eyes and instead focused on the distraction of Lenny's sinful fingers dancing a path up and down his spine. "Trust me, I'm sleeping all day tomorrow. Cass has banned me from every site until the evening."

"Well, I'm banning you too, just in case you're thinking of not listening to him, and I've already told Steph not to bother you."

"She still getting on Jimbo's case?"

"Yup. Debs says they hate each other, which means they're probably shagging, right?"

"They've managed not to as long as I've known them, and I ain't never hated you."

Lenny's grin turned wicked. "Good, 'cause you fuck me well enough as it is. Don't think I could handle you angry." He checked his phone. "Shit, I've got to go."

Nero grumbled. "Yeah, yeah. You're staying with Jake, though, right? I don't want you wandering around by yourself later."

"Later? Jesus, Nero, I wandered around London on my own just fine my whole life until—well, you know. But that's done with now. You don't have to worry about me, I promise."

"Humour me."

"Okay, okay. If we're not done by midnight, I'll stay with Jake again."

"Make it eleven."

Lenny huffed. "Okay, but only because you're fit as fuck when you go all daddy-bear on me."

Daddy-bear? Fuck that. But Nero didn't argue—how could he when Lenny put his hands on his chest and kissed the shit out of him? How could he do anything but kiss him back and growl gruff words of love he'd never uttered to another soul?

Then Lenny left. Nero watched him go, weaving through the restaurant, guiding Jake, who seemed to be having trouble keeping his often-wayward arms in check. Letting Lenny leave his side was always hard, but for some reason today it hurt more than usual, like they were parting for months, instead of a night that would pass in a flash of industrial pans of artisan bread dough. Nero raised his hand to his chest, like he could push the piece of his heart Lenny had taken with him back in.

But it was no good. Being without Lenny was torture, and the only way to survive it was to work like a dog until it was over.

It was past dawn the following morning when Nero drifted home under a cloud of flour and fatigue. He let himself into the flat, half-hoping to find Lenny in bed. Disappointment warred with relief when he found the sheets unslept in. Lenny had, for once, done as he was told and stayed with Jake, but *Christ*, Nero missed him.

A shower and an abandoned cuppa followed, and Nero fell asleep to the sound of the bin lorries rumbling up and down the streets below. He woke sometime later to a still-empty bed, a pounding heart, and a blank phone. *Shit.* Groggy, he stumbled up and plugged it into the wall. He shivered as a cool breeze filtered through the open windows, but the goose bumps tingling his naked flesh remained as he returned to bed, and under the covers, he couldn't get warm. A hot shower was tempting, but his body was too weary to move, and he drifted back to sleep with an odd air of foreboding colouring his dreams.

Not that he remembered his dreams when he finally woke up at midday, and he took that to be a good thing. Sleeping beside Lenny every night had driven away some of his demons, but they often came back when he was alone—when they sensed weakness in the void Lenny had left behind. Not today, though. Today, Nero stepped into the shower with a smile, and his mind a long way from the treacherous path he'd taken to get to a place where the mere thought of a man had him grinning like a pig in shit.

Brutal banging on the front door broke into his Lenny-themed daze. Nero frowned and peered around the shower curtain, like he imagined he could see through walls. *Idiot.* He waited a moment to see if whichever fucktard it was from downstairs took the hint, but the banging continued until he got to the door, cursing and a towel around his waist. "What the—"

Cass burst into the flat, eyes wild. "Have the old bill been here?"

Nero flinched. "What?"

"Fuck, Nero, we've been calling and calling you, and the bar downstairs. The *coppers*. Did they find you?"

"Find me? Why would they be looking for me?"

"Tom sent them. Nero, something's happened to Lenny. I don't know what, or where, just that the police found Tom at the office and sent him to the Royal Free Hospital. His phone cut out halfway through his message, but he said he'd sent the coppers here to find you."

Nero's heart stopped. He shot back to the bedroom and wrenched his phone free from the charger. Blood roaring in his ears, he swiped at the screen and called Lenny, even as Cass followed him into the bedroom and told him there was no point.

"It's dead, mate, and he don't have voice mail, does he?" Cass said.

A legacy of Lenny's attempt to disappear. *Fuck.* Nero fought the urge to hurl his phone at the wall. "What about Jake? Have you called him?"

"Course I have. He said Lenny left this morning to come back to you, so whatever's gone down happened between here and there."

"Shit." Nero grabbed his jeans from the floor and yanked them up his legs. "Tom's phone's dead too?"

"Yup. He just said to find you and get you to the hospital. I'm so fucking sorry, mate. I don't know anything else."

Nero whirled around the room, searching for a T-shirt. "It's that fucking bloke, I know it is."

Cass's silence spoke volumes. Nero flew at him. "What are you not telling me?"

"Whoa." Cass coughed as his back hit the wall, driving the breath from his lungs. "*Nero*, take it easy. You ain't no good to anyone if you lose your shit."

"Tell me."

Cass winced. "I'm trying. Let me go so I can breathe, will ya?"

Nero released Cass, breathing hard enough for the both of them. "I can see in your eyes it ain't good."

"Before he got cut off, Tom said that Gareth Harvey got bail a week ago. The coppers were supposed to warn Lenny, but it slipped through the net. And . . ."

"*Cass.*"

"They lost track of him. He's been AWOL for three days."

Gareth Harvey. Finally, a name, but it meant nothing as Nero's legs gave way. He sank onto the bed beside him and pressed his fists against his eyes, trying to contain his worst nightmare as it galloped off, taking with it every good dream he'd ever had. "He's got him, hasn't he? He's fucking got him."

"We don't know that." Cass dropped down in front of Nero, his hands on Nero's knees. "The two things might not be connected. Tom didn't say they were."

"But he got cut off."

"Yes, but . . ." Cass's voice fell away.

Nero stared hard at him, searching for something, anything to ground him, but he found nothing but concern and worry that seemed to have rendered him immobile.

"Nero." Cass grasped Nero's shoulders and shook him slightly. "Listen to me, we don't know nothing for certain. Lenny coulda tripped on the Tube and got himself a little bump like Jake did last year, or punched a copper . . . anything. We don't know shit until we get to that hospital, so let's *go*."

Cass's attempt at reassurance fell flat, but two words punctured the panicked haze Nero was drowning in: *let's go*.

He lurched up and grabbed a T-shirt, then followed Cass to the front door, pausing only long enough to stamp into his shoes. Outside, they dashed across the street to where Cass's car was parked on a double yellow line. A parking warden was filling out a ticket. Cass blew past her and jumped in the car, peeling away as she pointed her camera at his number plate.

The journey north to Hampstead was a car ride Nero couldn't describe. Cass drove like the retired joyrider he was, swerving in and out of the dense London traffic, but even with his best efforts, he couldn't avoid the gridlock on Pond Street, the road leading up to the hospital.

He swung into a bus stop, ignoring the rage of a black cab behind him. "Go. Run. You'll get there quicker on foot."

Nero was already halfway out the car. He left the door open and sprinted up the road, shoulder barging anyone who got in his way. The Royal Free wasn't a hospital he knew, and as he charged towards the main entrance he realised he had no idea where to go. A&E? The fucking morgue?

He burst through the revolving door, searching for Tom's sandy-blond hair, and any sign of the police. At first glance, he found nothing, and the panic already crippling him increased to the point where he could hardly breathe. White dots danced in front of his eyes. He spun around again and again, until finally he focused enough to see a reception desk.

The woman behind the desk was staring at him like he'd fallen from Mars. "Who are you looking for?"

"Lenny Mitchell. Is he okay?"

"I can't tell you that until you tell me who you are."

"Nero Fierro."

The woman nodded and searched her chaotic work station. "There is a message here somewhere . . ."

Nero balled his hands into fists. "Is he okay?"

A phone rang. "Just a moment, sir—"

The woman started talking into the receiver attached to her head. Nero wanted to rip it from her and throw it at the wall.

"Please. You have to tell me if he's okay."

The woman put her hand over the receiver and reached behind a computer monitor. She passed Nero a scrap of paper and a tangled coil of leather, and then gestured to a set of double doors. *Through there,* she mouthed.

And then she went back to her phone call.

Nausea roiled in Nero's gut as he tried to make sense of the artisan jewellery he'd never seen before—a necklace and a bracelet—but they weren't Lenny's, were they? At first glance, he was certain not, but as he peered closer and turned the pendant over and over, his heart said different. He stared at the brushed silver tiger, so tightly entwined with a butterfly-themed sugar skull. Goddammit, it *was* Lenny *and* Nero, forged together, like they had been ever since Nero had found Lenny squatting on his couch. "Where did you get these?"

The woman glanced up impatiently. "They've got your name on. Says here that you should have them."

"Says where?"

But the woman merely pointed again to the double doors and buzzed him in.

Nero shoved his way through the doors the moment there was room enough, his brain echoing with the last time he'd heard those ominous four words: *"You should have these, Nero. Your granddad always wanted to give them to you. We just never found the right time."*

Rosa Fierro slid two cameo rings across the plastic prison table. "They aren't worth much, but perhaps you can use them to start a new life when you get out of this place."

If only. The rings had been stolen from his cell a few days later, and Feltham YOI hadn't been—still wasn't by all accounts—the kind of place where anyone gave a shit. Even Nero hadn't cared much. What good would a couple of rings have been when the only man he'd ever looked up to was gone, taking his wife with him just a few months later? And all that remained now was the reason they had been given to him in the first place—because *Tito* was dead.

Oh god.

He's dead.

Lenny's dead.

Nero moved blindly into the emergency department. He gave Lenny's name at another reception desk and, like magic, more doors opened, but he felt no relief, only panic-laced grief—grief that he *deserved*. After all, losing Lenny was no more than Nero deserved. He'd taken a man's life with no remorse. What right did he have to expect his own to remain so vibrant?

His heart had never hurt so much, even when they'd told him Tito had died. His hand flew to his chest, like he could push the pain back, like he could plug the widening cracks before they fissured, and broke him apart. *Lenny, please. I love you.*

"Nero?" Tom's voice was distant, like Nero was underwater, and his hand on Nero's arm was surreal.

Nero pulled away from the unfamiliar touch. "Don't."

Tom ignored him and grabbed his other arm. "*Nero.* Come on. You need to come with me."

CHAPTER NINETEEN

He's not dead. Nero stood in the small waiting room, cramped with coppers, hospital staff, and Tom, talking in the soft, respectful tones that washed over Nero as he missed every word . . . all but three: *he's not dead.*

The relief that washed over Nero was dizzying, and he couldn't bring himself to feel like a dick for jumping to such dramatic conclusions. Besides, if his belated take on what had landed Lenny in hospital was anything to go by, his fears hadn't been that far-fetched.

"Do you know when he'll be discharged?" Tom asked the doctor standing close to Nero.

"In the morning, I'd imagine. We need to stitch his leg and observe that bump to his head. I'm not anticipating any problems, though. He's in good shape, considering."

"Considering what?"

Tom and the doctor swivelled their eyes to Nero, staring at him like he'd grown horns. Perhaps he had. Tom thanked the doctor and took Nero's arm, guiding him out of the room he'd steered him into just minutes before when he'd found him wandering the corridor, lost in a haze of grief that had turned out to be wonderfully misplaced. "I forget how feral you and Cass get around authority. Come on. Let's get you a cuppa."

"I don't want tea. I want Lenny."

"I know, but the police are with him at the moment, and then he needs to rest. Just come and sit for a few minutes, and let me explain what's happened. That way you can save Lenny the trouble, eh?"

The logic broke through the addled haze in Nero's mind. He reclaimed his arm and followed Tom to a vending machine at the end of the corridor. "Start at the beginning, 'cause it don't make no fucking sense to me."

"I don't know the beginning, Nero. I just know that Gareth Harvey was given bail when he shouldn't have been, and allowed to go missing, which left him able to come after Lenny, and the other people he'd formed obsessions with. Lenny fought him off, but the police won't tell me what happened to the others, which leads me to believe they weren't so lucky."

The haze returned, darker this time. Nero dropped into a nearby chair and steeled himself for the specifics he'd somehow managed not to hear the first time—the details that had passed him by after he'd realised Lenny was alive and in no danger of being otherwise. "This happened in Hampstead?"

"Yes. Lenny left Jake around eleven, presumably on his way to wherever you were—he didn't tell Jake where he was going—but he was attacked outside the Tube station. There was a struggle, and he hit his head, but he fought long enough for security to come to his aid. He was unconscious for a while, which is why they called me—I was listed as his emergency contact when I intervened on Lenny's behalf a few months back."

Shivers of rage rippled down Nero's spine. "I want to stamp on that bloke's head."

"Understandable, but you won't get the chance. He's been arrested, and I was given the impression he probably won't be released for a very long time."

"They said that last time."

"Actually, they didn't, but they also failed to inform Lenny when Gareth Harvey was granted bail, so they aren't entirely blameless."

Nero couldn't speak, though he was furiously certain that there was something Tom wasn't saying. Tom sighed and laid his hand on Nero's shoulder.

"Listen, I know you're angry with the police, and they made a mistake that ultimately they'll have to pay for. For you, and Lenny, the important thing is that he's going to be okay. Let someone else sort out the rest of it."

"Someone like who? You?"

"If it's necessary, yes. It's my job to take care of you all, *including* you, as much as you don't want me to."

Nero leaned forward, his elbows on his knees. A mottled blemish on the shiny hospital floor sucked his gaze in like a vortex. "Why are you nice to me when I do nothing but fuck you off?"

"Because who you are doesn't change who I am, and it doesn't stop me liking you, even when you do your best to make yourself thoroughly unlikable. Now, drink this tea and get yourself together. I expected Lenny to go into shock, not you."

Dick, but Nero didn't mean it. He drank the weird vending-machine tea and listened as Tom explained the finer details of Lenny's injuries, and how he'd sustained them—a blow to the head, and a gash in his leg that needed extensive stitching, a broken finger from punching his assailant hard enough to fracture his own bones. *He's the tiger, not me.*

The thought made Nero smile and remember the leather and silver jewellery stuffed in his pocket. He retrieved it and held it out to Tom. "How did the receptionist get this?"

"I gave it to her," Tom said. "The paramedics found it in Lenny's pocket, and I thought it might reassure you when you arrived."

Nero didn't have the heart to tell him how epically his good intentions had been wasted on Nero's morbid imagination. He stood, drawn to Lenny, just as a nurse approached and waved him forward.

"The police are gone," she said. "You can sit with Lenny now."

Nero's imagination was clearly having a field day. He followed the nurse to a bed and peered around the curtains, half expecting to find Lenny stricken and wired up to a million machines. The reality was almost benign. Were it not for the slight graze on Lenny's cheek, and the bandages on his hand and leg, he could've been asleep at home, in Nero's bed—in *their* bed. Head flung to the side, hair flopping in his face, how many times had Nero seen Lenny like this?

Not enough.

Nero took Lenny's uninjured hand. Lenny's eyes opened, unfocused and devoid of emotion, until he saw Nero and gifted him with a watery smile.

"Hey."

Nero leaned over the bed. "Hey, yourself. How are you feeling?"

"All the better for seeing your pretty face."

"Very funny. Wanna humour me a moment?"

Lenny poked his tongue out. "I'm fine, if you must know. Hungover and stoned on codeine, but other than that, I'm fine. Can we go home now?"

"Nope." Nero helped Lenny sit up. "Tom says we have to wait for the doctor to clear that bump to your head."

"Since when do you listen to Tom?"

"Since I realised him doing his big-boss-manager-thang was the only reason I knew that something had happened to you. Without him, you could've been killed and I'd have been the last to know."

Lenny's playful belligerence faded. "Is that why you look like you're about to shit a brick?"

That was one way of putting it. Nero had barely held it together since the moment Cass had banged on his door, and now Lenny was right in front of him, apparently well enough to take the piss out of him . . . *Fuck*. Nero's relief made his legs feel like they belonged to someone else.

He sat down abruptly, still clutching Lenny's hand. "Don't laugh at me. Being civilised about this shit is sending me fucking insane."

Lenny said nothing, just slid silently from the bed and into Nero's lap. He wrapped his arms around Nero's neck and pressed his face to his chest. Nero buried his face in Lenny's shoulder. His T-shirt smelled of Cass. Nero pulled back, frowning, until he focused on the faded Judas Priest logo that was actually more likely to be Jake's. "That's not yours."

"I know. I was in such a hurry to come home this morning that I stole Jake's clothes."

"Fucking Hampstead." Nero's hands curled into fists.

Lenny flinched and reclaimed the hand Nero had wrenched from his. "Am I missing something?"

The irrational rage darkening Nero's vision evaporated as abruptly as it had arrived. He knocked his forehead against Lenny's shoulder and then raised his head. "No, just remind me to twat Cass for buying that stupid bloody flat, will you?"

Lenny left eyebrow twitched, like it always did when Nero's best efforts at communication fell short.

"They used to rent the place," Nero said. "For Tom, when Cass lived at Pippa's and they treated the house like some kind of mecca instead of their home. They were supposed to get rid of it, but they ended up buying it instead, 'cause they can never leave shit alone—"

"Whoa." Lenny cut Nero off. "Come on. Please don't be angry, Nero . . . not with them, or me, and not with yourself, okay? There's nothing you could've done. He would've got to me eventually."

Nero would never get over how startling it was to love someone who read his thoughts so absolutely, but Lenny was wrong about one thing. "I'm not angry."

"Liar."

Nero shook his head. "I feel *guilty*, not angry . . . guilty that I wasn't with you, that I couldn't protect you, but I'm not angry—at least, not how I used to be. Years gone by, I wouldn't be at your bedside right now. I'd be out on the street, tearing up anyone who crossed my path until I found the bastard who hurt you, like the rage in me mattered more than anything else."

"How you feel *does* matter."

"I know, but I don't have it in me to be so angry anymore."

Lenny dragged his thumb over Nero's cheekbone. "You're different, even since I last saw you."

"I'm different *because* you saw me, Lenny."

This time, Lenny's silence was loaded with the understanding and empathy that had saved Nero's soul more than Lenny would ever know, and his gentle sigh felt like a dying summer breeze. "You know, I've been lying here trying to figure out if today actually happened? It blew up so fast, it doesn't seem real."

"I thought you were dead. Turns out I'm a bit of a drama queen."

"Not really." Lenny shook his head. "He said he was going to kill me, he was shouting it—*screaming*—all this weird shit about chosen ones. He had a knife, an old one, like an antique. I thought he was going to stab me, so I punched him in the face."

"And broke your finger." Nero brushed his palm gently over Lenny's taped-up fingers. "We're going to have to work on that."

"Punching?"

"Me and Cass are quite good at it. No broken fingers between us."

"When was the last time you punched someone?"

"Can't remember. Cass punches people." Nero pointed to the map of faded scars on his knuckles. "I punch walls."

"Fair enough. Can we leave now?"

"How about we wait for that doctor?"

Lenny scowled. "How about we fuck the doctor off and get going? We've got a restaurant to open tonight, remember?"

TST's imminent grand opening had slipped Nero's mind. "They'll manage without us."

"How? If Tom and Cass are both here? Jake can't do it on his own."

Nero retrieved his phone from his pocket to text Cass. A message was already there, informing him that Cass and Tom had left the hospital, were headed to Vauxhall, and to call them anytime. "See? They've got this."

Lenny's frown deepened. "It's not about *them*."

Isn't it?

It took Nero a moment to compute Lenny's cryptic mutiny, but when the lightbulb came, it was blinding. The Stray Tiger, was it him, or Lenny? Or were they one and the same, pouring their hearts and souls into each other? And was that the point? That separately they were drifters, but together they'd made a home?

Nero had no idea. He pulled the tangle of leather and silver from his pocket and dropped it into Lenny's damaged hand.

Lenny's eyes briefly widened, and then he smiled ruefully. "Where on earth did you get those? I've been carrying them around for weeks, waiting for the right moment to give them to you."

"They ain't both for me." Nero gently fastened the bracelet around Lenny's wrist, and then hung the necklace around his own neck. "I *love* you, Lenny, now let's get out of here and open a motherfucking restaurant."

EPILOGUE

Six Months Later

H ampstead tube station still felt strange. Often, Lenny found himself standing across the road from it, staring through the crowds of commuters, and trying to picture the day he'd punched a man hard enough to break his own bones. Punched *him*. Ended *him*, and the nightmare he'd lived in for so long.

Not that he'd been living the nightmare when it happened, because by then he'd been in that blissful, wonderful haze of complacency where he'd honestly believed the danger was over, that *he*—Gareth Harvey—was safely locked up. Oh, how wrong he'd been. In the month that followed the attack on Lenny, details had emerged of the injuries he'd inflicted on his other victims, horrors Lenny still saw when his mind drifted if something—or someone—didn't distract him.

It was Jake today. He fizzed like a firework and jostled Lenny's arm. "Come on—*wankers*—stop staring. People will think you've caught my crazy."

"You're not crazy," Lenny retorted.

"Nah, I just look it, eh?" Jake tilted his head to one side and pulled a face.

Lenny resisted the impulse to shove him, like he might've done Nero, and instead took Jake's arm, and casually guided him across the road, though his attempts at subtlety were pointless. Jake always knew when he was being handled. Lenny released him. "Are you going home now?"

"Home? Hmm? Oh, *home* home? Yeah. I'm meeting Cass at Euston." Jake fished his Oyster card from his back pocket. "What about you?"

"I'm going to drag Nero from the kitchen and go to bed, unless you need me for anything else?"

"Nah, go home, mate. And thanks for today. I know I keep calling you a bell job, but what I actually mean is that you make my life a million times easier."

Lenny beamed, though he'd learned long ago that Jake's vocal tics, however brutal, weren't personal, and affected *Jake* more than anyone else. "It's no worries. I like being your PA. It keeps me out of trouble."

"Does it balls, but at least it's the good kind of trouble, if that shit-eating grin I keep seeing on Nero is anything to go by."

Lenny couldn't argue with that. He saw Jake onto the right train and then made his way home to Vauxhall, to the newly renovated flat he and Nero had moved into just a few weeks ago. The door was at the back of the building, but Lenny couldn't resist taking the alternative route through TST, absorbing the dying bustle of the bakery as it shut up shop for the night, and then the renewed buzz as the business moved seamlessly to the vibrant pizza restaurant.

Nero was easy to spot, dressed in the black chef jacket Lenny had bought him for his birthday, circling the pizza oven like a wolf protecting its young. Lenny took a moment to gaze at him before Nero sensed his presence and turned around. Working for Urban Soul, Lenny had seen many chefs come and go, but none were as glorious to watch at work as Nero. The instinctive way he moved around the kitchen was a special kind of alchemy, and some days Lenny truly missed the heady summer days they'd spent holed up in Pippa's kitchen. *Some* days, because he could live without the smell of cooking clinging to his skin.

"Are you hungry, or just eyeing me up?" Nero said without looking around. "'Cause if it's the first, I've got just the thing."

"Oh yeah?"

"Yeah." Nero slid a pizza out of the oven and beckoned Lenny forward. "Spelt and spinach, your favourite."

And it was. The wheat-free pizza base TST had fast become famous for was to die for, and paired with spinach, manchego, and

Spanish manzanillo olives, it was the closest thing to heaven Lenny had ever eaten outside of a tub of ice cream. Lenny tore off a piece and stuffed it in his mouth. "It's almost like you knew I was coming."

"Almost." Nero expertly slid a few more pizzas and calzones out of the furnace-hot oven. "Or I might've seen you dancing up the road in a world of your own."

Oh. Lenny should've known. While he liked to meander through life with his head in the clouds, Nero was a man who missed nothing, and Lenny had yet to truly surprise him. "Are you going to be done by the time I eat this?"

"Depends how fast you eat it."

"You know how fast I can eat. Don't play games with me. You promised you'd come home with me tonight."

"Then why are you asking when I'll be done?" Nero finally looked at Lenny, and his eyes blazed. "Eat your dinner, birthday boy. I'm all yours."

"It's not my birthday till tomorrow."

"So?"

God, I love him. Lenny swallowed a blissed-out sigh and walloped back his pizza while Nero handed the kitchen to Jolen, who'd come over from Pippa's to be Nero's second sous chef. Then they left together, walking hand-in-hand through the packed restaurant they'd made their own. Urban Soul had built the foundations, but there was no doubt that the Stray Tiger had evolved into a vision that encapsulated Nero's soulful, seasonal menu and merged it with Lenny's eclectic artwork splashed on every available surface. The pizza restaurant combined with the artisan bakery had become one of Vauxhall's most popular food spots, and Lenny couldn't deny how proud he was of that fact.

Nero let them into the upstairs flat—a cool, white space that was still devoid of many creature comforts, aside from the mountain of Lenny's books that Tom had delivered a few days ago. Moving day had been enlightening. It was only when they'd packed up to leave Shepherd's Bush that Lenny had realised Nero had even fewer worldly possessions than he did, something he was planning to rectify if they ever stopped fucking long enough to go shopping, which, apparently, wasn't happening today.

Lenny shut the door behind him and unbuttoned his coat. Nero helped him, and made short work of stripping them both. Then he stood back and flatted himself against the wall behind him, arms open wide, giving Lenny his cue to take over.

He wants me to fuck him. Lenny's pulse quickened. The first time he'd pushed Nero back on the bed and eased inside him had been an emotional night. Nero had cried, and Lenny had held him tight, and taught him that pain wasn't inevitable, and that the void in his heart could be filled with love. Since that night, Lenny had fucked Nero over and over, and it just got better. Nero had proved a versatile lover—a rough top, a submissive bottom, and everything in between—and tonight he was Lenny's for the taking.

They stumbled to the bedroom, the only sounds in the flat their tripping footsteps and breathless gasps. Lenny's cock throbbed as Nero knelt before him and took him in his mouth, and he saw stars as teeth scraped skin.

He couldn't take it for long. Groaning, he tugged Nero to his feet and kissed him roughly, pushing backward to the bed. They tumbled onto it, scrambling, rolling, grabbing any part of each other they could reach, until Lenny had Nero where he wanted him, on his stomach, his arms behind his back, and his face mushed into the pillow. Nero liked it like this, slow and rough, Lenny's cock thrusting into him, driving him into the mattress until he came so hard Lenny briefly feared something was wrong.

After, they lay panting, tightly entwined in each other, while Nero dozed and Lenny gazed out over the city. It hadn't taken long for Vauxhall to feel like home, but that wasn't a surprise. Cass could call him a stray as much as he liked, but holed up the bakery with Nero in his arms, Lenny was the happiest bloke in the world. And finally, he was home.

NERO

Lenny scowled, looking, thanks in part to his turquoise hair, like a stroppy teenager. "Where are we going?"

"Berkhamsted," Nero said. "Now get on the fucking train."

Lenny glowered some more, but he got on the train and flung himself into an empty seat. "I don't see why we have to go all the way to the Dragonfly to see Gloria. She comes to see Efe often enough."

Nero shrugged. He was running out of things to say about his fictitious meeting with the head chef of Urban Soul's Berkhamsted bistro, and Lenny's obvious hurt feelings that Nero would do such a thing on his birthday were hard to take. "She's got those jerked sweet potatoes she brought us last week on the menu this week if it's any consolation."

Lenny sighed. "It shouldn't be, but it is."

"I don't get why you're so upset. You said you didn't want to do anything tonight."

"Uh-huh." Lenny pulled his phone from his pocket and became instantly engrossed in the Urban Soul Twitter account he'd taken over from Jake.

The conversation was apparently done. Nero left him to it and sat back in his seat, contemplating a twenty-minute catnap, but Lenny's conciliatory hand on his thigh—squeezing—kept him awake, like Lenny did most nights when they crawled into bed.

A bolt of heat zipped through Nero's veins. He'd always known he'd get off on having a man inside him, but that man being *Lenny*? Jesus. The only thing that came close was when they switched—

"Nero?"

"Hmm?" Nero looked down at Lenny, who'd lolled his head on Nero's shoulder. "Sorry, what?"

Lenny laughed. "And you call me a dreamer. I said, 'Is it Berko we get off at, or Hemel Hempstead?'"

"Berko." Nero glanced out the window as the train passed through Watford Junction. "Won't be long."

And indeed it wasn't. The train rolled into Berkhamsted a few minutes later, and Nero guided a grumbling Lenny off and through the station until they hit the canal path that led to their real destination.

"It's posh round here." Lenny looked around at the well-kept houses and neat gardens. "Is this where Tom's from?"

"Never asked. Cass seems to like it well enough, though." Nero cut across the lock. "Come on."

Lenny frowned. "I thought the Dragonfly was on the high street?"

"It is."

"So why are we headed in the opposite direction?"

"How do you know what direction the high street is? You've never been here."

Lenny inclined his head at a nearby sign. "Can read, though, innit? And isn't this where the bosses live?"

Balls. Oh well. Nero pointed down the street. "The house is down there. They wanted to see you on your birthday, so I said we'd drop in."

"Drop in?"

"For fuck's sake!" Nero finally lost patience with the daft secret that had been forced on him by a mischievous Cass. "There's a few people there, okay? From work. They wanted to surprise you, if you'd just do what you're fucking told and get in there."

Lenny burst out laughing. "I knew you'd crack. Do you honestly think I didn't know you were up to something? Man, I thought you'd at least hold out until we got to the doorstep."

"You knew?"

"Course I knew. Why else would you voluntarily take a Saturday night off work?"

"Because it's your birthday?"

"I already told you I don't give a fuck about shit like that any more than you do."

"Yeah, but I *really* don't give a fuck about my birthday. I saw your face when Spanks came in with that cake this morning. Made your day."

"That's 'cause I like cake."

"Whatever. I heard a rumour that there's cake in that house too, if you want to go in and have a look? You'll have to act surprised though."

Lenny sighed. "You're an arsehole, you know that?"

"Yes."

"And I love you. You know that too, right?"

Nero pulled Lenny close and kissed the tip of his nose. "Yes, and that's why I took tonight off, 'cause there's nowhere else I'd rather be."

Lenny admitted defeat and they walked, hand in hand as always, into the big Victorian house that Tom, Cass, and Jake called home. The house had changed a lot since Nero had first visited eight long years ago, and the small reception rooms had been knocked through into a space large enough to hold the two dozen friends and colleagues who'd taken Lenny in as one of their own. Lenny's faux surprise was flawless, and it wasn't long before he was stolen from Nero's side and dragged to the ad hoc dance floor in the middle of the room.

Nero let him go and retreated to the sidelines, rum in hand, and watched, awed as ever, as Lenny owned the room, dancing up a storm like Nero had never seen until Lenny had turned his world upside down. Damn, the boy could move. Was that shit even legal?

"Your boy's got stones." Cass appeared at Nero's side, echoing Nero's thoughts as Jake joined Lenny: "They look good together."

"Hands off. You've got two of your own."

Cass chuckled. "Don't I know it? They're more than I deserve."

"No, they ain't."

"If you say so."

Cass flashed Nero a wink, reminding him of their shared past, as if Nero could forget. And he didn't want to forget. His mind drifted to a dull winter morning a few weeks ago, when he'd found himself in Hackney, staring at the new-build block of maisonettes that had replaced the house he'd burned down. The sight of it had nearly brought him to his knees, but Lenny had pulled him back. Lenny *always* pulled him back.

The night went on. Drinks flowed, camaraderie and friendship solidified. It was the early hours of the morning by the time things quieted enough for Nero to drag Lenny outside to show him the real reason he'd let Cass talk him into the party.

"Where are we going?" Lenny stumbled tipsily behind Nero, swigging from a bottle of vodka, and clutching a bowl of Hackney-brown-biscuit ice cream. "You taking me down the garden for a quickie?"

The idea was tempting, but for once there was something far more pressing than fucking around. Nero led Lenny to the garage at the bottom of the garden and unlocked the sliding doors. "Are you ready for your present?"

Lenny shoved the last of his ice cream in his beautiful mouth. "Not a lawn mower, is it?"

"Not quite. Close your eyes." Lenny obeyed while Nero turned the lights on in the garage and dragged the dustsheets off the present he hoped would make Lenny smile that blinding smile Nero liked to pretend was just for him. "Okay, you can open them."

Lenny opened his eyes. Blinked. Opened them again. "What the *fuck*? Oh my God, is this . . . Shit, it can't be. Is this that rusty old bus you found in Vauxhall?"

"The very same." Nero grinned hard enough make his face ache and gestured with both arms to the once-dilapidated bus that was now a shiny, refurbished mobile kitchen. "Me and Tom struck a deal. He funded the conversion on the condition that we—me and you—make it pay by showing the world what Urban Soul's about."

Lenny moved closer, apparently transfixed by the crazy unicorn-themed logo Jake had taken from Lenny's rough designs all those months ago, and painted on the bonnet. "The Urban Vegan?"

"Yup. Fancied a challenge. Up for it?"

"You're not giving up meat."

It wasn't a question, but Nero shook his head anyway. "Fuck no, but Tom wants to save the world, and I don't mind helping him."

"You *like* helping him."

If you say so. Nero just smiled. "Cass wants us to take it to some festivals this summer, if we can get organised in time. The bus is good to go, we just need a menu . . . and I'll need you to help me cook."

"Cook? At a bunch of hippie festivals? Fuck yeah. This is the best present ever."

"Seriously?" Nero dangled the keys for Lenny to snatch. "I was kinda worried it was a bit like buying your wife a Hoover."

"It's perfect . . . and it's fucking green. I love it!"

Lenny unlocked the passenger door and climbed in. Nero followed him and shoved him over to the driver's side. "I ain't suggesting you take it for a spin now, but you're insured to drive it home in the morning."

"Really?"

"Yep. Sorted it this afternoon."

"Wow." Lenny put his hands on the steering wheel. "What gear have we got in the back?"

"A flat grill, a fryer . . . a bread oven. A gas hob we can boil with. It's small, but we can make it work."

"We can make anything work, can't we?"

The double meaning wasn't lost on Nero. He leaned across and scooped Lenny into the kind of embrace that Lenny would be lucky to escape from intact. "I love you."

Lenny didn't say it back. Didn't need to. His fingers tangled in the leather cord around Nero's neck said enough.

Nero absorbed the moment, and then drew back a little, inclining his head at the driver's-side sun visor. "Pull that down. Jake said he left something in it for you."

Lenny flipped the sun visor. An envelope fell into his lap. He opened it and peered inside, retrieving another smaller envelope. "What's this?"

Nero shrugged. "No idea."

"Liar."

Whatever. Nero watched as Lenny tore the envelope open and whooped at what he found inside.

"Glastonbury tickets? Oh, wow . . . they're vendor tickets, for the bus. Access all areas. Oh, man." Lenny laid his head on the steering wheel. "What did I do to deserve all this?"

"The impossible," Nero said. "Cass told me just yesterday that you've made me a much nicer person."

"Bollocks. You're the nicest person I've ever met underneath that grumpy façade . . . Ooh, hang on, there's more." Lenny withdrew yet another envelope from inside the first. "It's got your name on it."

"What?"

Lenny handed it over. "It's not for me. It's for you."

Frowning, Nero opened the envelope and revealed a stapled legal document with the Urban Soul logo on the front. "What the fuck?"

"Read it," Lenny said, his voice muffled as he bent double to peer at who knew what under his seat. "Maybe it's a new contract or something. You're due a pay rise."

Nero hardly heard him as the first page of the document began to sink in. He flipped quickly through the pages, scanning for any sign that he'd misunderstood, but there was none. Cass had done the unthinkable, and Nero could barely believe it.

"What is it?"

"Cass signed TST over to me . . . I think."

"*What?*"

Nero shook his head and read the document again. "I don't understand."

Lenny pried the paperwork from Nero's hands. "The brand name remains with Urban Soul, but the business—the bakery and the restaurant—belong to you. It's yours. He's giving it to you."

"Fucking bastard." Nero started to get out of the bus.

Lenny grabbed him. "Don't you dare."

"Dare what?"

"Go in there and throw it back in his face. He's giving it to you because you've earned it, and because who *he* is, who *they* are. Don't hustle in there and disrespect what they stand for, what *you* stand for."

"I don't stand for getting shit for nothing."

"It's not for nothing, Nero. It's for you . . . for eight years of hard work and loyalty. Did you honestly think they were going to let you set up a dozen businesses for them and not give you anything in return?"

"They pay me, don't they?" But the fight in Nero faded as he realised that this was a fight he'd never win. A fight that Jake had lost too. "Fucking bastards."

"Uh-huh. Same bastards who gave me a bus for my birthday, eh?"

"Fuck off."

Lenny laughed and laughed and laughed, until Nero pounced on him and kissed the hell out of him to shut him up.

They parted, eventually, flushed and breathless, but the mirth in Lenny's eyes remained, and Nero couldn't contain his own grin. "I'm going to take the summer off."

Lenny blinked. "Am I dreaming?"

"Maybe, are your dreams good or bad?"

"If you're implying that we can take this van around the world this summer, Nero, then my dreams are everything I've ever wanted. How about you?"

Nero smiled. "You are my dreams. I just never knew it."

Explore more of the *Urban Soul* universe:
riptidepublishing.com/titles/universe/urban-soul

"[T]astefully erotic [but] more smart
than smutty." —*Publishers Weekly*

MISF!TS

GARRETT LEIGH

Dear Reader,

Thank you for reading Garrett Leigh's *Strays*!

We know your time is precious and you have many, many entertainment options, so it means a lot that you've chosen to spend your time reading. We really hope you enjoyed it.

We'd be honored if you'd consider posting a review—good or bad—on sites like **Amazon, Barnes & Noble, Kobo, Goodreads, Twitter, Facebook, Tumblr,** and your blog or website. We'd also be honored if you told your friends and family about this book. Word of mouth is a book's lifeblood!

For more information on upcoming releases, author interviews, blog tours, contests, giveaways, and more, please sign up for our weekly, spam-free newsletter and visit us around the web:

Newsletter: tinyurl.com/RiptideSignup
Twitter: twitter.com/RiptideBooks
Facebook: facebook.com/RiptidePublishing
Goodreads: tinyurl.com/RiptideOnGoodreads
Tumblr: riptidepublishing.tumblr.com

Thank you so much for Reading the Rainbow!

RiptidePublishing.com

ACKNOWLEDGEMENTS

Thanks, as always, to my wonderful editor, Caz. Your patience and kindness knows no bounds. And to Alex, for wading through the British slang with enough hilarity for copy edits to be one of my favourite things.

ALSO BY GARRETT LEIGH

ABOUT THE AUTHOR

NOTE: The best way to keep up to date with the day-to-day chaos that is Garrett is to join her Facebook fan group, Garrett's Den: facebook.com/groups/garrettsden.

Garrett Leigh is an award-winning British writer and book designer, currently working for Dreamspinner Press, Loose Id, Riptide Publishing, and Fox Love Press.

Garrett's debut novel, *Slide*, won Best Bisexual Debut at the 2014 Rainbow Book Awards, and her polyamorous novel, *Misfits* was a finalist in the 2016 LAMBDA awards.

When not writing, Garrett can generally be found procrastinating on Twitter, cooking up a storm, or sitting on her behind doing as little as possible, all the while shouting at her menagerie of children and animals and attempting to tame her unruly and wonderful FOX.

Garrett is also an award winning cover artist, taking the silver medal at the Benjamin Franklin Book Awards in 2016. She designs for various publishing houses and independent authors at blackjazzdesign.com, and co-owns the specialist stock site moonstockphotography.com.

For cover art, please visit blackjazzdesign.com or email blackjazzdesign@gmail.com

Website: www.garrettleigh.com
Facebook: facebook.com/garrettleighbooks
Twitter: twitter.com/Garrett_Leigh
Instagram: instagram.com/garrett_leigh

Enjoy more stories like
Strays
at RiptidePublishing.com!

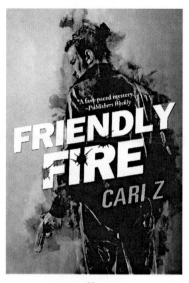